THE JUNKYARD DICK

GILLESPIE LAMB

Black Rose Writing | Texas

ISBN: 978-1-68513-017-6
PUBLISHED BY BLACK ROSE WRITING
www.blackrosewriting.com

Printed in the United States of America
Suggested Retail Price (SRP) $19.95

The Junkyard Dick is printed in Garamond Premier Pro

*As a planet-friendly publisher, Black Rose Writing does its best to eliminate unnecessary waste to reduce paper usage and energy costs, while never compromising the reading experience. As a result, the final word count vs. page count may not meet common expectations.

"I am grateful for God-given talents, parent-instilled values including work ethic, and freedom of opportunity to try new things. These are blessings that can make life interesting."

–Gillespie Lamb

THE
JUNKYARD
DICK

PROLOGUE

Pablo Munoz sensed danger. In a heartbeat, the surrounding pasture had changed character and threatened him. He turned and scurried away, ducking from instinct to lower his profile, though he hadn't seen anyone else in the field.

He covered no more than forty feet in his flight when a blow to his lower back knocked him off stride and to the ground. Gasping now, his fears crystallized, Pablo scrambled to his feet in panic. *Estupido! Idiota!*

He still couldn't see a threat, but the pain in his back became intense, doubling him over in agony. He straightened and pivoted back toward the fence, stumbling forward, bleeding and hurting.

The impact of a second bullet sent him face-first to the ground, where he sprawled like a dropped marionette. Clothing disheveled. Arms and legs askew. Mouth open and caked with dirt. Dust puffed up around him and hung in the air like an ephemeral tombstone. Then it, too, died.

CHAPTER ONE

When Roque Zamarripa arrived on his motorcycle bearing news of a fatal shooting, I knew my river sojourn was over. I had planned to loiter another hour in the clear Nueces River, disporting myself like a vagrant on a hot Texas Monday. The cool water under the rural highway bridge lured splashers and swimmers nearly every summer day. This day, it had attracted me.

But my buddy knew me. He never doubted that I would lose interest in lazing in the Nueces—delightsome as it was—if handed a chance to investigate a crime. As usual, he was right.

My penchant for crime investigation was well-known and a mystery in itself. Anyone examining my family tree would find no detective ancestors hidden among the branches, not even a beat-walking cop. The fascination with criminal acts couldn't be blamed on DNA or family tradition.

For that matter, owning a salvage yard couldn't be easily explained. I hadn't inherited it, nor otherwise followed a family member into the recyclable junk business, so why *was* I in salvage? Another mystery. It wasn't for the glamor, certainly. Nor did the fact that I enjoyed the work feel like sufficient justification most days.

But crime-solving, well, that was a whole other matter. I loved it without reservation. My zeal didn't rise to the level of passion, perhaps, but almost. Only discovering a garaged 1953 Studebaker coupe in restorable condition might satisfy me more than fingering a perpetrator. Snag a *murderer*? The very idea thrilled me.

3

I'd heard the baritone of Roque's motorcycle engine change pitch as it slowed on the highway approach to the bridge. The shiny red motorbike turned off the highway and glided down the turnoff toward me. It reached the bottom of the slope and idled across a concrete low-water crossing. The rain-starved summer river gathered itself upstream and flowed through the crossing's culverts, one of which fed the pool where I loitered.

Roque eased to a stop near me, killed the engine, and removed his helmet. He brushed a palm across his thick, black head of hair and looked apologetic. "Senor Tak Sweedner, I presume," he said loud enough for me to hear above the trickling river.

"Yes?" I asked, lolling on the water's surface.

"I hope I'm not disturbing your retreat from the cares of the world."

"You are." I sensed my vagrancy was about to end.

"I am so sorry. That is, I'm so sorry I don't own a salvage yard so I, too, could play in the river when everyone else was trying to make a living."

"I'll make a deal with you, Roque," I said, dropping my feet and sitting upright in the water, legs scissoring nearer the rocky bottom. "I'll trade thirty acres of salvage yard for three hundred acres of the Zamarripa ranch."

Roque put the helmet on the tank in front of him and propped his arms on his hips. His brown forearms flexed with strength. "And what would you do with three hundred acres of south Texas ranchland, *amigo*? You couldn't raise a single cow on it."

"Let me worry about that. Is it a deal?"

"I'll have to talk to my father."

"Oh, that's right. It's your *father's* ranch. I need to speak to *el jefe*." I lay forward and stroked through the water toward my friend. A moment later, my feet touched bottom, and I stood and stepped onto the pavement. My luminescent orange trunks glowed in the midday sun.

"Your swimsuit should be outlawed. It violates some community standard, I'm sure," Roque said. It wasn't the first time he'd panned the trunks, so I ignored the remark. I dried off with a sun-warmed towel, including swiping my shaved head and toweling my bearded face.

Roque waited silently, which was out of the ordinary. He wasn't taciturn by nature and seemed more sober than the situation called for, so I sobered up as well. "What can I do for you, Roque?"

"My father and I have a problem we'd like you to check out, Tak. One of our ranch hands, Pablo Munoz, went missing over the weekend. His body was found this morning."

"A body. Found where?"

"On the solar farm being built on Peyton Ruskey's ranch property just across the north fence from our place. You know where I'm talking about?"

I'd noticed the work site that morning from the highway on the north edge of the valley, solar panels glimmering in slanting sunlight. I nodded. "How'd the man die?"

"From a bullet." Roque hesitated and sighed. "Two bullets, actually, both of which entered his back. A searcher found him on the ground next to a solar panel. It's very disturbing because we can't imagine why anyone would shoot Pablo once, let alone twice."

I dropped the towel to the pavement and stood on it, the soles of my feet experiencing relief from sunbaked concrete. Tugging Arizona jeans up and over the still-wet orange suit, I pulled a T-shirt down over my head and slipped my feet into well-worn boots. I put my sweat-stained straw hat on my head and indicated that I was ready to leave. "Yep, a bullet in the back could be accidental. Two bullets usually isn't. Let's go see."

•   •   •

I followed Roque along the two-lane highway in my four-wheel-drive pickup. We reached the Zamarripa ranch in three minutes of travel down three miles of Texas Rt. 55. The ranch rides the rolling foothills just below the Balcones Escarpment. The geological transition in Texas between the High Plains of the Edwards Plateau and the fertile farmland of the upper Rio Grande Valley to the south was termed Hill Country. Eons of erosion created the small mountains that marked the drop between higher and lower elevations. The Zamarripa ranch sprawled across the southern end of these hills.

The two vehicles sped through a ranch entranceway that was modest by Texas standards. Eighteen feet overhead, a rough-hewn live oak pole supported by sturdy rock pillars spanned the unpaved driveway. An oak panel suspended from the pole announced "ZAMARRIPA RANCH." Burned into the panel on either side of the name was the ranch's sleepy Z brand—*ZZZ*. A gray-and-brown Cooper's hawk perched atop the panel and eyed us as we passed beneath.

The Ford truck's heavy front-end grille cut through the dust kicked up by the Honda with almost the same ease it deflected the bodies of white tail and mule deer foolish enough to dart in front of it. Highway collisions with the graceful animals never were pretty.

A hundred yards from the highway, Roque pulled over. He climbed off the bike, hung his helmet on the handlebar, ambled to the pickup and climbed in. "Take the first roadway to the left," he said and rolled down his window.

I took orders from Roque because he was my best friend and a good guy. We grew into adulthood together and somewhere along the way I concluded he was the superior human being. While I didn't feel inferior to him, exactly, my respect for him knew no bounds. "I'm sorry about Pablo."

Roque nodded. "He was just an ordinary guy, but he deserved better."

My buddy was an empathetic soul, feeling pain in others. I supposed his sensitivity helped him in his writing, for Roque aspired to be an author, which I admired as an avid reader. He had earned a literature degree at the university in Austin. but did most of his writing after full days of running the family's ranching operation. Staying close to Roque seemed a good idea in case he ever cashed in on a best-seller and needed an indigent write-off.

The slightly rutted path we were traveling wound among blackbrush and persimmon shrubs before descending into a shallow arroyo and rising on the other side. At the top, the path veered right to run east alongside a four-wire barbed fence. The solar panel field came into view, and I could see a construction crew drilling into leveled ground, erecting the short steel poles that supported the panels.

"Here is good," Roque said, so I parked the truck next to the fence. We exited through the passenger side door, clambered into the bed of the truck and, leaning on the top of a fence post, hopped over the fence. Dust kicked up where we landed on rain-starved dirt. Roque led the way through the field of panels to an area cordoned off with yellow tape. We ducked under the tape and approached the death scene.

The ground was trampled, presumably by law enforcement officers, coroner's office people, and assorted other emergency responders. I could picture them swarming over the site, taking profuse notes, wearing out their digital cameras shooting from every angle. I hoped any clues near the body had been retrieved before the official invasion obliterated them. A spray-painted yellow silhouette on the ground marked where the body had been.

"Judging from the position of arms and legs, it doesn't appear Pablo was hiding or standing still," I said, gesturing toward the painted outline. "It looks like he fell in a heap."

"He had no reason to be in this area," Roque said, "other than curiosity. We don't have any cattle over on our side of the fence, so he had no work-related reason to be anywhere near here. What's more, he was an easy-going guy and unlikely to have had any murderous enemies."

I said nothing to that. How many easy-going, friendly people were murdered in the world in the last hour alone? I stood and looked west across the shimmering panels to the work party, then scanned the field, pivoting till I faced north. "What's that building?"

Roque looked where I was pointing. "I don't know."

Fifty yards away stood a wood-framed, one-story shed, perhaps twenty feet square. It was built near the base of a long incline from the hill's crest. The enclosed wall facing us was at least two feet taller than the wall on the uphill side. A sloping roof topped the walls. If it had windows or a doorway, they were on the other side. "That's too new to be an old line-camp building."

"I imagine it was thrown up to keep construction equipment and supplies overnight. I can't see any other purpose for it," Roque said.

"Hey!" The shout startled us. A man in a hardhat strode in our direction from the far end of the solar field. He wanted our attention, obviously, so we moved to meet him. The man threw up an arm and shouted again. "What are you doing here? This is a construction site."

7

When we drew nearer, Roque explained their presence. "It's also a murder site. It was *my* employee whose body was found this morning. I brought my private investigator here to examine the area." He flashed his most ingratiating smile. The expression on the man's face softened somewhat. Roque added, "We won't tarry. Sorry to disturb your work."

"Well... OK. I will have to ask you to leave though. It's hard enough keeping the crew focused after the discovery of a body. Having curious people poking around makes things worse."

"You're the project foreman?" I asked.

"I am," the man said and squared away to face me. "Bill Evans. You are?"

"Tak Sweedner. Tell me, Bill, is that your tool shed over there?"

"That?" he asked, pointing toward the building. "No. It belongs to Ruskey ranch, a line shack or something. We carry our equipment in and out each day."

We apologized for the interruption and walked back to the fence, climbing over it and re-entering the truck. I noticed Evans stood in place and watched us, hands on hips. As I started the truck engine, he continued to look our way, like a watchdog making sure its barking had scared away an intruder.

"I'm a private investigator, am I?"

"Very private, as in amateur and unlicensed," Roque said. "I figured 'private investigator' would impress him more than 'junkyard operator and river-loiterer.'"

CHAPTER TWO

"Did you check before you crawled under there, Billy?" I yelled as I strode up to the rusting hulk of a 1973 Chevrolet half-ton pickup, its axles resting on concrete blocks. The vintage vehicle sat near the middle of several acres of junked trucks and cars. No one was in sight, but a pair of worn boot soles protruded from beneath the truck's running board. One of the boots waggled in response.

"You did check? Or you're in death throes from a rattler bite?" The boot waggled again. "I'll take that to mean you're still alive."

Western diamondback rattlesnakes weren't as common as Texas lore might suggest, but sightings of them were not rare. The reptile wanted to be left alone as a rule, but if someone crawled into a shaded space where one of the snakes was cooling, or stepped on one slithering across a path, a rattler would strike. The bite wasn't fatal, generally, but neither was it a love nip.

"Who needs a piece of this antique?" I asked, stooping to peer under the truck, my straw hat falling to the ground. As I retrieved the hat, the boots began to scoot out from beneath the frame followed by a dirty pair of coveralls. A toolbox was shoved out. Finally, the arms and head of a lanky young man with long hair appeared, his lower lip swollen by a slug of chewing tobacco. He stood, dusted off the seat and back of his coveralls, and faced me.

"I always check first for snakes, boss. Your orders," he said and spat sideways. He held up a U-joint wrenched free from the truck. "Butch Randolph needs this for his old pickup. He insists on driving that wreck instead of parking it under a live oak."

Billy Wilson spat again as he picked up his toolbox. We walked back toward the office at the front of the property, sauntering along and chatting in the same spirit. I hired Billy right out of high school three years before and had never regretted it. The young man was one of those people blessed with instinctive mechanical understanding. What's more, his native intellect extended to puzzling out electronic mysteries that stumped me.

Last year, I had persuaded Billy to enroll in the automotive technology program on the Uvalde campus of Southwest Texas Junior College. I knew it would mean the eventual loss of a valuable employee, but the kid was too likeable and talented to squander his life pulling parts from junkers.

"Looks like you've been swimming," Billy said.

"How did you know that?"

"Either that or you wet your pants."

I was surprised the damp swimming suit still showed through on the jeans. "It's been a tough week. I needed a dip."

"Heck, you shoulda said something," Billy pulled a can of tobacco from a hip pocket. "I'd have given you a dip and you wouldn't have had to drive all the way to the river."

• • •

The rest of the afternoon at Sweedner Salvage was uneventful, yet productive. One customer followed up a call and purchased a transmission removed from an older model GMC. Another bought several sheets of galvanized metal picked up at auction after a manufacturer went out of business. A third needed several lengths of copper tubing salvaged last year from a demolished hotel. Commerce downstream from showrooms still can turn a nickel.

Near the end of the day, office manager and rollback-truck driver Tomas Gonzales sprawled in an office chair, as did Billy and I. Billy meticulously wiped grime from his fingernails. All day every day, Billy worked with rusty, oily, greasy materials, yet he was conscientious about hygiene, including regular shampooing of his long hair. The kid had good instincts, except when it came to sticking tobacco in his mouth.

"Tak, you'll be glad to know that so far this month, we're taking in more money than you're paying out," Tomas said. "I consider that a good trend."

"I'd agree with that. See the trend continues, will you?" I leaned back with my legs outstretched, feet on a desktop, and played a succession of chords on an old acoustical guitar kept in the office. The guys were used to me strumming and humming at odd times of the day. It was a perk of being boss.

Today I plucked chords and sang to myself about "old cars and new gals, bright stars and best pals." I liked to make up ditties—to describe them as songs would be a stretch—and had composed them for so long, I couldn't remember *not* doing it. "You hear about the murder up at the solar farm?" I asked between strums.

They had. Tomas said he'd known Pablo through mutual friends and couldn't imagine someone getting angry enough at the man to shoot him. "He was a gentle guy, more interested in birds and nature than women and beer, which usually is what gets a man shot."

"A bird lover?" I lay the guitar on my lap. I didn't attribute bird-loving to men of south Texas, generally speaking. Shooting doves in season, sure. Beyond that, I'd never met a local man with avian interests. "What kinds of birds?"

"Oh, you know. Storks. Falcons. Songbirds. I'm told he liked to prowl around in pastures and river bottoms just to watch rarer birds in their natural habitat."

"Interesting," I began to strum the guitar again, but my mind was on birds.

At closing, I swung shut the gate to the salvage yard and mulled Pablo's reputed habit of birdwatching. Maybe in his sneaking around on the Ruskey place in search of a rare owl or some wildfowl, Pablo had stumbled onto poachers bagging protected wildlife and been silenced before he could report it. While that was possible, such tragedies usually came from inadvertent discovery of a meth lab, which I doubted happened in this case.

My route home took me east on Hwy. 90 for three miles before turning north and bumping across Burlington Northern-Santa Fe railroad tracks. The stretch of railway was among the busiest in the state. On some days, westbound or eastbound trains a mile long rumbled along the tracks, one after another, a few minutes apart.

More than once, I'd sat at the crossing and counted the usual string of one hundred boxcars and flatcars, the shipping containers stacked two-high. Their rumbling passage sometimes touched my inner hobo and left me feeling hamstrung by routine and obligation.

A half-mile north of the tracks, I navigated a short, curving lane and pulled into the carport on my thirty-five-acre home place at the base of a shrub-covered hill. A brown-bodied, black-faced boxer greeted me, barking and hopping up to rest his front paws on my stomach after I stepped from the cab. "Otis, I'm glad to see you, too. Have you chased away any burglars today? You have? Good boy."

The dog trotted alongside me around the truck to the front porch. He panted with excitement. I picked up a stainless-steel bowl, banged it against a porch post to empty it of fouled water, and refilled it from a hydrant off the end of the porch.

Otis watched with the intensity of an animal that hadn't had a lick of water all day, which I knew to be untrue. After I replaced the bowl on the porch floor, the dog lapped up the water. Otis was a sloppy drinker and messy eater, but an incomparable companion. I loved the dog.

The modest home had belonged to a favorite bachelor uncle, my father's brother Portis, who until his death at 79 managed the 10,000-acre Perry ranch. The ranch was a cattle operation with a few hundred tilled acres for growing feed. It was a penny-ante organization compared to the Nunley brothers' 300,000-acre spread or the Briscoe family's half-million-acre holdings. Still, Portis Sweedner was a respected cow man, and I remembered him with fondness.

Only after Uncle Portis died five years ago did I learn he had left me his one-story house and surrounding acreage. The bequest surprised the heck out of me, a gift from one bachelor to another. I was moved when learning of it, because Uncle Portis hadn't even hinted at bequeathing the property to me and thanking him became impossible after his death. Being a good steward of the property was my only way to demonstrate gratitude.

I hung my hat from a three-peg hat rack on the kitchen wall and poured a tall glass of iced tea from a pitcher in the refrigerator. I carried it to a lounge chair in the den, sat, leaned back, and sighed. Like most evenings.

For a full minute, I sipped the tea and relaxed while scanning the room, which still was furnished with my uncle's belongings. The furniture was in good condition, but eclectic. There was no theme other than, "Make Yourself Comfortable." I told people I hadn't yet replaced the furnishings because Uncle Portis had such good taste in home design, but the truth was I saw no real reason to do so.

On a side table was a short stack of books, fiction in most cases. I liked history and biography well enough, but when I sank into the soft chair at the end of the day, I was ready to escape life and enter worlds of adventure, mystery and imagination. I had the bad habit of reading more than one novel at a time. The current stack included a Walter Longmire contemporary whodunit, an Arkady Renko Russian detective story, and a character Western, *Monte Walsh*.

My best acoustical guitar was propped next to the chair. I set the container of tea on the floor and picked up the instrument. After tuning it, I soon accompanied myself on a melody I'd been working on over the last week, a bluesy tune keyed to minor chords. The blues seemed to come to me naturally these days. I couldn't remember the last time I'd composed an upbeat, happy song and resisted exploring what that meant.

After several minutes, I resettled the guitar by the chair and plucked a cell phone from its holster on my belt. I scrolled through the contacts list and punched a number not called for quite a while. The clock on the opposite wall read almost six o'clock. Moments later, a female voice sounded in my ear.

"Hi, Emma. This is Tak."

"Tak!" the enthusiastic response brought a smile to my face. "I was just thinking about you. I heard there was a murder up there. Are you on it?"

The allusion to my detective work pleased me. "Heard about it, huh? I figured you were too busy digging up bones to pay attention to such things."

Emma Townsend laughed. I loved her laugh. It was energetic and genuine and never verged on shrillness. I imagined she was smiling at that moment, running her fingers through her brunette hair and swiveling on a stool as she talked. "I don't just dig up bones. I dig through trash pits, too. Archaeologists have many skills." She laughed again.

Despite her self-deprecation, Emma's scientific interests were not a few. Her inquisitive mind ranged across the anthropological sciences. I wanted to explore that field of knowledge with her. "How free *are* you these days? You have time to run up here and walk around a pasture with me?"

"Maybe run through a pasture with you. I don't have time to walk." I listened to her lament about being overworked. Emma was a non-tenured adjunct professor in the anthropology department at Texas A&M. Having discovered a love of archaeology as a Uvalde High School summer intern, she had earned a bachelor of arts in anthropology with an archaeology track. Her professors were so impressed upon her graduation they had offered her a staff position. The woman was on the path to a full professorship.

She had married an A&M baseball player who proved to be big-league only as a womanizer. She had divorced him three years before. My story was similar—marrying young and disappointingly, unable to piece my marriage back together after discovering my wife's philandering, and now a self-proclaimed "old bachelor" just like Uncle Portis. Though Emma and I never had dated, we were friends of a special order.

"Actually, my request is in connection with the murder," I said. She fell silent and I heard a surprise intake of breath. "I'm thinking someone might have killed Pablo Munoz because he saw something he shouldn't have, maybe someone stealing an ancient shard. I'm told Pablo liked rare birds, so maybe he bumped into a hunter with a bagful of endangered species. You know a little about birds, don't you?"

She remained silent a moment, as if considering the situation. "I do. I'm an amateur ornithologist. I would love to walk a pasture with you, Tak. How soon can we get started?"

The tingle I felt at her response surprised me. "Heck, if you can make it here tomorrow, we can catch up over supper and then head out first thing the next morning. No rain in the forecast. We can skinny dip in the Nueces if you want."

"Uh huh. See you tomorrow."

Ending the call, I finished my tea and mulled my good fortune. *Friends are a blessing*, I thought, still grinning. Then I heard Otis scraping on the door and hoping to be fed. "Especially four-legged friends like you, Otis," I said loud enough for the dog to hear. "I'm coming."

CHAPTER THREE

Emma arrived in Uvalde the next day almost at closing time and caught me still at work. Tomas had pointed in the direction where he believed I was working at that moment, and she found me after meandering through my world of cars and trucks.

She strode past whimsical hand-lettered signs on weathered plywood, the signage designating sections of parked vehicles. She first passed through an area reserved for Ford Motor Company products—*Ford Country*. It contained Mercury sedans, Pinto station wagons, numerous vintages of F-150s and other vintage Ford vehicles parked in weeds on either side of the service road. The next section was dubbed *GM Land* for General Motors cars and trucks, obviously, and just beyond that, *Chrysler Fields*.

She found me in *Othersville*, where I was loading onto a flatbed truck a pastel green Studebaker Lark two-door station wagon. I lowered the car onto the truck bed, pulled the hydraulic lifting forks from under the vehicle's frame, and backed away my Hitachi wheel loader. I waved at Emma. "Climb aboard!"

Emma jogged over and stepped up on the first rung of the ladder hanging between the wheel loader's huge tires. I grabbed her extended hand and helped her up and onto the machine's platform. With her clinging to the railing, I raised the front forks from the ground and steered it toward the shop.

"That was an old Studebaker, right?" Emma said loud enough to be heard above the engine's roar. "I knew someone in college who drove a hardtop model."

"You're right!" I said. "I'm surprised you could identify it. It's sort of a rare car. A collector in Austin decided he just had to have it."

The wheel loader rumbled through *GM Land* before I angled off along a different lane. We skirted two foreign car-themed areas, *Rising Sun Acres* and *Euro Borough*, and entered an area full of building materials. Electrical steel conduit was mounded over here, rows of iron pipe over there, steel barrels stacked three-high off to the side.

I parked the big orange machine at the rear of the shop and switched off the engine. We each backed down the ladder. "Welcome to the world of still-valuable junk," I said.

The self-deprecating comment reflected my chronic uneasiness about the cultural status of salvage yard dealers. I couldn't rid myself of the gnawing feeling the work was not a reputable calling. I enjoyed the daily routines and the pace of it, and the enterprise provided me sufficient money to live on. Yet at moments like this, with a true professional standing beside me, I again questioned my career choice.

We chit-chatted our way into the office area. Tomas was snapping off the lights as we entered. He and Billy knew Emma and friendly greetings were exchanged before she and I led the way out the front door.

The flatbed truck driver pulled into the yard as we exited the building. The driver jumped out of the cab to check straps holding the Studebaker firmly in place. Persuaded the car wasn't going to fall off on its trip north to the state capital, he climbed back behind the wheel and drove out of the yard. Emma and I followed in my pickup, leaving her car locked up in the yard. Destination: Zach's Steak Barn.

The place was crowded, but we found a booth. As usual, the food surpassed expectations, which was extraordinary considering how hungry we were. My bacon-wrapped filet mignon was better than usual, it seemed to me. Emma described her grilled shrimp as perfect. We also consumed a small loaf of bread lathered with honey-whipped butter and some sweet chocolate mousse. We had been a ravenous pair.

Throughout the meal, we talked like old friends do, and continued our conversation after the food was consumed. Her soft voice pleased my ear. When we noticed a waitress drumming her fingers on a low wall near the booth and frowning at us, we felt embarrassed about taking the booth out of circulation. After leaving a tip larger than I might have otherwise, we left the restaurant and I offered Emma a timeless line. "Your place or mine?"

She smiled at that. "Mom would be disappointed if I came to town and didn't spend the night with her. Thanks for the offer though."

A few minutes later and a couple of miles across town, her mother greeted us on the front walk of a low-roofed ranch house on West Mesquite Street. A mature live oak crowned the middle of the street. Uvalde liked its trees, and city fathers had decided a long time ago to sacrifice safe vehicular movement to statuesque greenery whenever they could. Consequently, several streets had pavement surrounding the trunk of one, sometimes two, tall shade trees.

Emma's mother had shared some of her best genes with her daughter. She was still a slender and attractive woman of sixty-something. Mother and daughter hugged. I doffed my Western hat and clasped hands with the woman for an instant, then handed a small travel bag to Emma and waved goodbye. "See you around nine." The drive back home seemed lonelier than usual.

Before Emma had arrived, I'd called NewAge Solar to ask if an investigative colleague and I could walk through pasture acreage at the construction site. I'd made the call to avoid another confrontation with the solar project supervisor. The executive sitting in his office in far-off Dallas sounded hesitant until I told him I was visiting the site at the behest of the Zamarripa family, which was *very* upset about the death of its employee.

That refocused the conversation. The executive didn't want the local community perturbed just as the company was coming to town. After promising we would not disrupt construction, I was given permission to explore the property. The supervisor would be so informed.

So, at ten the next morning, Emma and I in my truck bounced across a cattle guard at the western edge of the solar company property and followed a curving path back to the work site. I parked the truck at the end of the project farthest from the work crew. Before we stepped out, I pointed out to Emma where Pablo's body had been found and the possible locations of his shooter. It was all speculation, of course, but the coroner had reported the body hadn't been dumped on the property. Pablo had died where he fell.

We exited the truck into a blazing sun, each of us clad in jeans, T-shirts, and wide-brimmed hats. Emma shouldered a lightweight backpack. We walked north along the edge of the solar complex to where the leveled field began its climb to the adjacent hilltop, the rise peaking perhaps a hundred-and-fifty yards away. Scrub trees and underbrush gave the hillside a rough complexion.

The crease between the level field and the rise to the north sharpened as it meandered east, becoming a serious gully before broadening into a broad rift between a pair of hills. After planning our route and reminding one another to keep an eye out for rattlesnakes, we began a silent walk east, eyes to the ground, staying about ten feet apart.

Emma stopped now and again to bend over and examine a rock or the pattern of erosion in the hard pan, her archaeological training showing. I could hear her talk to herself. I was skirting a bush when she stopped to ask, "What are we looking for again?"

"Anything that catches your eye. If something catches your eye, it is apt to be out of place or to have been disturbed," I said. "A welter of footprints. A dropped glove. Or something less subtle like a hunting rifle."

"I wish you'd told me earlier," she said and looked behind her. "I saw a carbine back there under a bush. I guess we can check it out later."

"Uh huh. Right. I should be asking *you* what we're looking for," I said. "You're the trained scientist." I was enjoying this stroll through the pasture with Emma, even though the reason we were there couldn't have been more serious.

The vertical rise from the edge of the solar field grew steeper as we reached the line shack that I'd noticed on my first visit. I walked around the building and found a door on the north side with a padlock on a clasp. I shook the door, but the lock rattled and remained in place.

Because the shed's vertical plywood sheeting extended clear to the ground, rain had washed dirt up onto the panels on the uphill side. Each side of the shed was the same—plywood sheets running to the ground.

"An odd way to finish a wall," I said to Emma who had walked over for a closer look. "No crawl space under the floor."

"Don't you imagine it was enclosed to repel rattlers looking for a cool place to sleep?"

"Probably right. Makes sense. I would have." My eyes followed faint tire tracks leading away from the door and up and across the hill to the north. "The shed must be used for *something*. A four-wheeler is visiting it often enough to leave a trail." I considered walking the trail to see where it led, but concluded it was a diversion from our objective.

We resumed our positions and our journey along the bottom of the slope. I scuffled along an outcropping of rock that extended eastward from the shed for twenty yards. Emma inspected the ground to my right. As we neared the active construction area, we tried to downplay our presence, eyes to the ground and looking straight ahead. I heard a loud comment or two from crew members, an indication that we had been spotted, but we ignored the spike of interest. Soon we were past the crew and Emma entered the deeper part of the draw.

She dropped down into the ditch that appeared to be three feet deep. She knelt and moved her face close to the exposed embankment looking for anomalies. After a moment, she continued ahead, with me following along on higher ground adjacent to the gully. Twenty-five yards farther on, the draw widened and flattened somewhat, and the land sloped upward on both sides into flanking hills.

I was seeing nothing interesting on my path. Emma stayed in the rut where it cut through the center of the low area. A rock outcropping formed one side of the broadened gully, which deepened to four or five feet. Emma dipped lower as she moved east. Moments later, I realized she wasn't in my peripheral vision at all.

"What are you seeing?" I asked after spotting her standing still and peering intently. She waved me over. I sidled up to the gully and dropped into it. When I reached her, she pointed at the rocky slope on the gully's north side. An opening maybe two feet wide and a foot high framed a black hole in the embankment.

Emma swung her backpack off her shoulders and pulled a flashlight from a side pocket. She switched it on and aimed it in the hole, which swallowed up the light. I leaned toward the opening with her. Neither of us could see an opposite wall or a bottom. It might have been twenty feet deep or two thousand feet deep.

"That's an *old* opening, isn't it?" I asked.

She nodded. "Not real old," she said, and felt along the lower lip of the hole. "It's worn down but not like openings exposed to weather for hundreds of years. This is Devil's River limestone, which is notorious for creating karst caves. Water eroded the rock over tens of thousands of years and eventually flooded the space. When water tables dropped, as they periodically did, the pools drained away. Ceiling material in the emptied passageways couldn't support itself and collapsed, creating a cavern."

"Like Kickapoo Cavern," I said, citing one of the more famous ones in south Texas.

"Like Kickapoo Cavern." She shined the beam of her flashlight into the darkness, peering up and down. "When the edge of a cavern near the surface collapses inward, an opening is created and that's what happened here."

She sniffed the air near the opening and turned to me. "Smell that."

I did. Ammonia.

"A bat colony probably lives here," she said. "A hole this size wouldn't accommodate the comings and goings of a colony of millions, like at Devil's Sinkhole on the plateau, but I bet this cavern has more than a few bats in it."

I leaned back on the gully wall next to the opening, tipped back my hat, and wiped my forehead with an arm. "So, what does this tell us about the murder?"

Emma laughed and placed her flashlight back in the backpack. "Not a thing, Tak. Oh, maybe the gun was tossed in there after the murder. Maybe some other incriminating evidence is on the floor of the cavern amid the guano. Good luck retrieving it. Probably, though, this is just a hole in the ground."

CHAPTER FOUR

We rested against the gully embankment for a few minutes and admired the little canyon. I could see a handful of bluebonnets and paintbrush blooms in the distance. Black-eyed Susan blooms dotted the slope directly in front of us. A month ago, the hill would have been a riot of color from spring blossoms. Now the beauty was more subtle—rugged terrain punctuated by hardy bushes set against a blue-gray backdrop of higher hills.

We decided to walk ahead another fifty yards and then turn back and travel a parallel route farther north of the gully. On the return trip, we searched with the same care we had on our first sweep of the area but found nothing helpful to the investigation. I felt an inkling of frustration. As we crossed the four-wheeler track on the slope above the shed, I again was intrigued by it, but we continued past.

When we reached our starting point, we were sweaty and hungry. So, I suggested we interrupt our search and get something to eat. Emma agreed without hesitation. Her face glistened with perspiration, and she waved her hat in front of her face for relief. We walked over to the truck and left the ranch, driving north on Hwy. 55.

A mile or so this side of Camp Wood, we rolled into the gravel parking lot of a lakefront convenience store and snack shop where we bought chicken salad sandwiches. I got a Sprite and she a Corona beer and we carried everything to a table in the shade of a tall Shumard red oak at the edge of the parking area. The surrounding area was a series of hills—small mountains, really—bordering the Nueces River, the source of the small manmade lake

Several travel trailers were parked in a grove at lake's edge. As we looked, a man sitting in an outboard near the shore pulled the starter rope on his motor and pointed a jon boat toward the middle of the lake. I didn't especially envy him because fishing always seemed a chore to me. Being on the lake was appealing, though.

"To our venture," Emma said, raising the bottle of Corona toward me as I sat across the table from her. I lay my hat on the table and clicked my can of pop against the bottle.

"Not a beer drinker, huh?" she asked, tipping her bottle.

"Not much."

"You're Mormon, aren't you?" she asked, and took a bite of her sandwich. That caught me by surprise.

"I was," I said, and then felt a need to say more. "Or I guess I still am. I'm not much of a churchgoer, though."

She didn't pursue the subject and conversation died for a minute. We enjoyed the tree's shade and the chance to relax in it after several hours of walking uneven ground in May sunshine. In south Texas, May can be hot. The temperature at that moment must have hovered near ninety degrees.

After consuming half of her sandwich, Emma broke the silence. "I've forgotten how you got the name Tak."

I finished a bite. "Well, there are two stories. I was named for a grandfather on my mother's side, his first name being Bartak, which got shortened to Tak. On the other hand, my father is said to have seen me charging around as a young boy and to have declared that I had a revved-up tachometer, and tachometer became Tak. Both stories are true."

"Interesting. Though I don't think of you as 'revved up,'" Emma said and pursed her lips in a quizzical expression. "More like smooth-running. Or firing on all cylinders."

"OK, maybe I should go by 'Smoothie.'"

"I'd stick with 'Tak.'"

We ate some more. Emma was well-mannered, lifting food or bottle to her lips with natural grace, nothing pretentious nor self-conscious about it. I could see a person of any social station feeling at ease sharing a dinner table with Emma Townsend.

"So, after the supervisor and his crew leave for the day," I offered, after a moment of silence and chewing, "we'll go back and scout out the area around the solar panels. It can't hurt to look. To be truthful, Emma, I'm not getting good vibrations about our search."

"The cavern opening might be significant," Emma said. "Did the solar company know a cavern was part of the ranch property? Maybe they wouldn't have bought it if they'd known."

I considered that. "But they surely had someone walk the property, and the opening wasn't exactly hidden. Wouldn't you think an environmental impact statement of some kind was involved?" Emma agreed that was likely.

"I think we should assume we didn't discover anything today that the solar folks didn't already know about," I said. "The question is, did Pablo discover something that *nobody* knows about? Nobody but the murderer."

We fell silent. "Has it occurred to you, Tak, that Pablo might have been shot *accidentally*?" Emma asked. "Or gunned down by some guy wanting to pursue Pablo's wife? Or maybe killed by someone who doesn't like Latinos in general? People are murdered all the time for reasons that really aren't mysterious."

"I know. That's true," I said, pleased that she'd seen the obvious. "If the Zamarripas hadn't asked me to look into it, I wouldn't have considered the killing extraordinary." We lounged sideways on either side of the picnic table, our legs stretched out on the benches. "But the family *did* ask so I felt obligated to explore the matter until I was satisfied it was a pointless shooting."

We lingered in the shade for another twenty minutes, catching up on mutual friends from the area and enjoying Emma's stories about faculty life on campus. It sounded challenging and satisfying. Who knew anthropologists lived such an interesting life! Working a junkyard was less intriguing, I admitted to myself with chagrin.

Because I didn't want to hassle with the work supervisor once we returned, we killed a little more time. After dumping our plates and empty containers in a trash can, we wandered to the lake. There, we dawdled, tossing pebbles into the clear water and watching the fisherman in the boat reel in a bass large enough to justify the time expended casting for it. When my wristwatch read half past three, we returned to the truck and drove back south.

No workers were around when we arrived, so we explored the ground under the field of panels. Toward the middle of the area, I spotted a dead bird, but closer examination showed it to be a common blackbird. Pablo hadn't been killed over it. At the base of an upright pole, Emma thought she might have found an artifact, but what appeared to be an ancient chipped and flaked arrowhead proved to be a naturally occurring sharp-edged stone.

We searched among the panels with the same care we did the open pasture area, making four sweeps in all, but after forty-five minutes of searching, nothing of consequence had caught our eye. In our final pass, I walked along the outer edge of the erected panels, feeling disconsolate about the day's work. I found myself near the shed and decided to take one more peek at the structure.

"I'll be right back," I told Emma and jogged over to the building. I circled it, tapping the bottom of the walls with the toe of one foot. The plywood seemed solid at every kick-point. It obviously was nailed securely to an interior frame—nailed rather than screwed, that is, because recharging a portable drill's batteries would have been a headache at the remote site.

Then I froze. A small engine had started nearby. I was sure of it. I looked up the slope in the direction of the four-wheeler path, so the sound must have pricked my ears from that direction. I listened, holding my breath to focus my senses. After a moment, I concluded that if an engine *had* been running, it no longer was. Nothing moved or glinted in sunshine at the top of the hill.

Because I was operating that morning in a detective state of mind, killing the engine seemed furtive. On an impulse, I began a jog up the hill along the path. I had no intention of going clear to the top, but I did hope to reach a point where I could identify the machine whose engine had been turned on and then off.

I almost reached the crest before I heard Emma calling. I looked back and saw her standing by the shed, waving her arms and yelling. I scanned the hilltop, saw nothing and nobody, and gave it up. After I reached the bottom again, I still panted from the uphill run, but Emma greeted me with a red face and a frown, as if *she* were the one who'd been running.

"Why were you going up there?" she asked, with wrinkled brow.

"I thought I heard an engine and was curious what it was. It seemed like a good idea to check it out, but I should have told you what I was doing."

Emma stood with hands on hips. She seemed calmer, her face less flushed. "Well, we can come back and check out the hill tomorrow if you want."

"Probably nothing to check. I just wondered who was up there." She shrugged and we headed for the truck.

Back in Uvalde, I dropped her at her mother's house so she could enjoy the evening with family, then I drove home. Though I hadn't planned to spend more time with Emma, I nonetheless was discouraged at the prospect of an evening alone. Otis was happy to see me though.

The following morning, Emma came out of the door as my truck pulled to the curb in front of the house. She turned to give her mother one more hug and then strode toward me with a loose-limbed gait that I continued to find wonderful. I had envisioned it on the drive to Uvalde, in fact. She almost hopped up into the truck and gifted me with what I took to be a flirtatious smile.

"Pretty warm already," she said, snapping on her seatbelt. "Though I don't know how warm exactly. Mom's window thermometer is broken. Has been for a while. It doesn't matter. Warm is warm."

"True enough."

"Did you have a good night?" she asked.

"No, unless you call feeding a dog and watching an old movie a good night."

"You should've stayed for supper. Mom scolded me for not inviting you. I told her I suspected you'd had enough Townsends for one day."

I glanced at her as I steered the truck onto the highway. "I might have been able to suffer another hour of you. You should listen to your mother more often."

She hesitated and then responded in kind. "Well, I'm sorry, too. Maybe we should search more pastures together."

By the time she'd tossed her travel bag and backpack into the rear seat of her car and crawled under the wheel, an unspoken agreement had been reached: We would get together again soon. I felt upbeat as she drove away.

. . .

"How can I help you?" I asked a dark-haired man wearing a red checkered shirt with rolled-up sleeves, faded jeans, boots, and a sweat-stained Western felt hat. He'd clomped to the counter during the lunch hour. Billy and Tomas were eating lunch somewhere in town, leaving me to handle the counter traffic.

"You got any Chevy trucks back there?" the man asked, a sour expression twisting his words. Probably in his 30s, he was of slender build and, judging from his tool-toughened hands and sun-dried face, a ranch hand. He seemed to sweat more than was justified by the temperature reading. Some do.

"A few. What year? What part?"

"1985, '86, somewhere in there. I'm not sure what I need. I'll have to look."

I've told Tomas and Billy not to leave the counter untended, but I had done so before and so had they. Small town and all that, plus it was my prerogative as owner to bend the rules. From a desk drawer, I took out a hand-lettered sign, "Back in a Texas Minute," and hung it from the front of the counter. The man followed me out though the overhead door at the rear of the shop, and we headed for *GM Land*.

"Truck break down? Or are you rebuilding one?"

"Broke down."

I tried a couple other conversational openers, but the man seemed untalkative and I quit trying. I could finish the transaction faster without conversation, anyway. We walked to a row of Chevrolet pickups of 1980s vintage. He looked them over and pointed to a faded red '85 C-10 with an eight-foot bed. It sat in a patch of weeds two rows from the service road.

"Why is it always the one farthest from the road?" I said, grinning, without raising so much as a smile from the man. Sourpuss. We made our way through knee-high weeds and grass. When we reached the trunk's tailgate, I turned and gestured for the man to look for himself.

He stepped past me, walked to one of the doors and wrenched it open. He fumbled inside before stepping back and gesturing for me to look at something. "I think this is it," he said, stepping back from the door.

I eased past him and peered inside the cab, not knowing what he was referring to. "What are you looking..."

The door slammed against my shoulder, bouncing my head off the frame and knocking me sideways. The blow stunned me. I automatically pushed back against the door, feeling a little dizzy, and raised an arm in instinctive response to a loss of balance. When I felt something sting my shoulder, I realized I was being attacked.

I lunged against the door more violently and turned to see the man rearing back again with a tire iron, probably taken from the cab. I threw myself at his chest, deflecting the iron's blow, and struck him in the neck with my fist. The man's hat flew off, but he gathered himself and again swung the tire iron. I dodged but it thudded against my head, anyway, and left me weak-kneed. I staggered around some more and threw fists at him, hoping to connect.

Once more, I felt the iron smack against the side of my head. I recovered and lunged at him, delivering a frenzy of punches. I was operating in pure survival mode at that point and had nothing to lose. When I threw my weight against my assailant yet again, he fell backward, throwing the iron at me as he dropped. I flinched when the tool banged off my shoulder and clattered against the side of the truck.

My ears rang and I stood there panting as he regained his footing and stared at me. I returned the stare as best I could and tried to anticipate what the guy would do next. He surprised me when he turned away, stumbled through the weeds, and ran down the road toward the shop. I didn't move and listened to my ragged breath.

It suddenly seemed important to yell something just to keep him running instead of turning back to finish the job. I took a deep breath, a trembling one, and mustered all the malevolence I could. "You *better* run, you son-of-a-bitch!"

Then I blacked out.

CHAPTER FIVE

The ladybug walked the stem of goosegrass, taking her time, working her way along a main shoot of the weed before coming to an intersecting stem and deciding to veer off on it, a small adventure. *Wonder where this stem leads?* I gleaned vicarious pleasure from her journey until a shout from nearby distracted me.

"Tak! Tak! Where the heck are you?" It sounded like Tomas. What was he doing yelling at the top of his voice? When I tried to respond, my voice was so faint I doubted anyone heard me except the ladybug.

"Tak! Doggone it, are you back here somewhere?" Tomas' voice sounded again, nearer than before.

I took a deep breath and winced when pain streaked through my shoulder. The painful sensation brought me back to the moment. I remembered where I was... and why. I needed help. "Tomas!" I shouted, or believed I had. Maybe I had grunted. I tried again. "Tomas!"

The next thing I knew, Tomas was stomping up to me through the weeds and falling on his hands and knees to peer into my face. "Hang in there, Tak. You're going to be OK." Then he stood and shrieked for Billy to call 911. He refused to let me sit up for fear I would lose consciousness or something. "*Solo descansa, amigo.*"

I didn't protest and lay unmoving in the weeds. He pulled out a blue working man's handkerchief from a rear pocket and slid it under my head so my face wouldn't rest directly on vegetation. The next instant, or so it seemed, EMT personnel were there and nearly as considerate as Tomas had been. They took my vital signs and talked to me with great deference as they rolled me on my back and eased me onto a stretcher.

"You don't have to be so gentle," I whispered to them, feeling more assured minute by minute that I hadn't been hurt. The emergency personnel didn't buy it, though, and treated me as an invalid, which I admitted to myself I might have been right at that moment. My head sure pounded.

Tomas and Billy walked beside the stretcher as I was carried to the yard where an ambulance waited. A Uvalde police officer accompanied us. He had examined the tire tool and the attacker's hat, picking it up by its brim in one gloved hand. I described my attacker as best I could, sharing details about the man's clothing, the color of his hair, his height and weight, and so on. "He might have a black eye tomorrow or a gouge on his cheek. I think I hit him pretty hard."

"Any idea why he attacked you?" the officer asked. I did have an idea but decided not to share it.

· · ·

The following two days and one night in the hospital were tedious. Sleeping. Being poked and tested and scanned. Then more sleep interrupted each hour by nurses making sure I hadn't lapsed into a coma. On the second day, the attending physician told me all the tests indicated I hadn't suffered a concussion thanks to my efforts to ward off the blows.

My shoulder was bruised deep beneath the skin and my head was swollen on the left side, but otherwise I seemed uninjured. The official diagnosis was that I would survive without permanent injury if I took it easy for the next week. Taking it easy was an appealing prescription because I seemed to have no energy. It was all I could do to lie in bed and stare at a flat screen on the opposite wall, watching the screen flicker without engaging with the images or voices.

Whenever my mind searched for a thought, the first one I found always was of the attack. The innocent search for a truck part that preceded it. The unexpected battering. The warmth of blood flowing on my face. Ringing ears. The recurring memories intrigued me at first, then became intrusive and, in the end, frightened me more than I cared to admit.

Friends visited and distracted me, including Bill Castillo from church. Bishop Bill Castillo, that is, long-time leader of the local Church of Jesus Christ of Latter-day Saints congregation. "See? See?" he said, with garrulous melodrama, as we shook hands in greeting. "This is what happens when you don't come to church."

"If I'd known that, bishop, I'd never have skipped a Sunday." We shared a laugh. I hadn't been to church for a couple of years, but Castillo stopped by to see me every few weeks anyway just to check on his back-sliding friend. "Come to give me a blessing?"

"I will if you need one," he said, pausing to see if I would ask for one. I didn't, and he moved on. "What did you do to warrant such a beating?"

I was noncommittal about that, but we visited for twenty minutes. About mutual friends in the congregation. About memories of my parents, both taken prematurely, Dad by leukemia, Mom by a drunk driver. Before moseying out the door, he offered a prayer of thanks for my survival. I felt better for his visit.

A horrified call from Emma turned pleasant once I calmed down the woman. "Everyone knows I have a hard head, Emma. I'm lucky the man targeted it."

"Well, you'd be better served with a thick head of hair," she said, trying to lighten the conversation. "Seriously, Tak, I cried after Mom called. I was terribly upset."

"Crying over me? I'm flattered." She fell silent and I knew she thought I was being flip, so I brought up what I had concluded was the heart of the matter. "I think the attack was a retaliation for our snooping."

Emma still didn't respond. "The thing that got Pablo killed got me banged up. I'm sure of it. It can't have been anything else. That being the case, I don't want you anywhere near Uvalde right now, Emma, or near that solar farm, not until we get to the bottom of this."

"I'm not worried about me, and I doubt you're right about why you were jumped. I think you just ran into a crazy man. You better let the sheriff do the snooping from now on. I mean it." She offered me solace for a quarter of an hour before ending the call.

Later, as I lay in bed wondering why nurses in white always seemed extra attractive, I remembered what Emma had said about turning things over to the sheriff. It wasn't a bad idea. The murder was in the sheriff's jurisdiction. The police weren't making much headway on the assault. Fingerprints on the tire iron weren't on file anywhere. The man's hat bore no identifying marks. DNA material in the sweatband would nail the attacker if the police ever found him, but probably they wouldn't.

If the assailant indeed was a ranch hand, which I felt certain he was, that didn't narrow the field much. Plenty of hired hands in south Texas fit the man's general description, and hired hands came and went all the time, including in and out of Mexico. Unless I bumped into the man in the grocery aisles of HEB and wrestled him to the floor, the chances of catching him were slim.

The sheriff, on the other hand, had more sources on ranches where the guy lives...or lived, for I felt certain he'd taken flight by then. Whoever had sent him to club me surely had sent him across the border for safekeeping. I was confident he was gone.

In the end, I didn't dwell on the idea of involving the sheriff because I had so little to share with him. Intuitive conclusions are just hunches and the sheriff had better things to do with his time than play hunches. I did not have enough evidence to bother the sheriff. Period.

On the second day of the hospitalization, Roque echoed Emma's suggestion, but with a twist: The elder Zamarripa was close to Sheriff Phillipe Rodriquez. "I could ask Dad to have a quiet conversation with the sheriff, ask him to check out the shed."

I rubbed the bandage on the side of my head. Light pressure on the wound soothed me "On what grounds?"

"He wouldn't need any grounds. He's investigating a murder, for gosh sakes! In fact, I imagine the sheriff already has plans to check it out."

"Go ahead and ask," I said, still rubbing my head. "It's worth a shot."

So, two days later, while I recuperated at home with Otis, the sheriff secured permission from NewAge to visit the property. He then approached

Peyton Ruskey at his Uvalde home and asked to inspect his locked shed. According to Roque, Ruskey hadn't hesitated for a milli-second before agreeing to the visit. He'd led a small convoy to the ranch property, with the sheriff and a deputy in one car and Roque in another.

Roque said the rancher had chatted and joked as the three men exited their vehicles and walked across the pasture to the building. Ruskey unlocked and threw open the door. Inside, covering half of the shed's plywood floor, were salt blocks and bags of cattle supplement. Roque, the deputy, and Rodriquez poked among the livestock feed. They walked from wall to wall in the shed's open area and found nothing but dust and cobwebs.

"But why is the stuff there? He doesn't have any cattle in that pasture," I asked Roque when he called with the report.

"Actually, he does," Roque explained. "Well, no, not in the pasture where the solar work is going on, but in the next pasture over. A small herd. He said he had needed a new line shack for supplemental rations, so he'd built and stocked one. He did so after being contacted by NewAge because he didn't believe the deal would go through. When the transaction *did* happen, he was stuck with four-wheeling the stuff to the next pasture as it was needed."

Roque added, chuckling, "It was funny how embarrassed Ruskey seemed about building the shed. He called it a real goof. When the supplement's gone, he'll raze the building, or leave it for NewAge."

So, there it was. I still had nothing. A big fat zero. Peyton Ruskey had been near the top of my suspect list and now I had no list at all. In sheer annoyance, I decided to do what any ordinary person would under the circumstances.

The next morning, I showered, slowly dressed myself in a clean outfit, and drove into Uvalde. There I met Roque. We climbed into his almost-brand-new four-door Chevy pickup and headed for the casino in the border town of Eagle Pass. Maybe fanning a few cards, pulling a few levers, and tossing dice would expunge my sense of failure.

CHAPTER SIX

"We oughta do this more often," Roque said from behind the wheel, sipping from a plastic cup of coffee. "Let's not wait till the next time you're attacked." I managed a faint smile.

In truth, our gambling getaway was a semi-annual event, spring and fall. Neither of us put much trust or money on games of chance, so the outings were a lark. We each considered a hundred dollars a major investment in anything, which is why we never carried more than that into the gambling facility. If we were lucky, fine, but we weren't going to bet a bundle on it.

Kickapoo Lucky Eagle Casino hugged the Rio Grande on the south edge of Eagle Pass. The town was the first U.S. settlement on the border river, dating to the 1840s. It shared the metropolitan area with Piedras Negras on the Mexican side, a city three or four times bigger. One ton of cartel cocaine was alleged to enter the U.S. through Eagle Pass each month, so the casino fit right into the winner-take-all, loser-loses-everything local scene.

I was having difficulty getting comfortable in the truck's soft leather seat. I knew Roque could sense my discomfort from my body language. I wasn't sprawled in the seat as usual nor gesturing as much in conversation. It was as if a slug filled the passenger seat, without the slime.

"Thanks for this, Roque," I said. "I know I'm not very good company right now. I appreciate you treating me to a getaway." He smiled and said nothing.

Exotic livestock grazed on hunting ranches alongside the highway—the graceful ibex and oryx, the rugged wildebeest—but today I didn't gripe as usual about their plight. I seldom hunted, certainly not African game reestablished on Texas ranches, but Roque did stalk the animals whenever a benefactor took him along. Today, neither of us wanted to banter about the merits and demerits of importing animals from Africa for sport-killing.

"Shoulder bothering you? Head hurt?" Roque asked. I moved my head from side to side and fiddled with the wheat-colored Stetson straw hat on my lap. Only by coincidence was it a gambler-style hat. I favored the style for all dress-up occasions.

"I'm OK. How's Pablo's family doing?"

"OK. The funeral was loud, with some wailing. He was only a couple of years older than you and me, you know. Too young to die." Roque's voice betrayed bottled-up emotion that surprised me. I noticed he gripped the wheel tighter than was necessary to keep the truck on course.

"You seem a little emotional. Were you close to him?"

"No, but Maria is pretty good friends with Pablo's wife, Alicia. They see each other at least once a week. Shopping. Girls night out, *en un bar de musica*. Girlfriend stuff. She's hurting for Alicia."

"Sorry." That explained the tension. If Roque's long-time girlfriend was upset, he was sure to be upset. I looked out at the countryside and eased my shoulder into a more comfortable position against the seatback.

The stymied investigation weighed on me, even though the probe was in its early days. My failure to make sense of the murder wasn't more acceptable to me just because law enforcement agencies weren't having more luck. Whiffing at the plate was not something I did in the cases I took on and it bothered me. My local crime-solving rep, such as it was, had been built on succeeding where others failed.

I had figured out, after police couldn't, who stole Bill Ferguson's pickup—a spiteful neighbor who sold it in Mexico. I determined who poached a prize deer on Stu Bender's private hunting preserve—the grandson of a California client, who was terribly embarrassed by the episode. I deductively identified who shot Bill Merriman's stallion—a drugged-up teenager. Small potato crimes, sure, but solvable ones, and I'd solved them when others hadn't.

I called myself a puzzler, puzzling out unknowns the way some people resolved software glitches. Logically. One piece at a time. It was an instinctual gift and I'd been successful often enough to have earned the respect of local cops, who sometimes inelegantly called me "The Junkyard Dick."

They were comfortable with me nosing around a crime scene. I did so only when asked and only half a dozen times a year. After all, most crimes were committed by obvious suspects. There was no mystery involved in them, no Sherlock Holmes deductions required.

That wasn't true this time.

It was possible, of course, that someone just passing through on his way to hunt bighorn sheep in New Mexico decided to practice scoping in his rifle on a distant target and happened to sight in Pablo Munoz. If that described what happened, the murder might never be solved. Yet I was willing to bet a local deer-hunting weapon had fired the .270-caliber bullets that slammed into Pablo, not the gun of some transient hunter.

"I wish we'd found a .270 shell in the pasture," I said aloud, though I had intended only to think it.

"Don't worry about it, Tak. Not today. The point of gambling is to turn off your mind and lose yourself in a quest for instant riches. *Vacia tu mente, amigo.*" Roque grinned. "Empty your mind." I knew his advice was sound.

• • •

The casino's parking lot was half full, a good showing for a Saturday morning. Three chartered buses from San Antonio lined one side of the lot. One of the bus drivers stepped out of his high-riding tinted-window machine, closed the folding door, and trudged toward the casino entrance.

The building was understated in its architecture, but it contained sufficient square footage to house the most popular gambling venues. Its entranceway opened into a large room with bright orange carpet laced with swirling patterns that dazzled the eyes.

"You have your swimsuit made from that carpet?" Roque asked.

"Not bright enough."

We wandered through alleys of electronic gaming machines, probably thousands of them, occasionally pausing to drop in a quarter and pull a lever.

At one machine with glittering lights across the top, we stopped long enough for Roque to sit, feed in quarters, and try to coax the machine to line up apples and kumquats or whatever. The fruit refused to cooperate, and we soon gave it up. A gray-haired woman in a baggy outfit filled the seat as soon as Roque vacated it.

After a futile hour of tempting Lady Luck to give us instant treasure, we treated ourselves to lunch at a Mexican food grille, one of a half-dozen bars and buffets in the building. We built burritos at a counter, sat together at a round table, and ate the stuffed tortillas with a side salad and Cokes. When we returned to the gaming area, the floor was more crowded. It looked like another busload or two of sport gamblers had arrived.

Bingo tables were full. We strolled by them without much interest and entered the poker room, where we had a choice of two games—Limit Texas Hold 'Em, or No Limit Texas Hold 'Em. We sat at one of three Limit tables, each making the minimum fifty-dollar buy-in. With a pot of five hundred dollars at stake, we peeked at our hole cards with high hopes. I had a seven of clubs and a three of hearts. A straight in the making, maybe, but that wasn't going to win much.

Roque was not blessed with a poker face, and I read disappointment all over it. I could tell we each were going to lose our fifty bucks at this table. Fifteen minutes later, we had. "Stupid cards never line up right for me," Roque muttered, sucking from a second can of Coke.

A crowd at a No Limit table got loud so we strolled that way to watch. As we approached the playing area, Roque grabbed my arm, almost spilling his Coke as he did so. I winced and he apologized for wrenching my shoulder. "But looky there," he whispered and gestured with the can.

A man sitting sideways to us at the table made most of the noise, yelling about an errant deal. I wasn't all that interested in the scene. Disappointed card players frequently erupted in displeasure. The dealer seemed unperturbed as well, conditioned to poor losers, though this loser seemed to persist in his complaint longer than most.

"That," said Roque, eyebrows raised, "is someone you know, at least by reputation. Meet Peyton Ruskey."

Just that quick, I was interested. Ruskey was a stocky, red-faced man wearing tinted sunglasses and a black felt hat with a narrow brim. He argued the dealer wasn't shuffling the cards enough between hands. His proof was that he kept receiving unplayable combinations of cards. Were his complaint valid, every losing poker player would have a case.

"Poker is a game built on odds and the odds are astronomical that I would not be given a single face card in four hands," he said with venom in his voice. "I'm not saying you're cheating. I'm saying you're doing an awful job of shuffling!"

A rust-red jacket hung across the back of his chair. Thick arms protruded from his short-sleeved, checkered and multi-colored shirt. He wasn't anyone's stereotype of a smooth gambler. He looked like what he was: a rancher come to the tables to strike it rich. Ruskey pounded once more on the table, pushed back his chair, and stood in undisguised disgust.

"Next time I'll sit at a table where you aren't dealing!" he yelled and snatched up his coat. He strode away from the table headed in our direction. He started to veer around us, then stopped short and stared at Roque, whom he had seen just the day before when Roque and the sheriff had rummaged through his shed. "What are you doing here, Zamarripa? Checking on me?!"

Roque stammered something about their meeting being a coincidence. It felt like the whole roomful of people watched the confrontation. I feared that Ruskey would swing at Roque with me in no physical condition to intervene.

"Two days two meetings? That's more than a coincidence," Ruskey yelled, glaring at Roque and then at me and back to Roque. "You think if you follow me around—you and your snooping friend—that you'll find something connecting me to Pablo? Leave me alone, ya hear?"

"And *you* stay away from my property," he shouted at me, pointing a finger, "or I'll sic the sheriff on you. Both of you!"

He stomped past us and a room that had fallen silent began to resume its chatter. I heard chips again clattering into the center of a table. Roque and I walked from the poker area with as much nonchalance as we could. We only regained our composure after reentering the busy gaming machine alleys. Roque pointed to a lounging area, and we sat on a buttoned-down padded bench.

"Wow!" Roque said, adding a *whoosh* for emphasis. "I didn't see that coming."

I revisited the verbal assault in my mind. It was clear that Ruskey had been surprised to see us and was upset by our presence. I couldn't imagine it was all that uncommon for Uvalde residents to run into each other in the popular casino, yet Ruskey had reacted to seeing us with the same violent spirit he'd exhibited toward the dealer.

"I have a question for you, Roque. I've never seen Peyton Ruskey before today. Not that I know of. So... tell me: How would he recognize me as someone who's been 'snooping' around his property?" I watched Roque's face as he processed the question. He sat up straight and stared back at me.

"That's right," I said. "He must have *seen* me checking out his shack. From the top of the hill. He must have been on his four-wheeler when I thought I heard an engine running. Had I kept running up the hill, I'd have run into *him*—not that his presence would have been incriminating. It was his property, after all. Still, if you'll recall, that occurred one day before someone pounded me with a tire iron. I'm beginning to think Mr. Ruskey sees me as a threat."

"*Vaya!* I think we have run into a man full of guilt," Roque said.

I looked around the room. My thoughts rolled like the apples, grapes and oranges on the electronic machines. *If I can get things lined up in my mind,* I thought with new confidence, *I still might hit the jackpot.*

CHAPTER SEVEN

After a few minutes of reflecting on the run-in with Ruskey, we moseyed toward the entranceway. An older man looked spiffy in slacks and a sport coat as he gambled away his Social Security allotment. As we passed the slot machine where he was seated, he hollered. Both Roque and I jumped sideways, still jittery after the confrontation.

It turned out the guy was celebrating a win. Quarters began to bounce down a metal tube into a collection bowl at the bottom, some of them careening onto the fluorescent carpet. The man kept yelling in jubilation as he cupped the bowl to contain the quarters. He laughed like he'd won a million dollars. It was more like a hundred, in all probability, but a win is a win. We congratulated him, picked up the handful of quarters on the carpet, and handed them over.

"My lucky day!" he exulted. I was thinking the same thing.

We continued on our way and just before exiting the building, Roque stopped without preamble and asked me to hold on a minute. He turned and headed back into the room, disappearing down another alley. What was this, a run for another Coke?

While I waited, I wandered among the slot machines and marveled at the marketing of this thing called gaming and formerly called gambling. Slot machines were a hoot. Bright lights. Colorful images. Buoyant language. All of it a gratuitous distraction from reality. All of it hiding six-hundred-to-one-odds. Slot a dollar six hundred times, actuaries tell us, and a person *might* win back six hundred dollars. Crazy.

Yet universal belief in beating the odds was reinforced every time a person bought one lottery ticket and won a million dollars or dropped four quarters into a slot and won five hundred dollars. The positive way to look at it was that gamblers weren't dumb. Their hope was boundless, that's all. Was there something wrong with giving people a reason to hope? I supposed not, unless the kids were home hungry.

I saw Roque striding toward me. He wiggled his eyebrows. I knew what *that* meant and it wasn't that he was flirting.

"Have I got something to tell you!" he said and walked on past me. I followed him out the door and across the parking lot to his truck. My shoulder was stiff and aching and my head had begun to pound again. I looked forward to resting in the truck's comfortable seat for a couple of hours.

Several more buses lined the lot, a reflection on the human condition. There it was a beautiful, clear, warm Texas Saturday in May and hundreds of people were choosing to spend it indoors in a glittery world of artifice and false hope. So be it.

"Okay, mystery man," I said, easing myself onto a leather seat warmed by the sunshine, "what's the revelation? Reveal all and quit your gloating."

He wrinkled his brow. "*Quien? Yo?* Revelation? I'm no prophet, but I'm a pretty good detective. So, one detective to another, here's the deal." He started the truck, let the air conditioning kick in and eased out of the crowded parking lot before he said more.

He told me he had remembered seeing another person at the table with Ruskey, an ag equipment sales rep from Del Rio who'd sold a tractor or two to the Zamarripas. After the run-in with Ruskey, Roque had been way more interested in leaving the poker hall than in saying hello to the guy.

When he returned to the poker room moments before, Roque had found the man just stepping away from the table. "Apparently, he made a little money playing the cards today, a couple hundred dollars. He said he's had better days. But here's what's interesting: He doubted Ruskey ever experienced a worse day. It seems our friend dropped more than five thousand buckaroos today. That's five thousand, as in a five followed by three zeroes."

I slapped my hat against my knee. "Five thousand bucks! Your friend was sure about the size of the loss?"

"Yes, sir, because when Ruskey sat down he bragged about how much he had in chips. He said it in a way that was meant to intimidate his fellow players, to let them know he was serious about winning. And then they all watched the big pile of chips dwindle, little by little, hand after hand."

I thought about it. "That may have been some of the money NewAge paid him for his land." Roque turned onto the highway leading northeast to Uvalde and gunned the engine. The ride home was going to seem shorter because they had something new to talk about.

Roque nodded. "Probably. But all of us in the neighborhood know Ruskey ranch is marginal in its profitability. He's never had the money for the capital investments that make cattle operations productive. He gets by. My salesman friend says Ruskey paid off some of his equipment debt after the sale, but not all of it. He seriously doubts Ruskey has thousands of dollars lying around to lose in poker games."

"So, this was a real loss."

Roque shook his head. "That's the even more interesting thing. My friend says Ruskey seemed upset about getting poor hands, very upset, as we saw, but reacted casually to the money disappearing. After the first couple of hands, Ruskey said something like, 'There's more where that came from.' He was mad about the cards dealt him, but not particularly upset about losing the money."

Neither of us spoke for the next mile as we tried to plumb Ruskey's frame of mind.

"Does your sales rep regularly play cards at the casino?"

"He must. He says he's shared a table with Ruskey before, mostly over the last month or so."

"So, this is a recent habit, Ruskey's gambling?"

"*Tal vez.* Maybe."

A few miles farther on, the speculation about Ruskey petered out and conversation turned to the progress of Roque's latest novel, or, rather, his lack of progress. Roque was reluctant to talk about his writing, which I respected. He and I both remembered the wife of a local restaurant owner who referred to herself in public as a writer even though her authorship amounted to a few rhymes published in a local church publication.

Roque's mantra was, "Write. Don't talk about writing." He spoke more freely about it with me than with most of his friends. Before we reached Uvalde, he confessed he was struggling. "I guess you could call it writer's block, but deep down I think it might be me not having anything to say. Either that or a lack of talent to say it." He shrugged.

"Well, it's not a talent problem," I said and reached across to squeeze his upper arm in reassurance. "I've read your stuff, Roque. And I've read enough contemporary and classic writers to compare your writing and theirs. You express yourself well. Heck, I'm so confident of your eventual success, I'll pay you right now for a copy of your first novel."

"*Gracias,* Tak."

"But if you're having a mental block," I continued, "you need to get over it, or get around it, or whatever. Lots of good writers run into walls. Maybe it's a plot problem. Maybe you need to tinker with the plot."

His book was set in south Texas and was a contemporary tale of a young man from the Texas panhandle trying to make a life for himself and his bride in San Antonio. Roque had shown me a snippet of an early chapter where the main character, named Tolson, was working a second job as a bouncer at a raucous dance hall-bar. The character was a Jehovah's Witness and the chapter concerned his wrestle to reconcile religious convictions with the need to pay the rent.

"No, I believe the story is structured well, plotted well," he said, glancing my way. "I believe in the characters. They've become real to me. They're almost friends of mine. But I'm having trouble telling their stories. It feels too contrived.... Ah, you don't want to hear all this."

I looked at Roque who refused to look across the seat at me. He was a proud man and upset.

"Listen, my friend, if you believe in your story and in your characters, just let them tell it. Relax instead of beating up on yourself. Writing isn't easy, but there's no expiration date on creativity. You have years to polish your novel. Your *first* novel. They say the second one comes easier. Don't worry about it."

He didn't say anything, but he looked full of thought. I was glad I'd given him reason to think.

• • •

After Roque dropped me off at my truck, I bought milk and yellow corn tortillas at HEB and headed for home. On an impulse, I turned into the drive-through at Whataburger and ordered a double-meat Whataburger Jr. and French fries for me, and a Justaburger for Otis. I knew I shouldn't have gotten the fattening fries. In a magnificent demonstration of willpower, I ate only half of them before clearing the city limits.

I arrived home before seven o'clock to a leaping welcome from Otis. In my absence, he once again had protected the place from armadillos and feral pigs, and squirrels didn't appear to have invaded the house. The dog clearly was worth his weight in hamburger.

"Here you go, buddy. You're a wonderful watchdog. I don't know what I'd do without you looking out for the property." I separated the buns from the meat and pickles and pieced them all. Otis could consume a Justaburger in two slurpy bites, as if the animal had picked up on my eating habits. I was trying to teach him to be more disciplined and was pleased when he needed five gulps to down the disassembled hamburger.

As I keyed opened the door, the dog was slurping fresh water before heading to the end of the porch for a quick nap. Eating always seemed to wear him out.

I set the bag of food on the table by the chair and poured myself a plastic container of iced tea. After carrying it to the easy chair, I slumped into it, and sighed as if needing to recover from a long day of physical exertion. I rotated an upper arm and felt the bruise release a little more of its grip on my shoulder. My head still ached under the bandage.

I ate the hamburger with all the satisfaction of a hungry boy eating a Christmas day meal while gazing at opened presents. Clearly, the sandwich didn't warrant such over-the-top celebration. My juvenile sensory system regularly victimized me, picking up on simple sensations and magnifying them into feelings of wondrous well-being.

Can life get any better than this? I mused half-seriously, biting into the hamburger and sipping cold tea. After reflection, I appended the thought: *I sure hope so.*

CHAPTER EIGHT

The incessant cooing of turtle doves awakened me, a sure sign I had overslept. I listened a while to the lovebirds and then moved to the edge of the twin bed. Because prudent Uncle Portis slept alone, he didn't splurge all those years ago on a queen-sized bed. I still was weighing whether to switch out his twin bed for something larger. I might never have another sleeping partner but rolling over in bed was easier on a wider mattress.

I set my feet on the rug next to the bed, hands on knees, and felt a momentary impulse to hop up and drive to church. I hadn't had that feeling in a while. The attack in the salvage yard precipitated the change, I supposed, the blows to my head a painful reminder of mortality. And the bishop's visit had comforted me more than I might have expected.

But no church today. I dressed in lounging clothes, feeling pleased that my shoulder was freer of pain. The bathroom mirror showed my head to be less swollen under the bandage and the bruises a lighter shade of ugly. My stubby whiskers didn't need trimming back, or anyway I put off doing so. I poured a bowl of cornflakes and took it to the front porch. While Otis crunched through a morning ration of bagged food, I sat in Uncle Portis' rocking chair, eating and thinking.

Bees swarmed the white blossoms of the magnolia tree next to the front of the house. The nectar-gathering insects darted in and out of the blooms, full of industry. They made me feel even lazier sitting in the shade of my west-facing porch, rocking back and forth without evident purpose. Of course, rocking back and forth *never* actually gets one anywhere, but this morning's rocking struck me as particularly pointless.

I scratched behind the dog's ears when it strolled over for companionship. We were a lazy pair. His eyes pleaded with me for a walk. So, I carried the bowl inside, rinsed it, grabbed a hat, and we headed out to the pasture behind the house. Otis trotted ahead and periodically ran back to jump against me and trot away again. A fun, fun dog.

I unhooked the pasture gate for us, and we moseyed north into my thirty-five acres of south Texas soil. We moved past clumps of blackbrush and sumac, through stretches of buffalo grass, and under a live oak whose branches seemed to defy gravity in their undulating horizontal reach. I admired several Beauty Berry shrubs near the western edge of the property that were favorites of wandering white-tailed deer. Certain times of the year, hungry deer virtually stripped the plants of their lavender fruit.

Otis padded down the bank of a dry gulch that foamed with runoff after heavy rains, but normally was no more than a pleasing variant in the landscape, cutting southeast across flat terrain. The dog poked its head into a guajillo thicket on the other side. The bush wasn't good for livestock but was great for honeybees. Preserving it was my contribution to the local honey industry.

Otis lifted his leg to fertilize the bush and we began to walk the gulch back toward the house. A black-tailed jackrabbit sprang from hiding and Otis gave chase for half a minute before returning to my side with tongue lolling from the side of his muzzle.

The Sunday morning quiet began to disappear in an approaching racket and then a full-fledged roar. I looked up to see a bright-yellow needle-nosed spray plane winging straight at me at an altitude of perhaps a hundred feet. I threw up my hands and the pilot wagged his wings once before roaring past and dipping lower above the soybean field across the road. I watched as a slice of the field was dusted. The pilot pulled up at the other end of his pass, banked around, and headed back in my direction.

It was either Harvey or Chili in the pilot's seat because I knew the plane was homebased at the Uvalde airport. While it was unusual for it to be in the air on a Sunday, the fertile valley's farmers sometimes had urgent need of an application of insecticide or a topdressing of fertilizer. The plane roared overhead while Otis and I continued our walk.

I never relaxed entirely in a pasture out of respect for rattlesnakes. Otis usually gave me early warning when he spotted one, barking and jumping around. Because he'd experienced the rattlers coiling in self-defense and springing at him, he always protested their presence at a safe distance.

The snakes seemed to feel at home in the little pasture. Because it was under-grazed, it offered extra cover and was close enough to ranch buildings to attract the spillover of rodents and other yummy rattler fare. The rattlers and I had an understanding: They didn't show up around the house and I didn't go after them in the pasture.

The dog and I passed a thorny amargosa shrub and a pair of short mesquite trees that I made a mental note to remove in the near future. It was a philosophical thing. I'd never understood why God in His wisdom had placed so many thorny and prickly plants in this part of the world. I felt the same about rose bushes. What was the point of mixing delicate blossoms and wounding spikes?

Thirty yards from the gate, the property's old well beckoned me. It pre-dated my uncle's ownership of the property and still had the original cranking mechanism to pull buckets of water to the surface. I peered into the well and could see the bottom some fifteen feet below, dusty dry as ever. I hoped to look into it one day and find a pool of water.

Several steps farther ahead, something glinted in the grass and I stopped, stepped back, and located the source of the reflected light. A spent cartridge, one of several nine-mm shells littering the ground from handgun target practice. I hadn't been shooting for several weeks, but the brass still was shiny.

I picked it up and rolled it between thumb and finger as I strolled. Then and there I decided to return to the scene of the crime against Pablo, to the pasture by the solar field. I would walk it with a dozen other people and put eyes on the ground. If two or more bullets were fired from a rifle in the direction of Pablo, chances are at least one of the shells hadn't been recovered by the shooter.

Back at the house, Otis and I stanched our thirst, and I took the guitar to the still shady porch and began plunking. Danged bluesy chords kept coming from the instrument. I was determined to compose an upbeat, happy song. Maybe something about walking the dog in the pasture on a Sunday morning, though that still struck me as melancholy. The cell phone sounded.

"Hi, Tak. What're you doing?" Emma.

"Otis and I have taken a walking tour of my acreage and are back on the front porch talking about it. What are you doing?" She said she was packing a bag and preparing to drive to Uvalde for a couple of weeks. The news left me tongue-tied.

"Hello? Did you fall out of your rocker?"

I was having none of her impishness. "You shouldn't come here, Emma. As much as I'd like to see you, this isn't a good time. There's something going on here and you don't need to be involved in it." It was a churlish response, but I couldn't help it.

This time Emma was the one slow to respond. "You sound like a dad admonishing his daughter. I'm pretty sure you're not old enough to be my father."

"Well..."

"Well, nothing!" she said, not at all impishly. "I appreciate your concern for my safety. That's sweet of you. But I have two weeks of vacation coming and I'm going to spend it with Mom. Plus, I'm thinking you need my help to solve this murder, that is, if you persist in diving into it. I don't suppose you're prepared to admit needing my help."

We bantered a bit, but I was softening. I would love having her around, but it was quite clear that serious players were involved in the shooting of Pablo. She was too nice a gal to get "bumped off" for being in the wrong place at the wrong time, and I told her so.

"Hey, I'll decide what reason justifies getting 'bumped off.' In fact, I've already decided that helping solve Pablo's murder is an entirely worthwhile reason. So, like it or not, I'm coming home. Listen to me! I can't believe it! I'm practically *asking* you if I can visit my own mother!"

I hesitated. "Well, I am not going to involve you any further in my investigation. Maybe take you to a movie or something now and then. That's the best I can do."

"Hell no! I'm your Girl Friday or whatever they used to call it. Your right-hand man. I'm your helper and you damned well better let me help."

"You cuss like a detective, I'll give you that." And then we both walked back our truculence and agreed to disagree about the wisdom of her helping me. She would arrive that afternoon. I told her I would stop by her mom's place that evening to welcome her back.

After the call ended, I picked up the guitar and began to strum and hum while I ran the conversation through my mind. I guffawed then, because I realized my plunking was chirpy and that I hummed a frolicsome melody. Where had the melancholy gone?

• • •

I held off driving to Emma's mother's place until after seven p.m., making some phone calls and then piddling around the house. Sweeping floors. Hauling rugs outside and shaking them. The volume of dust that erupted from each rug was an indictment of my housekeeping. But, hey, I kept my kitchen sink clear of dirty dishes and my bed made.

On the off chance that Emma might stop by sometime in the next week, I decided to wash the pane of glass on the front door and knock down cobwebs in the corners of the ceiling. I even laundered the bed sheets for no real reason other than being caught up in a cleaning expedition. The house needed a good airing and the possibility of a visit by Emma was an excuse to do it.

In late afternoon, I showered and dressed in clean jeans and a collared shirt. Otis sent me off with excited barking. Even he seemed to like the idea of a budding relationship with Emma. I bumped across the railroad tracks and onto the highway and headed for town. In Uvalde, I pulled into the salvage yard.

There's something spooky about being alone in an auto junkyard in the quiet of Sunday evenings, a place where the souls of Packards and Pacers cry out for remembrance and everything is moldering from rust to dust, like the Bible more-or-less says. I had long felt that way, and today as I unlocked the front door of the office, I also felt antsy. Would someone be waiting for me behind the door?

Ridiculous notion. Nevertheless, I banged the door against the wall when I swung it open and glanced behind it as I stepped through. I hated that the attack on me earlier in the week had robbed me of some more innocence.

On a shelf behind the counter, I found what I sought. Wrapping it in brown paper, I tied twine around it, fashioned a large bow and left the office with the package in hand. When I stepped back into the sunshine of the yard, a flush of relief swept over me, which rankled me anew. *I should be able to feel safe in my own place of business!*

Across town, Emma greeted me and glanced at the package. I joined her and her mother in a living room just off the foyer of the house. The couch I sat on was a rich blue with brocaded flowers on its cushions and back. It seemed almost new compared to the rest of the room's well-worn furniture and I imagined the sofa being worn out by friends and family visiting a congenial host.

"I suppose you're going to keep us guessing about what's in that package?" Emma said, folding one leg under her as she sat in a soft armchair.

"Well, it's a small gift I thought you might be able to utilize, Mrs. Townsend," I said, handing the package to Emma's mother. She returned my smile, untied the twine, and lay open the paper. Her face brightened.

"It's a dial window thermometer, probably fifty years old," I said, "a Conant Custom Brass unit made in Vermont. I found it awhile back in a box of junk from a hardware store. Its readings seem to be accurate."

"How nice, Tak! Thank you very much. Emma must have told you mine was broken." She glanced over at Emma and then raised the thermometer for a closer look. "Of course, I see it only gives readings up to one hundred twenty degrees Fahrenheit. Think that's high enough for south Texas?" We all smiled at that, and I accepted her thanks and Emma's gratitude for my thoughtfulness.

"You even provided screws for mounting it outside a window," Emma said. "Do you have a screwdriver small enough for those screws, Mom?" I lifted a screwdriver from my shirt pocket, and we laughed some more.

CHAPTER NINE

Ninety minutes later, after affixing the swiveling thermometer to the wall outside the kitchen window and checking it for visibility from inside, I again warned Emma about the potential for violence. I admonished her for putting herself in harm's way. She patted me on my shoulder and shook her head. "I can take care of myself." I had tried.

In parting, I reassured Mrs. Townsend that I would not let her daughter get herself in trouble, and Emma walked me to the curb. She moved with the easy-going confidence of a woman actively being courted.

This was the moment where a woman was in control. She could say yes to more involvement or say no, string a man along or snip away his last fragile hope for romance. The options belonged to the woman. I wouldn't go so far as to characterize Emma's attitude at that moment as smug, or gloating, but I was smitten, and she darned well knew it.

"Thanks, Tak, for that thoughtful gift. Mom really appreciates it and so do I. I don't care what everyone says, you're a nice guy."

"Yep, everyone else has a bad read on me. So, you're coming back to the pasture with us?"

"You bet. That's why I'm here," she said with enthusiasm and touched my arm. The touch felt good.

"I'll call you tomorrow," I said, walked around the truck, slid in, waved goodbye and drove away, missing the woman already and looking forward to another pasture search with her.

• • •

I had arranged for a search party. Roque and a sheriff's deputy I knew were enthusiastic about the idea, Roque dubbing the search party a "posse." We would walk the area around where Pablo's body was found in search of a spent rifle cartridge. At least two shots had been fired, probably from somewhere higher on the solar farm acreage. If we found just one shell that hadn't been recovered by the shooter, we would have a solid piece of evidence to begin tracking a murder weapon.

The search was unlikely to produce anything, of course. I knew the odds, which were higher than anything gamblers faced at the casino. It was akin to looking for the proverbial needle in a haystack. Nevertheless, it was a box in the investigation process that needed to be checked.

I could have marshaled a search party by calling on friends, but I wanted official sanction in case a spent cartridge was discovered. The fact is, a found casing would need to be bagged by someone with authority—like a deputy—and the location officially marked. Found evidence without official certification was no more valuable in a courtroom than hearsay. I was told the sheriff had been considering such a grid-by-grid search and supported the initiative.

So, at nine a.m. the next day, Emma and I and ten other men and women who agreed to help were clumped together at the west end of the NewAge property listening to Sheriff's Deputy Miguel Santiago explain how he wanted us to proceed.

"We walk slowly in a straight line so that the plane of discovery is clearly defined. In front of the line is unknown. Behind is clean. If one or more people in the line must work their way around a bush or a tree, everyone should take notice, and the line at that moment will move forward no faster than those slowed by the bush. Understood? Whatever you do, don't leave your place. Maintain the integrity of the search line."

Santiago spoke with the authority of one whose previous searches had succeeded in locating discarded murder weapons, incriminating personal effects, and, yes, bodies. "We walk five feet apart and each person is responsible for the five feet to his or her right. Got that? Those five feet belong to you. Don't worry about what's left of you. Someone else is scouring that area. All right? It's important that we proceed methodically."

I stood by Emma and Roque at the edge of the group and said nothing. This was the deputy's show. He knew what he was doing. We then formed a line, and I found a place next to Emma. Roque was near the other end of the string of people.

We lined up at the west edge of the solar panels and began a sixty-foot-wide eastward sweep. Movement was ragged at first and then grew more uniform. The tension ordinary people were feeling about being part of something extraordinary died away within a few minutes. Each person realized he could do it and the search took on aspects of a personal mission.

We swept west to the front entrance, pivoted north, and returned east along a parallel path sixty feet wide. Back and forth the group moved, eyes on the ground. Between sweeps, everyone sipped from water bottles or canteens.

We all were keyed up, of course, and when someone came across the skull of a rabbit, conversation ensued before dying away. A crumpled beer can spiked on a thornbush was a source of chit-chat for a few steps. A spent shotgun shell raised a holler from the woman who found it. The deputy duly marked the location with a yellow-ribboned wooden stick and bagged the shell, but no one thought it relevant to the search.

Our first sweep to the east carried us between the shed and the edge of the solar panel field. As we passed the construction crew, the superintendent worked hard to keep the crew laboring. He had been told about the search party. We entered the shallow canyon beyond the solar panels and the searcher passing nearest the cavern opening glanced at it but continued ahead. The group had been forewarned about the sight. Emma and I exchanged knowing looks.

Our searches continued as we scrutinized the gentle slope north of the solar panels. We ended a rotation at the western fence when the noon hour was nearly upon us and marked the line for the next search before taking a break. Two of the searchers walked to their SUV and drove it over to us. Cold beer and water and sandwiches were dispersed from the rear cargo area.

People sat in the shade of the SUV or moved to a grassy area where they could rest comfortably in the sun.

Emma sat on the ground in the shade, her back to a rear tire, jeaned legs stretched out in front. She sipped a cold can of beer and closed her eyes. I watched her from a few feet away where I stood with Roque. I wiped the cold plastic water bottle against my neck and shivered at the touch of it, then drank about half the bottle, some water dribbling onto my beard.

"Whaddya think?" Roque asked and bit into a turkey and lettuce sandwich. His T-shirt was soaked through, as was mine. I chewed and swallowed some of my sandwich.

"I think everyone's doing a great job of keeping their eyes on the ground. We've made real progress in eliminating possible shooting locations," I said. "Could we have missed something? Sure. But we're almost as likely to have *not* missed something. I'm glad we're doing it."

"You ought to tell Miguel that, so he can commend everyone," he said.

"Tell me what?" Santiago spoke from behind, clapped a hand on my shoulder, and stepped between us. A few days ago, his friendly shoulder gesture would have stung.

"Tak was just saying he thinks everyone is doing a good job. I suggested you tell them that just to keep up their spirits," Roque said.

The officer nodded. He looked hot. He wore a short-sleeved uniform shirt, but gun, radio, three-foot-long marking dowels and assorted other paraphernalia attached to his belt surely added discomfort on a ninety-degree day. His smile was bright as always, however, and his dark eyes twinkled. "I *will* tell them. They're doing a great job."

I took a sip of water. "Think we're going to find anything?"

The deputy shrugged. "I think we are going to look carefully. If I was the bad guy, I'd be worried. That's what I think."

The drinks and food revived the volunteers. Bottles and sandwich wrappings were collected and placed in the back of the SUV. After the deputy encouraged the searchers to stay focused, we began to re-form our line. Those who had been sitting got to their feet and fell into line, their faces showing determination. Conversation and laughter burbled up and down the line. Emma and I concluded we would rather be walking then standing still in the heat.

Two more passes followed, each of them crossing the four-wheeler trail running up the hill from the shed. The top of the slope came closer. Then Richard Rowen got a thorn in his boot.

His position was near the center of the group. He cried out when he discovered the thorn. It had penetrated most of the boot's sole just in front of the heel, but had stopped short of puncturing his foot, for which Rowen expressed gratitude.

So, we stood in place. I took the moment to gaze down the hill. The shed was some two-hundred feet below me and the solar panels another fifty feet or so away. The area where Pablo's body had fallen was to the left of the shed amid the panels.

"Long ways down there," Emma commented, following my gaze. "Are we out of range of a rifle shot?"

"Oh, no. A hundred or hundred and twenty yards isn't a long shot for a seasoned hunter. Someone scoping in on Pablo from here easily could have hit him. I couldn't, but I imagine some of the hunters in this line could."

Emma tilted back her hat and wiped her brow with a red handkerchief. She tucked the hanky in her hip pocket, her eyes locked on me the whole time. "You're not getting discouraged, are you?"

I shrugged. "Probably a little. Hope, you know, that's what keeps you going. Hope. We're going to run out of ground in another couple of sweeps and that will be that. I mean, the shot *could* have come from across the fence on Zamarripa land for all we know. I just hope we're looking in the right spot."

We now call it the lucky thorn, the three-inch spike that Rowen managed to step on at just the wrong angle so it flipped up and buried itself in his boot. After he sat, wiggled the thorn loose and yanked it out, he got to his feet and started to straighten up. Hands on knees, he stopped and stared at the ground in front of him. "I don't believe it. Look at this, deputy!"

Santiago was several paces away and walked without urgency to where Rowen was bent over with a big grin on his face. The deputy knelt and peered at the ground, then stood and shouted for everyone to stay in place.

"Looks like we have a rifle cartridge, but there may be others. So, stay right where you are. We'll continue the sweep in a moment."

Someone whooped, which made me smile. Others also cheered the discovery. Roque and I saluted each other from a distance. Emma was subdued, her exhaustion showing. We all stood more-or-less where we had stopped, particularly searchers on either side of Rowen. They stared at the ground in hopes of seeing a second cartridge.

Santiago picked up the shiny brass shell using a pen and sealed it in a bag. He drew out another three-foot-long wooden rod from his belt and punched it into the ground. The yellow banner atop it glistened in the sun. Then he circled Rowen several times, widening his walk each time around. The ground cover was rough enough that he could see no identifiable footprints.

The deputy instructed us to resume our search at half the pace we had been moving because another shot could have been fired either before or after the one that kicked out this shell. "We are in a sight-line here and it's critical we scrutinize the ground with extra care."

So, we did, creeping now, inches at a time. Breath wasn't bated. It was too hot for that, but hearts were beating slightly faster than normal, and nerves tingled. When Rowen shouted that he had found another one, Roque shouted back at him, "Dead-Eye Dick!" and the legend of Rowen the Cartridge Hunter was born.

Santiago said the casings were for .270 bullets, the same type of ammunition recovered from Pablo's body. I was elated. Especially interesting to me was that the shells were found just a few yards from the four-wheeler trail leading down to the shed.

CHAPTER TEN

We completed the sweep and made one more pass through the pasture without discovering anything noteworthy. Santiago dismissed his undeputized searchers and we celebrated our success. Finding what we were looking for felt like a triumph, especially when compared to the ho-hum tasks facing most of us the rest of the day.

As we broke up, I couldn't contain my satisfaction. I tossed my hat in the air and felt justified doing so. We descended the hill toward my truck. Emma still was subdued, obviously hot and tired. Roque gleefully punched my uninjured shoulder and grabbed Emma's arm, chiding her for not finding anything. I wanted to hug her as a reward for her efforts but decided to keep walking.

"Of course, we still don't know who fired the bullets," I said. "We still don't have the gun. What we found today helps, but it doesn't solve anything."

"You are such a party-pooper!" Roque responded. "Aren't the shells going to tell us something about the shooter? Couldn't they have fingerprints?"

"They could," I said, "but if they're Ruskey's fingerprints, for example, it's a big *so what*? This was *his* land. He might have been practice shooting here. Now if Ruskey has a .270 and a ballistics guy can match his rifle to the *bullets*, then we would have something."

Emma seemed to be reviving. "Hey, Roque's right. What we found is significant. I'm saying that as a certified archaeological detective."

"I see. Maybe the sheriff should just arrest Ruskey today and not bother to wait for actual evidence linking him to the murder," I said.

At the cattleguard, Roque roared away on his Honda motorbike. Emma and I rolled out to the highway and drove south toward Uvalde. The truck's air conditioner never worked well, but it worked well enough to cool our bodies a few degrees and cool our conversation, too. We rode along for a mile or so without saying anything of consequence. We were happy to be out of the sun and resting. Forensics was tiring work.

"You're hopeful again, aren't you, Tak?" She looked at me sideways, unsmiling and appearing a bit haggard. It occurred to me that professors of archaeology may not get out of their classrooms often enough to build up stamina, though Emma looked fit to me.

"I *am* hopeful. My working theory has been strengthened. I still have no idea why the shooter targeted Pablo. For all I know, it could have been a crime of prejudice. But those shells suggest it wasn't someone target-shooting from the highway on his way through Texas."

Emma said nothing. She turned to look out the side window and spoke without turning back toward me. "Makes me so sad. An ordinary and good guy being killed before he could live his simple life. So unfair."

As we entered town, Emma said she was too tired to do anything else with me today, so I dropped her at the curb at her mother's house. Before walking to the front door, she gave me a gentle smile and I rode to the salvage yard basking in the gentleness of it. I really would have preferred spending the rest of the day with her, but I couldn't have justified it. Work called.

When I entered the office, Tomas looked up from the counter with a surprised look. He hadn't expected me back today, which said something about my recent irregularity as a workplace colleague. He was pleased when I told him about the discovery of the shells. He related that a Munoz family member had asked him the night before if anyone was really looking for Pablo's killer. "You know, *really* looking." He had assured the person the investigation was still active.

"I bet you're feeling pretty good, aren't you?" he said to me.

I admitted I was and that I would have been extremely disappointed had we turned up nothing. "But needles are hard to find in haystacks, you know?

Thank goodness we had Dead-Eye Dick Rowen." I recounted the drama of Rowen's starring role in the search. The semi-retired high school math teacher and basketball coach was a gadfly. We knew he would never let the community forget what he'd done today.

Later, as closing time neared, I asked Tomas and Billy to hold on for a few minutes. Tomas shrugged. Billy was cool with it. I suspected their nonchalance masked excitement. They were hoping I would give them inside dope on the investigation. Tomas' wife pretty much worshipped her husband, and if he could take home a gossipy scoop about Pablo's murder, she'd be extra pleased with her man.

Billy sprawled across the counter wiping oily liquid from his fingers after washing them vigorously in a pan of solvent. I sometimes doubted he ever again would have clean hands. Oil and grease had left the skin with a gray cast that only a zombie might love.

"I appreciate you covering for me here lately, guys," I said, hopping up to sit on the counter. Billy took three steps back and dropped into a chair next to Tomas. "Me trying to help the Zamarripas, and then getting hurt and all, it's taking me out of the yard a lot more than I like. Thanks for picking up the slack."

"Well, you better get back on the stick, Tak, or me and Tomas may have to let you go," Billy deadpanned.

"And I won't blame you. I'll try to shape up. Thanks for the counsel there, Billy." Billy slapped Tomas on the arm and mock-whispered that maybe now was a good time to ask for a raise. Tomas rolled his eyes. I would miss that kid when he headed off to school.

"Anyway, first I wanted you to know that you're pretty much up to speed about the murder. You know what I know. The evidence we recovered today might shed some light on how the shooting occurred, but everything still is speculative. I'm interested in what the sheriff does next."

"Like what?" Tomas asked.

"I don't know, but somehow he needs to connect those shells to a gun. I'm not sure how he'll try to do that. The point is, the murder still is a mystery." We all shook our heads at the possibility of the murderer getting away with his crime.

"Second, I want to talk to you about security. About safety. *Your* safety. There's a bad guy or a team of bad guys in the Uvalde neighborhood, in case you haven't noticed. They've expressed their irritation to me for sticking my nose into their business."

Tomas raised his hand, not to ask for permission to speak, but to interrupt me. "You're convinced that's why the guy jumped you?"

"I don't think there's any question about it. I don't have a lot of enemies. The attack was a warning. Or maybe it was intended to shut me up. I was lucky." I meant it. If my attacker had been more competent, he would have dropped me with one good blow to the back of my head as I peered into the cab of the truck and then pounded in my skull as I lay there.

"Here's the bigger picture: The bad guys still are running loose. There's nothing to stop them from coming back. Do I think they *will* come back? No, I don't expect them to return. They couldn't cover up another attack as a simple robbery or something. It would just bring more heat on them."

"But..." I left the word hanging. I looked squarely in the eyes of Tomas and then Billy. "They *could* come back. I want you guys prepared."

I stepped down from the counter and walked to my desk, where I slid open a side drawer and pulled out my Ruger .357 revolver. I gripped it from the side and held it up to them like a badge. "You know I have this gun here, of course, and it's loaded. Six rounds."

I carried the revolver to the counter, placed it on a shelf under the countertop and covered it with a trade magazine. "I want the gun here for the time being, OK? You guys know how to shoot."

I leaned back against the counter. "So, tell me, Tomas, if a guy walks in here with a gun, points it at you, and tells you to hand over the cash box, what do you do?" We'd been through this before, but not since the attack.

"Give him the cash box."

"Absolutely. No heroics. Leave the gun alone. Heck, offer him some M&Ms from the bowl. Just do whatever you can to encourage him to take the money and leave without firing his weapon."

I looked at Billy, who was paying close attention. "On the other hand, once he's run out the door, you should pick up the revolver and have it handy while you're calling 911. You know, just in case he decides to come back in. Got that, Billy?"

"Got it, boss."

I hopped back up on the counter. "But here's a second scenario. Let's say a man walks in here with a smile on his face and says he wants to go back in the yard and look at some old Buick or something. For some reason you really can't explain, you don't like the situation. It feels threatening somehow. What do you do?"

Neither man spoke.

"You say, 'No.' You say, 'We're not showing any cars today. Please come back tomorrow.' If he gets upset, you politely tell him that you're sorry, but that's just the way it is. If he continues to press you, you ask him to leave. If he won't leave, *then* you reach under the counter and pick up the gun."

"Even if he walks in with a smile on his face?" Tomas looked quizzical.

"If you don't know the guy and you're not comfortable walking back into the yard with him, you say no. Even if he seems like a nice guy. We aren't going to take any chances. It's a judgment call and if, in your judgment, it doesn't feel right, just say no."

We left the office a few minutes later. At the gate, Billy waved good-naturedly and goosed the V-8 of his twenty-year-old Chevy pickup. He left a little rubber on the pavement as he zoomed away toward town. As Tomas drove by, he nodded with a somber expression.

I locked the gate and climbed in my truck. Before driving away, I evaluated the safety talk. Had it been melodramatic? Was I overreacting? I hoped so.

CHAPTER ELEVEN

One measure of the public's respect for Uvalde County Sheriff Phillipe Rodriquez was that after he swept into the office nearly twenty years ago, he'd faced no more than token opposition for re-election. Every few years, a deputy wanting the top job would make a run at him, but the outcome never had been in doubt.

His political success was founded on the man's good character. His integrity was plain to see.

Before his first bid for public office, he was Mr. Rodriquez to his non-Spanish-speaking acquaintances, and Senor Rodriquez to everyone else. His wife may have addressed him more casually than that, but no one else dared. They respected him too much to exhibit such familiarity.

His word was considered inviolate. If he said he would do something, he did it. If he didn't want to do something, you could bet he wouldn't. Abe Lincoln could have learned a thing or two about ethical behavior from Phillipe Rodriquez.

The truck farm he inherited from his father was well-run. His equipment wasn't the newest, but it was beautifully maintained. The three Rodriquez children didn't get into trouble during their school years and hadn't since. At times of mass at Sacred Heart Catholic Church, the family always could be found in a pew.

Did he support the community? Each year, the Rodriquez farm bought a goat or a hog at the annual junior livestock auction at the fairgrounds. In the July Fourth parade, the farm could be counted on to sponsor a float, usually a tractor-drawn wagon carrying smiling children surrounded by the farm's produce.

In short, Phillipe Rodriquez earned the respect of Uvalde County peers by living an above-board life. He managed to do so without coming across as a goody-goody-two-shoes. He was a sober, good man who could be counted on to act like the grown-up in any room.

The benefits of living that way were many, of course, beginning with a clear conscience. But for a professional lawman, none of the consequences of probity were more consequential than the deference shown him in courtrooms. Men and women wielding gavels and sitting in judgment accorded inordinate consideration to pleas for justice from Sheriff Rodriquez.

The sheriff opposed bail for a defendant? You could bet no bail would be forthcoming. The sheriff said he saw a defendant fire a handgun in the direction of the victim? The defendant's attorney could argue contrary ballistics evidence all he wanted, but the jury would believe the sheriff. We're talking Solomon-like trust in the man. No one really believed Rodriquez could walk on water, but they strongly suspected he could if he wanted to.

Felons paid him a modicum of respect by crossing the county line to indulge in their mischief. That way, in case something went wrong with their perfect crimes, they wouldn't have to face in a Uvalde County courtroom the man they call *el diablo*.

All of this public goodwill was put to the test when Deputy Santiago reported back to the sheriff after the hillside search. Two days after being handed two bagged .270-caliber shells from the slope above where a body was found with slugs of the same caliber, the sheriff publicly appealed for everyone in the county with matching rifles to bring the weapons to his office for testing. The hope was to match the identifying striker pattern on the head of the cartridges with the firing pin that struck it.

That was the moment when NRA members in good standing could be expected to start hollering about the government encroaching on their right to bear arms. The next step, they would argue, was confiscation of the weapons. I was as sympathetic to that argument as anyone in the county, even though I seldom took my Mossberg Patriot from the closet to hunt deer. I, too, was impatient with liberal knee-jerk repugnance for anything with a trigger. So, the sheriff's appeal was unprecedented.

"I'm not sure what he'll accomplish," I said to Roque as we ate in a favorite lunch place called Live Oak Gorditas. Situated on an alley about a block from the post office, the restaurant consisted of a covered porch area built around a trailer. The screened patio was enclosed with plastic in winter months. In a word, it wasn't fancy.

Roque and I sat across from one another at a picnic table and ate from Styrofoam containers. Today it was the delicacy of brisket fajita gorditas with browned rice. While the restaurant sounds like a temporary gig, the gig so far had lasted eighteen years.

"Process of elimination, *amigo*," Roque said. "Most people in the county trust the sheriff and will voluntarily drop by with their rifles. I hear they're doing exactly that. They know he will not glom onto the guns. The folks who *don't* cooperate by bringing their guns can expect a friendly visit from the sheriff to remind them of his request."

I swallowed some brisket and sipped water from a cup. "But he can't force them to hand over a rifle unless he has a legitimate reason to go after it."

"True," Roque said between bites of his gordita. "But if someone chooses not to bring to him a weapon after being asked amiably to do just that, the person becomes a suspect. The sheriff is a bulldog in going after suspects. Everyone knows it. Still, you're right. Absent incriminating evidence, he can't seize a gun for testing."

A man stepped through the doorway from the kitchen and walked among customers sitting at three tables. "Everything all right?" he asked over and over. He was assured he hadn't lost his touch at the grille.

We walked back to the courthouse, where we'd parked. The area was busy for downtowns in Walmart America. Two antique businesses that had been around for decades still opened their doors each day. Clustered around the post office were a barbershop, a beauty salon, lawyers' offices, the newspaper office, and so on. It wasn't dead. Even the old "opry house" on the corner still was home to professional and amateur productions.

The courthouse sat at the intersection of two of the longest highways in America—Rt. 83 which ran from Canada to Mexico, and U.S. 90 that extended east all the way to Florida. No parking was allowed on the highway sides of the courthouse and parking was at a premium on city streets bracketing the other two sides.

On the way to the restaurant, Roque had spotted an open space next to the building and decided to park while he could. The short walk helped each man burn a calorie or two.

"What's the girlfriend doing today?"

"If you're talking about Emma, who would laugh at your characterization of her as anyone's girlfriend, she and her mom are shopping in San Antonio," I said, uncomfortable at the idea of Roque assuming anything about the relationship. It was what it was, and to be perfectly honest, I wasn't sure what it was.

"Maria and I both think you're pretty sweet on her. And why shouldn't you be? She's a feisty catch."

"A feisty catch?! Now you're really stepping on her feminine independence. Some women equate feisty with bitchy, you know. Next you'll be calling her cute as a button."

We crossed U.S. 90 and walked onto the courthouse grounds. "Now that you mention it, she *is* cute as a button. A feisty little button at that," Roque said without shame. Frankly, I agreed.

Sheriff Rodriquez hadn't returned from lunch. We assured the receptionist we were early and perused old *Sports Illustrated* magazines in a waiting area. Derek Jeter still looked in his prime in the vintage issue I slipped from the stack next to my chair. Twenty minutes of catching up on outdated sports news was enough down-time for each of us, so we were more than ready for conversation when Rodriquez finally entered the office.

"Come on in, guys," he said. His inner office was furnished Texas lawman style, with a G.W. Graves saddle sitting on a mesquite stand just inside the door. Visiting children often were perched in the saddle for a photograph with the sheriff.

His desk was heavy and long with a lone star carved in the center of the front panel. Wall photos included Uvalde County landscapes and a gallery of former holders of the office. The only picture in the room of Rodriquez was with his family and it wasn't there for political effect: The photo faced him as he sat at the desk.

He lay his Western hat on a corner of the desktop and sank into a well-worn leather-upholstered swivel chair. His black hair was matted where the hat had compressed it and his bronze skin glistened. "Hot out there today, or maybe I'm just getting too old for heat."

"No, it's hot," I said. "It was a little warm in Live Oak Gorditas, too, but we suffered through it for the sake of the brisket."

The sheriff smiled. "Brisket is worth suffering for. So, I suspect you're wondering how the rifle search is going."

"Yep," said Roque. Remembering he was in the presence of a local institution, he added, "*Si, senor.*"

"What you really want to know is if Peyton Ruskey brought in his .270, right? Well, no and yes. No, he didn't volunteer it, which was fine. Voluntary is voluntary. So, I happened to stop by his place yesterday to inquire about it. Just a quick stop on my way somewhere else, you understand, as I explained to him."

We smiled and nodded. Following up with the handful of rifle holdouts was the tricky part. Only an amiable, no-nonsense public official like Rodriquez could hope to badger thin-skinned gun owners and get away with it.

"He didn't seem too surprised to see me and said he'd heard about my request for voluntary inspection of .270-caliber rifles. However, he assured me he owned no such weapon." Roque and I exchanged glances. We had been assured that Ruskey *did* have a rifle of that caliber, a Remington, having hunted with it in the company of other local hunters.

"But..." Rodriquez went on, raising his hand for emphasis, "he told me he *used* to own such a gun. It seems that he was in a hunting party in New Mexico last year when, quote unquote, 'some Mexican' who was in the party admired the weapon and offered to buy it. Because the guy made a good offer, at the end of the hunt, Ruskey sold his rifle. He doesn't have a name for the guy."

I frowned. "Convenient."

"You're a skeptical man, Tak. Cynical almost." He smiled at me. "Anyway, Ruskey said, 'Sorry, sheriff. Sure wish I could help.' I have to conclude that he *was* sorry."

Bad news. All other rifles of that caliber known by local gun shops and ammo dealers to belong to local residents had been checked without finding a match. Bottom line: The found cartridges were not going to help with the investigation. I leaned forward, dropped my ballcap on the floor, and rubbed my scalp vigorously in pure frustration.

"Don't be too disappointed, Tak," the sheriff said. "I didn't really expect to be handed the murder weapon. Did you? Who would be that dumb? But I did narrow the field of suspects dramatically. The only one giving me a cock-and-bull excuse was Senor Ruskey. That might not mean anything, but down along my spine I'm feeling it does."

I knew the feeling. "Thanks, sheriff. We'll keep plugging."

CHAPTER TWELVE

Nothing cleared my head like physical work. I'm told it was endorphins and serotonin doing their thing, maybe adrenalin, too. Psychologists credited the infusion of extra blood into the brain. All I knew was that when I strenuously labored at something, my mind and body seemed to surpass their potential. I thought quicker, if still not at blinding speed. My pain threshold rose. My legs and back seemed to grow strong enough to accomplish tasks I wouldn't even consider in daydreams. A work ethic was a wonderful possession.

I fully exercised it the day after the meeting with the sheriff, working at the yard in hopes of distracting myself from my disappointment. And at a critical moment, the body once again kicked into another gear. It happened when Billy pushed a tow truck lever the wrong way and let a cable sag at the end of the winch. I scrambled up onto the flatbed trailer, banging my shin, and pressed my chest and arms against a Cummins diesel engine block threatening to topple without the cable's support.

I knew I could not possibly prevail for more than five seconds against the dead weight of the massive engine block—endorphins or no endorphins. Yet there I was, trying to do the impossible.

Billy reversed the lever and tightened the cable and the oppressive force of the cast iron lifted from my chest. Relief swept through me. Winch cable still in place, I then wrestled the block more securely into an old tire cushioning it on the trailer. Billy slackened the cable at my signal, and I unhooked it. The block stood upright in its makeshift rubber collar. I dropped to the ground while the new owner of the engine block strapped it securely in place for transport.

"Sorry, Tak. I goofed," Billy said.

"That's OK, Billy," I said. "No harm." I limped into the shop on a sore shin knowing I'd averted a serious injury by sheer luck. Had the massive casting pitched onto me, it would have crushed every bone it encountered. A classic example of workplace injury from stupidity.

After gulping down water from a refrigerated bottle, I rejoined Billy on the concrete apron at the rear of the shop. We poured sawdust absorbent on several oil spills, and he systematically pushed it together with a broom. Then he swept the length of the concrete, gathering little debris for all the dust he kicked up. Billy swept as conscientiously as he cleaned his fingernails.

I put away hand tools and rags in designated drawers in our rolling tool chest and pushed the chest into the shop. The day had been a good one for the books. A body shop bought two Mustang bumper grille assemblies. Tomas hauled in an abandoned 1983 Chevy El Camino for which I'd paid a thousand dollars and hoped to piece out for three times that much. I closed a sale on the refurbished Ford 8N tractor parked by the front gate.

"We made some money today, Billy. I may have earned enough to keep you around another week."

He stopped sweeping. "Then it's a good thing I didn't let that Cummins fall on you."

"It's always good not to kill your employer. There's no future in that sort of thing."

"I suppose," he said and resumed sweeping.

Three heavy plastic livestock water tanks filled one area of the shop. The tanks had been repurposed as storage bins for aluminum, brass, and copper yanked from junk cars and appliances. Salvaged auto batteries lined two-by-eight shelves against one wall, the current low price of lead devaluing them. Scrapped catalytic converters, the emissions devices lined with valuable platinum and palladium, were in a locked cabinet.

These common pieces of machinery were my economic salvation. The whole premise behind selling a salvaged vehicle piece by piece was that individual parts were worth more than the whole. Marketing intact vehicles was only a byproduct of salvage yards. Parts were the main attraction.

I had explained the economics of this to Billy when he began working for me. Sitting at a desk, we'd stripped out a 2001 Volvo trash truck that at that moment sat in weeds at the rear of the yard. T-boned at an intersection, the truck had been hauled to the yard and awaited official abandonment papers from an insurer. On paper, I walked him through the dismantling.

"I paid five-hundred dollars for that truck. So that's my total investment, five-hundred dollars. You with me so far?" I asked. On yellow legal-sized paper, I penciled in "Investment—$500" and started a second column labeled "Revenue."

"The truck has six virtually new—heck, they might be brand new—twenty-two-inch tires. I can get four-hundred dollars apiece for them. The copper in the radiator will bring me at least a hundred dollars. The truck's two batteries at thirty-five cents a pound will bring in probably seventy dollars. You still with me?"

Billy seemed engaged in my impromptu salvage yard economics lesson.

"Volvo builds a good motor and the one in the truck runs perfectly. I can get a thousand bucks for it, I'm sure. Because the transmission is sound, some mechanic will be happy to pay me seven-hundred dollars and turn around and install it for twice that much. The rear end and other drivetrain parts will sell for around eight-hundred, maybe eight-hundred-and-fifty dollars."

The "Revenue" list on the paper lengthened. Billy spat tobacco juice into a Styrofoam cup and winked at me. "That old truck's gonna make you rich."

"We're not done yet," I said. "We still have the frame and body. The collision dented the debris container and bent the frame, so the truck's trash-hauling days are over. But I can have it crushed and sold as scrap metal. It weighs 15,600 pounds. At a hundred-and-fifty dollars a ton, that's another eleven-hundred-plus dollars."

I toted up the numbers and jotted down the total "Revenue" stat: "$6,170."

Billy gave me a thumbs-up. "That's something. Spend five-hundred bucks and make more than six grand."

I tossed the pencil on the desk and sat back in my chair. "Well, I still have to pay the tow truck driver and guys like you to piece out the truck, but the point is, there's money in junked vehicles. When you're removing something from an ugly old sedan, what you're doing is salvaging a valuable part for reuse. Take pride in your reclamation job. It's an environmental work. It also helps people keep their old cars running."

"Thanks, boss. You made a good point. I'll quit kicking fenders when I get frustrated."

We grinned at each other. "I'd appreciate it."

• • •

After Billy and I finished cleaning the shop, I joined Thomas in the office. He worked at the computer while I sat at my desk and flipped through papers without really seeing them. My endorphins were settling down and I felt lethargic. The absence of progress in identifying Pablo's murderer weighed on me like the cast iron block. I was annoyed with myself almost to the point of being angry.

"Some call it a horse face," said Tomas without preamble, "but I would call what you're wearing right now a long face. Any particular reason for it?"

I protested the description "A horse face? That's flattering. No, I'm just reviewing in my mind the murder investigation and not finding anything new. I need something new."

Tomas swiveled in his seat to face me. He dropped his big hands onto his thighs. His expression at that moment I would describe as a judge face, someone who'd just heard a convicted thief blame his thievery on his upbringing. "I don't recall you being appointed to solve anything. If I'm not mistaken, you appointed yourself. Here's an idea: Why don't you appoint someone else—say, the sheriff?—and spend your days figuring out how to raise the price of scrap metal. What we're getting paid for our steel is a crime."

I could only shrug in response. "True. Crime-solving is an avocation. Steel-selling pays the bills. I seem to have misplaced my priorities. Thanks for helping me find them again."

Tomas stood and walked over to lean on the counter. "Tak, we're all grateful for your detective skills and particularly in this case. Pablo's family is really suffering the loss of its son and husband and father. But you need to ease up on yourself."

"Yep."

"No, I mean it. You're running a business that you created and shaped into an enterprising little company. It took guts and smarts to make it go."

"Don't forget work ethic. I'm proud of my work ethic," I said, and tried to laugh but it sounded more like a whimper. "Though you wouldn't know it from my record of late. Missed a lot of days."

"And your work ethic," Tomas said. "I'm proud to be a part of Sweedner Salvage. I hope you know that."

His remarks hung in the air. Awkward was the feeling you got after an employee has extolled the very enterprise you were having trouble respecting as a worthwhile career. I cleared my throat and my mind. "Tomas, thanks. You're a terrific partner here. And you're right. I shouldn't appoint myself 'Solver of the Mystery.' I should let the sheriff track down the killer."

"Well, you're a good solver, but you're not a full-time solver and this case probably needs someone on it 24-7. You can't do that and run a business, too. Cut yourself some slack. You're doing the best you can."

Long after Tomas had volunteered his advice and returned to his computer, I flipped through the same papers, again without seeing them. *You're a businessman. An entrepreneur. You're good at buying and selling. Maybe that's enough.* Tomas was right. The project was too large for me.

"Yep, Tomas. You're spot on," I said, interrupting his work. "We have a business to run. Thanks for the reminder."

He grunted and I returned to the papers, this time in earnest. They soon had my complete attention. Not until we locked up and I headed home did I concede what I was feeling, something gnawing at me down deep. Disappointment. The thought of pulling back from the case disappointed me. I imagined it disappointed Tomas, too.

CHAPTER THIRTEEN

Emma and I decided to drown my disappointment in the clear water of Devil's River State Natural Area. I'd half-jokingly suggested an overnight visit there, a place reputed to have the clearest river water in Texas, which was saying something. To my surprise, she jumped at the idea.

"That's a rich archaeological area. I'd love to go back. Separate tents, though," she said, charming me with a smile. I called ahead and reserved a primitive camp spot for the following weekend.

The park was an hour north of Del Rio on the Mexican border. The drive there in my truck was pleasant enough, though the sun was in our eyes and my injured shoulder seemed to ache more than usual. From time to time, I shifted in the driver's seat to a more comfortable position, enjoying Emma's company despite the discomfort. She seemed happy to be returning to the park and, I hoped, to be doing so with me.

The camp site was at the end of a three-quarter-mile hike from a graveled parking lot. In late Friday afternoon sunshine, we trekked in with backpacks and two single tents. She also carried her father's fishing rod and reel. My tent was on a strap across my shoulder, and I carried my cast iron Dutch oven in one hand and a small ice chest full of cold drinks in the other. After a half mile, I regretted having brought the oven.

I stopped periodically to shift the burdens from arm to arm. My still-healing shoulder ached, but the pain seemed to vanish when we topped a small hill and looked down at the river running at the base of high, rocky bluffs. A rugged limestone rapids area rumbled and splashed in the distance. Immediately in front of us, a broad span of water sparkled in the sunlight.

On our side of the river, I recognized the boulder that overlooked what park literature described as "a perfect swimming hole."

We set up our one-person tents in a cleared area, my tent borrowed from Roque. It was tiny and I fretted that I would feel claustrophobic before dawn. Emma had hers up before I did and gathered sticks from the brushy area outside the camp, dumping them in a rock-circled campfire spot. She had assured me she was not a novice camper and didn't look like one.

Set-up chores done, we made our way down to the river with the fishing rod and a stringer. We counted on catching supper. Emma seemed excited as we neared the river's edge, its water moving past us at an easy pace. "I can't believe I'm here again. This is such a pristine place. I love it."

It did seem untouched by human hands and feet, maybe even by human paddlers, though we could only surmise about that. "Maybe we can find something prehistoric that I can display at the office. You know, a mastodon foot or something." Emma shook her head at the dopey comment

From her late father's tackle box, she selected a skirted jig. The river's clear, moving water was said to be home to several varieties of game fish. We hoped they would be attracted to the jig. Neither of us fished often. However, before her father died at age fifty-nine of a heart condition, Emma had gone with him enough times to learn what lures worked where.

She stuck out the tip of her tongue in concentration as she tied the lure to the end of the line, admiring her work when she completed it. I stepped away to give her casting space. She readied herself for the cast, positioning herself at the bank of the river and looking out into the moving water for a spot to plunk the lure. She flipped back the rod, then whipped it forward and sailed the lure maybe ten feet.

"Oops." She laughed at herself and reeled it back in. I liked her aplomb. Her second cast plopped the brown jig thirty feet or so away in a swirling pool downstream from where she stood. She cranked the lure back toward her, again lost in the moment. With her evident expertise, I fully expected to see the bobbing lure disappear at any moment after a finny eruption from beneath the surface. But that didn't happen. Nor did anything strike it the second time across the water.

My attention began to wander. Call me a slave to instant gratification, but fishing for me mostly was fun when fish were biting. From what I could tell, Emma was cut from better fisherman material and was content to cast and crank and cast and crank. While she did so, I admired the face of the bluffs across the river. Shadows deepened there as the sun reached for the western horizon.

"There you go!" Emma shouted and I looked back to see the line vibrating under the strain of a fish's frantic rush to escape. She played out the line for a moment and then yanked to set the hook and began to gather in the line. She walked backward and then forward as she reeled in the fish and indulged in trash talk with whatever she had hooked. "C'mon, buddy. Come to Momma. I've got you now."

She flashed a self-assured look at me then, as if to say, *I'm taking care of you, Tak. Don't worry.* A few seconds later, the struggling fish churned the water near the shore. And there it was, what looked to be a two-pound catfish, lying on its side, all of its energy spent in a futile attempt to escape. Emma reached forward, gripped the line, and pulled the fish upright from the water.

"I'm impressed," I said. The compliment was sincere. I seized the wiggling, slippery animal, re-gripping it a couple of times until I finally held it firmly enough to work the hook from its mouth. "Thanks a lot, Emma. Now I have to top this catch to hold my male head high. Real friends don't put pressure on friends that way."

"Poor baby." She took the whiskery fish from me to put it on the stringer and handed me the rod. "Go prove your manhood."

Was it possible to razz someone without saying a word? Emma managed it over the next six or eight minutes, mostly employing little shrugs, eye rolls, and smirks. Though I rather enjoyed the teasing, I also began to feel frustration building in me after a half dozen unrewarded casts. In desperation, I turned and flipped the lure upstream and slowly reeled it in as it floated past us.

Bingo! The line sank.

"About time."

I heard the derisive comment and flashed Emma a cocky smile. "Well, here was my thinking when you gave me the reel: If I landed something in an instant, it would diminish your joy at having caught the first one. I treat my friends better than that."

She shook her head. "Uh huh. The fact of the matter is, *friend*, you haven't actually landed *anything* yet, let alone something in the two-pound class. We'll see if you can finish what you started." She folded her arms and watched me work. I said a little prayer that the fish wouldn't get away.

And it didn't. A few moments later, a good-looking bass splashed in the water next to the bank. If anything, it was a mite heavier than Emma's catfish. I pulled it from the water and admired it extravagantly, turning it this way and that as it dangled in front of us. Emma just *harrumphed*, picked up the stringer with her fish on it, and walked away toward the campsite.

I followed and was glad she was in the lead. My relief that I had caught something at all washed over me and I was sure it showed.

She rummaged through her backpack for matches and skillfully started a smoky fire. I was camping with a confident Girl Scout. After the flames began to create a coal bed, she placed a skillet on the fire to melt some butter. Meanwhile, I knocked each fish in the head and gutted it. I did know how to fillet a catfish and soon had two skinless portions for the skillet. The de-scaled bass portions followed, and the skillet was crowded when Emma placed it on the fire a second time.

The fish were delicious even by Emma's higher culinary standards. She thought the catfish tastier than the bass, and I the reverse, but both were enjoyed. We followed that with peach-blueberry cobbler I had pre-mixed and cooked in the Dutch oven. Ice cream would have been the perfect topper, but we got by dribbling half-and-half on it.

"We didn't deny ourselves good eating by coming out here. That's for sure," Emma said. We were walking back toward the campsite from the river after rinsing the skillet and utensils in the stream. In the morning, we planned to fry eggs and bacon and finish off with more cobbler.

We stowed the utensils, banked the fire and sat ten feet from it with our backs against a small boulder. We watched the night come on, stars glimmering in the sky above the isolated park. We identified three constellations before losing interest in the overhead panorama.

"I don't want to ruin the evening, but I sure hope whoever had you roughed up didn't follow us out here," Emma said, half-seriously.

"Unless your mother told someone, there's no way anyone would know where we were headed. I sure as heck didn't see anyone following us on the road here. Did you?" She shook her head. "We're perfectly safe. I wouldn't have brought you here if I thought it would endanger you."

She looked skyward. "I'm not worried about me as much as I am about you. That man wanted to kill you, Tak." She looked over at me. "He wasn't playing around. You were supposed to be dead when he left the junkyard. Don't you agree?"

I could imagine more pleasant things to be talking about at that moment, but I couldn't think how to change the subject. "Probably. His intent was obvious. But if he has any brains at all, he'll back off. The fact is, we may never know who wanted me attacked, or who shot Pablo."

"I think the sheriff will find him," she said with conviction. "The guy is toast."

"Don't say that," I said and threw up my hands in mock horror. "If he's out there listening, he'll have to kill us now while we're sleeping!"

She picked up a small handful of dirt and underhanded it at me. The dust drifted in the flickering campfire light. "You aren't going to get me in your tent by telling me scary stories, mister. You can quit right now."

I leered at her. "Let me think of something scarier. Maybe something about rattlers."

We prattled and joked for another hour as flames became embers and then white ash. The mood turned melancholy, with references to her burdensome college debt, still years from being paid off, and my angst about not pursuing a more professional career. Just late-night talk. The darkness grew still around us and, after Emma's second yawn, I suggested we get some sleep, reluctant as I was to call it a night.

She walked away toward the river. After she returned, I did the same, relieving myself a short way off the trail, and then kneeling by the river to splash water in my face. We said our good-nights and I crawled into the tent. It was too short to stretch out, so I semi-curled on one side and peered out the screened flap at the sky. I doubted I would get much sleep.

CHAPTER FOURTEEN

I was wrong and only awakened the next morning when the sound of snapping sticks roused me. I looked out to see Emma steepling wood for a morning fire. She wore Bermuda shorts and a loose T-shirt, which I knew covered a swimming suit. We planned to check out that "perfect swimming hole" this morning.

I stretched my back muscles, which ached from sleeping on hard-packed ground. I slipped out of my shorts and into my swimming suit. I pulled jeans up over the suit, wriggled into a clean T-shirt, and unzipped the tent flap. Emma looked over.

"I thought I heard movement. Did you sleep well?" She stayed on her knees and kept fiddling with the sticks.

I stood and stretched my back before pulling on my boots. "I slept more than I thought I would."

She stood up from what had become a smoky fire beginning to crackle and sizzle. Her hair was tangled more than usual, her knees reddened from kneeling, one side of her T-shirt caught up on a hip. She ruffled her hair with one hand, conscious of her relatively unkempt state. I thought she looked terrific.

"Why is it people like you can hop up in the morning looking beautiful and the rest of us look bedraggled? There's something unfair about that," I said.

"What a nice thing to say," she responded with a smile. "My husband used to say that right before he slugged me. You're not going to slug me, are you?"

"I promised to be good," I said, and was delighted by the twinkle in her eyes. I wanted to hug her. "And I'm sorry you had an abusive husband."

She shrugged. "I survived. Are we swimming first and eating afterward?"

We elected to swim. We left the camp and made our way to the river, veering off to the left where we could climb the slope of the boulder and jump into the water. At the base of the boulder, we stripped down to our bathing suits. She had on a two-piece blue-and-green suit, a bikini, but not a severely cut one. It contained her gently curved seat, exposed a surprisingly firm-looking belly, and modestly covered breasts that could be described as fulfilling.

"Are you sure those trunks are orange enough?" she asked and spread her fingers in front of her face as if to fend off glare. Then she walked ahead of me to the lip of the boulder and looked down at the pool. "I hope it's deep enough."

Without warning, she leaped and yelled something inane on the way down. After splashing out of sight, she surfaced a moment later and swiped back her hair before looking up to where I stood.

"Wow. This feels wonderful!" she yelled and moved away with a backstroke, leaving me room to join her. I jumped and discovered after sinking into the water that she hadn't exaggerated about the delight awaiting me there.

Several feet below the surface where my descent ended, I could see the rocky bottom. A catfish glided away from me as I lingered a moment in the depths. The cool water was bracing. I propelled myself upward then and broke the surface.

Emma still was backstroking upstream. She stopped and looked at me after I let out a *whoop!* "Boy, this *is* wonderful?"

We frolicked for most of the next half hour. After she floated downstream to where I was, she splashed me with a sweep of her hand. I returned the favor. Then we dove for the bottom, each bringing up a smooth rock to prove we had reached it. Below the surface, the river was as quiet as it was crystalline. I dived a second time to enjoy the sensations once more.

We swam out into the river until the current began to pull us downstream whereupon we retreated, not wanting to be carried too far away. After being taunted into it by a competitive woman, I raced Emma from the base of the rock to a designated point thirty yards away.

About halfway to the finishing point, I began to pull away from her and imperceptibly slowed my strokes to let her draw nearer. The race ended in an approximate draw. In short, we grew tired playing in the water.

"You take another few laps by yourself and I'll go back and change," Emma said, stroking toward the shore. "Give me fifteen minutes. OK?"

I watched her leave the water. She made her way gracefully up the path to collect her clothes and then disappeared on her way to the campsite. I watched her walk away and felt possessive. She wasn't "my woman," by any stretch, but she was my buddy. I was ready to admit to myself that I hoped for more.

I lay back and floated on my back then, trying not to think about Emma being naked just over the hill. A moment later, I decided one more dive to the bottom was a good idea.

The eggs and bacon were satisfying in their greasiness, the cobbler just as good in the morning light as it had been the evening before. As we rinsed out the cookware one last time in the river, Emma talked about her previous trip to the natural area. She grew more excited as she described to me pictographs on a canyon wall a few miles up the river. She said they dated from 3000 BC

"They were kind of spooky," she said, squatting near the water and gesturing with a pot in one hand. "They depicted people with long upper bodies and short legs. Their arms were raised. You could see the fingers of the hands outstretched. One of the figures held a stick, maybe a cane or a scepter. From the arms of another dangled strips of cloth, or snakes, maybe. I couldn't tell."

She looked over at me. "I remember wondering what was going through the mind of the artist as he or she painted the picture on the rock. I felt a real connection to him, or her." She turned her attention back to washing and scrubbed a fork and spoon in the water.

"Three thousand years ago. I can't get my mind around that," I said and stood.

She rose, too. "That's the wonder of it all. They were people like us, living by the river and trying to figure out what the future held for them. Talking to each other about their lives, their fears. They were different than us, sure, but they weren't apes or something. My heart went out to them."

After we cleaned up the campsite, the walk out to the parking area with lightened gear was easier than the trek in. The truck was the only parked vehicle. After unloading equipment in the bed, I unlocked the passenger door and went around and unlocked my door.

I slumped in the driver's seat. A couple of hours of air-conditioned conversation with Emma was a pleasant prospect. She seemed ready to relax in relative comfort, too, though probably not as ready as I was. She was an outdoors gal. No question about that.

We rode the gravel road back to pavement, reached the main highway and headed southeast toward Del Rio. Heavy rains in the last week had spawned lots of color in the rolling terrain adjacent to the highway. Texas sage blossoms covered the slope of one hill, the purple blooms set off by the plant's silver-gray leaves. The spectacular sight interrupted our conversation as we zipped past it.

"Was all that color there yesterday? I don't remember it," I said.

"It might not have been. The blooms open quickly."

"I wonder if your pictograph artists got to enjoy purple sage."

She smiled. "We'll never know. Maybe they had something even more beautiful to brighten their lives."

Ten miles farther along, a thought popped into my mind. "Did your cavemen use karst caverns? Did they live in them or anything?"

Emma brightened. She liked talking archaeology. "They could have. The caverns were around. But the ceilings may have collapsed a time or two since then and buried any evidence of their habitation. Short of excavating the floors, we'll never know what's under the debris."

I considered that. "I actually was thinking about the hole in the ground at the solar panel farm. You say that hole isn't old enough to have attracted any interest from ancient tribes."

"Probably not. The opening might be older than what I suggested. There's a lot of evidence of more modern tribes using caverns. Midden piles and campfire traces are plentiful. But I doubt the hole you're talking about was accessed."

We arrived in Uvalde shortly after noon and Emma's mother insisted that I join them for lunch. We sat around a heavy-legged oak table in the dining room. Mrs. Townsend set a big plate of tuna sandwiches and cherry tomatoes in the middle, and we helped ourselves. I particularly savored the iced tea and drained most of a glassful before taking a single bite of sandwich.

Emma briefly ran down the outing for her mother, the swimming, the fishing, the deliciousness of the cooked fish and cobbler, the beauty of the river. "It really was quite idyllic. Even better than I remembered it from my earlier trip. Of course, I had better company this time."

"He's good company, is he?" her mother asked. "Did he attack you in your tent?"

"Twice," Emma said with a straight face. "I was going to talk to you about that later, Mom. Thank goodness my tent is so small one swift kick is all I needed to repel the attack. That plus my Mace."

"Poor darling," she said.

"I know," Emma said with a rueful expression.

"I meant Tak. He deserved better."

I smiled at that. I liked this woman. Emma smiled, too.

"Seriously, you have a pretty nice daughter, Mrs. Townsend. And we had a good time. Your husband taught her to fish like a pro. Did you teach her how to swim?"

And the hour passed, a comfortable coda to a terrific overnighter with a woman I was beginning to feel I needed to keep around me all the time. I still resisted the notion, but my resistance was peeling away.

Mother and daughter talked about a planned trip on Monday back to Del Rio to visit a favorite border shop. I told them I'd be on the road, too, driving a rollback truck to Rocksprings in the morning to load up an old Dodge pickup that's become something of a collector's item. "But the guy who owned it didn't know it was a collector's item, so I got it for a good price."

"What makes it a collector's item?" Emma asked.

"It's a 1973 Dodge Club Cab model. That's significant because it was the first truck to extend the cab to make more room behind the seats for packages, or suitcases, or little people. Being first gives it more value. I might get double what I paid for it."

"Good for you, Tak," Mrs. Townsend said. "Be careful driving up to the plateau."

CHAPTER FIFTEEN

Monday's sky was draped in dark gray clouds of an especially close weave. Nothing blue peeked through. It didn't look like the drape would turn sodden as the day progressed, but neither would I need sunglasses. I left the business yard about 8:30, drove around the north side of Uvalde, turned onto U.S. 83 to cross the railroad overpass and, on the other side, jogged west on Texas 55.

I settled back into the driver's seat. Not a stop light or sign separated me from Rocksprings some 70 miles away. Two small towns edged the two-lane highway before the pavement began the climb to the top of Edwards Plateau. I'd have to slow as I passed through the towns, maybe brake some, but those would be the only interruptions from highway speed.

Because the truck radio was broken, I would need to entertain myself. Singing was the answer. I concentrated on a ditty I'd begun to compose Sunday afternoon with the guitar. I called it, *The Girl in the Blue-and-Green Swimsuit.* I could have named it *Emma,* of course, but this way if things didn't work out, I could still sing it without embarrassment. You have to protect your heart as best you can.

As she plunged to the water, with aplomb and glee,
I quickly took stock of my yearning to be
with the girl in the blue-and-green swimsuit.

• • •

La de dah de dah. Time passed. Canyons just off the edge of the roadway were impressive as the highway neared the top of the plateau. Nearly vertical cliffs fell away from some stretches of the road, the longest drops falling directly to canyon floors where cattle grazed in places or, more often, not a living thing was in sight. Other canyon walls fell away more gently but the bottom was just as far down there.

I spotted a turkey vulture lazing on upswept winds above a picturesque canyon, the bird looking for something dead or dying. It reminded me of the story told by a motorcycling friend who once toppled his bike on a seldom-traveled road and pinned one of his legs beneath it. Before he was rescued two hours later, the biker watched a vulture circling above him, eventually joined by two more vultures, all of them gliding around and around as they eyed his predicament. They had recognized a human animal in distress, a potential carrion meal.

"They might have pecked out my eyes, but I knew they'd never chew through my leathers," the motorcyclist later boasted. Another good reason for bikers to wear leather coats and leggings: to protect themselves from vultures. I had to admit, I hadn't thought of that.

Finally, the road topped out and I drove through gently rolling range lands where Angus cattle, sheep, and Angora goats grazed. The sheep and goats ate weeds and proliferating seedlings, keeping those undesirable types of vegetation in check, whereas the cattle munched on short and tall grasses. The ecological impact of the herds was in harmony. The ecosystem worked well for the ranchers, and when prices for wool, mohair and beef were high enough, the economics worked, too.

I drove along the road through groves of oak and scattered mesquite. The Rocksprings airport outside town was quiet, unlike in hunting season when men and women with designs on whitetail deer or more exotic game flew to the plateau armed to hunt.

I slowed at the edge of Rocksprings and eventually came to the stoplight at the highway's Main Street intersection. After turning, I drove past the Edwards County courthouse, a structure built of rock with the statue of a goat on the grounds in front of it. A hundred-year-old hotel stood across the street.

Two blocks farther along, just past the wool and mohair auction barn, I turned left again and pulled to the side of the street in front of a low-roofed house with a rusty gate. Parked in front was the Dodge pickup I'd come to carry home. I pulled the flatbed forward and then backed up and positioned it for loading. As I dropped down from the cab, the seller walked out the front doorway of his house holding up keys to the vehicle.

"Hey, good to see you again." We shook hands and together loaded the Dodge, me doing the work and him watching. The rollback's bed hydraulically tilted and slid to the ground in the rear. All that was left for an operator to do was attach cables to the front of the vehicle being loaded and slowly winch it up the incline. Then the bed was raised, leveled, and repositioned.

Twenty minutes after arriving, I had chained the Dodge in place on the truck, exchanged papers, and crawled in the cab for the return trip. We waved once more and I eased away from the property with *my* Club Cab pickup riding high and proud for all to see.

At the highway stoplight, I pulled into a parking lot, got out and locked up. When the light changed, I crossed Main and then crossed the highway, too, and entered a restaurant called Kingburger. The owner sold more enchilada dishes and chicken-fried steak plates than hamburgers, but I always ordered a burger just to keep Whataburger executives on their toes. That's the American way.

"That your truck over there with the old pickup?" asked a leather-faced retiree as I squirted mustard on my hamburger. He wore a Western straw hat tilted back on his head and sat at an adjoining table, a thumb cocked in the direction of the parked truck. His plate was empty except for a lone French fry.

"It is. Taking it down to Uvalde. Want to buy it?"

"No, no," he said, shaking his head. "I used to have one just like it, though, except it was green. Great truck. Roomy, that was the thing."

I finished my burger while talking across the table to the man. We mostly compared notes on vintage trucks and reminisced about his goat-ranching days. When I was ready to leave, I knew I had given this hour of his life more satisfaction than what he'd anticipated before the conversation began.

I suppose that's the way I'll end up, I thought as I walked out the door. *Old and alone and mostly interested in talking about what I can remember of my heyday.*

I immediately was struck with the thought that I hadn't yet *experienced* a heyday. At least I hoped not. If I had, my remaining years on Earth were going to be spectacular in their dullness. I re-crossed the highway and street, frowning, reviewing my life, and concluding I was not impressed with the richness of my experience to date.

Driving out of town, I glimpsed in my rearview mirror a brown Dodge Ram 3500 with dual rear wheels pulling onto the highway a quarter-mile behind. I'd noticed the truck as I'd entered Rocksprings because it was a powerful model pickup that I knew was equipped with a Cummins diesel and enough torque to move a mountain. A heavy, black-painted grille protected its front end, the outer edges wrapping around front fenders a foot or more.

I felt a kinship with the powerful Dodge because I was carrying a forerunner of the brute on my flatbed. I wondered if the people in the truck felt the same. We both were headed south. I expected it to pass me before we got to the descending stretch of the highway where passing became more problematic. However, it maintained its distance and I soon forgot about it.

A second verse of *The Girl in the Blue-and-Green Swimsuit* was on my lips, but I soon was preoccupied with maintaining a safe speed as I began my descent on the Hill Country highway. The loaded truck had a high center of gravity and lots of dead weight now that the pickup was perched on its back. Speed was not my friend under those circumstances.

In an outside mirror, I noticed the Dodge Ram had pulled up directly behind me. Either the driver was admiring the old Dodge or otherwise was content to follow me down the slope. He stayed behind me through several turns. As I entered probably the sharpest switchback in the roadway, a *crack-boom* sounded, followed by shuddering in my steering wheel.

A moment later, the sound repeated itself and my wheel twitched in my hands as the truck lurched to the right. Tire blowouts! Talk about terrible timing. This was no place to have the steering go wobbly. I struggled to maintain control of the rollback, and braked and shifted to a lower gear to begin to slow and eventually stop the truck.

The Dodge Ram suddenly pulled out and into the opposing lane and raced forward, the driver apparently wanting no part of this potential smash-up. The driver gave me a wide berth, riding the other side of the center line as the big diesel roared and the front of the Dodge drew even with me.

I concentrated on shifting and braking and keeping a sure grip on the wheel as I swung the truck around the treacherous curve. The truck's rightward lean onto flattened rear tires was contributing to centrifugal forces trying to tip me over onto the shoulder. I fought to stay upright and was more aware of the sheer drop-off to my right than to the passing Dodge on my left.

Then my peripheral vision signaled that something was happening on the roadway, something my brain couldn't process and assign to a normal category. I looked over and was astonished to see the Ram hard upon me! The heavy pickup had veered sharply in my direction, its heavy grille on a trajectory to strike my left fender and front wheel.

Before it struck, I had a fleeting glance into the Ram's cab. I couldn't believe my eyes: The driver was steering his vehicle into the side of my truck on purpose. A man in the passenger seat braced himself for impact.

The collision jarred me. I was thrown against the door, the steering wheel almost twisting from my hands. I regained control of the wheel, but not until the rollback had begun to drift off the pavement at an angle I recognized was irreversible, not with that much momentum behind it. From instinct, I turned the wheel back toward the roadway. The loaded truck tipped right in response and began to roll over. I had lost the battle to stay upright. The ground seemed to tilt and the tumble down the long hillside began.

The noise of what followed was nearly as excruciating as the physical pummeling. I thought my eardrums would burst from the shrill screech of metal being wrenched apart. The booming of steel sheeting repeatedly being smashed against rock was so terrible it scared me all by itself.

Glass from the windshield sprayed me as it exploded under pressure. My eyes closed an instant before I felt my face pelted with the shards. Time and again, I was thrust against my seatbelt so hard that I expected the nylon either to part and send me flying or to bury itself in me like an extra diagonal rib. My jaw began to hurt after I banged my head against the door frame or the steering wheel or something unyielding while the truck and I tumbled and bounced.

The noise level finally reached a crescendo and began to recede and the jolting ride morphed into what seemed like a long, long skid. And then nothing.

CHAPTER SIXTEEN

I came to my senses with no idea of how long I'd been insensible. If my ears still worked, the world had gone silent around me. Wildlife had run or flown away or were crouched and perched in hiding after witnessing the thunderous spectacle of a disintegrating machine.

Minutes passed. I couldn't say how many. Wonderment robbed time of its urgency. I felt zero need to know the time of day. I was in a world of my own, anyway, content to sit and stare across the canyon at a nondescript hill on the other side. More minutes passed.

How interesting my life had become. My ho-hum existence had turned into a truck wreck, literally and otherwise. I was on someone's Do-In list and desperately wanted to get off it. The uneventful and boring days of a junk dealer held a new mystique for me.

There I was at the bottom of a hillside having been attacked a second time by persons unknown. When I'd dressed that morning and, later as I'd climbed into the rollback, I had not for a moment considered taking a precipitous shortcut home from Rocksprings. It had never occurred to me as I'd hummed and sung of Emma that this day might be my last. And without a heyday to show for it.

A twinge of pain, or perhaps the sound of oil or water dripping somewhere, brought me further awake. I lifted one arm to examine it and saw blood flowing from a puncture wound. I gently felt my sore jaw and my hand came away bloody. The beard seemed saturated with it. Then I looked out across the canyon one more time and gathered my thoughts.

This I knew for certain: I was thrilled to be bleeding and aching. From the angle that one foot was turned away from the bottom of my leg, I might have a broken ankle, but I still drew breath. I was in one piece. Hallelujah for all of that. I could move my neck, my arms and one leg, which meant I wasn't paralyzed. Terrific news! I could feel pain, including my ankle, which had begun to pulse, and I cherished the feeling.

I regained my senses and resolved to get out of the cab. The battered truck was sitting right side up but with its roof crushed to within an inch or two of the top of my head. A jagged piece of metal cleaved the space in the middle of the cab. One door was gone and the other hung from a hinge.

I peered down and concluded that a socket wrench toolbox stowed on the floor of the cab had become wedged against the heel of my foot. My seatbelt restrained me from moving the metal box. After unsnapping the belt, I slumped forward onto the wheel and felt a sharp new pain across my shoulder. I gripped the rear of the toolbox and shoved it to one side with a grunt, relieving pressure on my foot. The pain worsened immediately when blood flowed again through veins in the ankle.

I moved foot and ankle gingerly and concluded no bones were broken, so I slipped my hand under the leg, lifted it, and worked my way off the seat and out of the cab. The same instant my feet touched the ground, smoke reached my nostrils and I limped away to put some distance between myself and burning wreckage.

After a few limping strides, though, I could see it was the old Dodge pickup that was aflame. The ruined Club Cab had torn loose and been smashed into the embankment about a hundred feet above me. My investment was going up in smoke before my eyes.

Because the fire didn't seem to threaten me where I stood, I relaxed. I gathered my strength and worked my limbs and surveyed the mangled trucks. What a ruinous sight!

Then, with a *whomp!*, grass and shrubs around the burning pickup flared up and became a new menace. A grass fire could sweep down the hill and reach me in a few minutes. I looked around and considered my options. The rollback and I were a hundred yards down the hillside from the highway. I couldn't climb the slope without skirting around the fire and such a detour seemed daunting.

The rollback had skidded to a halt against a short mesquite tree growing from an earthen shelf that protruded about thirty feet from the slope. The tree and shelf had stopped our plunge to the canyon floor several hundred feet below.

The grass fire worked its way down the hill one bush at a time, and I needed to get out of its path. After limping to the edge of the drop-off, I saw a bluff virtually bare of burnable vegetation. It sloped gently away from the lip of the ledge. If necessary, I could slide part way down the bluff and be spared the worst of flames shooting overhead. It would be hot, and I might get singed, but probably not burned.

Satisfied with the fire escape plan, I eased myself down to sit on the edge of the bluff. I couldn't see the highway above me, which meant no potential rescuer up there could see me without stopping to peer over the edge. However, the smoky fire from the Dodge was sending a signal visible to all. A siren would sound before long as emergency vehicles responded to the report of an unidentified canyon blaze.

"What have I gotten myself into?" Talking to myself seemed a good way to fill some time and I had plenty to talk about. "What will they try next? I mean, c'mon, give me a break!"

I turned to scan the hilltop and roadway. Though I didn't expect to see a big brown Dodge Ram sitting on the edge of the highway and my assailants working their way down to finish me off, I still felt relieved when I didn't see that.

I had seen enough today. The sight of the driver steering that big black grille into the side of the rollback was seared in my memory. If that wasn't enough, I still could see the man in the passenger seat bracing himself for the collision and gripping the stock of a rifle. I had no doubt that weapon was used to shoot out the rollback's right rear tires.

I leaned forward and lay my head on forearms propped against my knees. Too much.

Help soon arrived, thanks to a woman rancher on a shopping trip to Uvalde. I later learned she saw the smoke, pulled over to determine what was burning, and called in the accident before driving on. Rocksprings volunteer firefighters responded a few minutes later. After signaling to them I was all right and was the only victim, I became a spectator.

They made their way down the steep slope and expertly knocked down the blaze before it ignited the rollback. Working in heavy, fire-proofed clothing with helmets and thick gloves, they pulled the heavy water-filled hoses into place and then struggled to control the bucking, spraying nozzle. Afterwards, already worn out from fighting the fire, they would have to pull the hoses back up the hill.

And all of that from men and women offering their services to the community without pay. I made a mental note to contribute something to the Rocksprings Fire Department.

The rollback was little more than a mass of metal, the frame undoubtedly twisted, the hydraulic lift system ruined, cab and engine mangled. Yet I was glad the fire hadn't consumed it because that meant the right rear tires, with their incriminating bullet holes, would be intact. The tires would be the starting place for Edwards County investigators in their probe of the Sweedner Salvage truck "accident."

EMS personnel worked their way down the hillside to me. "You're sure there was no one else in either truck?" one of them asked. Yes, I reassured them, I was the only accident victim. They cleaned and bandaged the cut on my arm and determined the facial cuts would heal quickly if kept clean. The jaw was bruised, not broken.

When four firefighters prepared to carry me back up the hill, I resisted. I knew I could struggle up the hillside if my life depended upon it, but the ankle wouldn't make it easy. In the end, I consented to be strapped on a stretcher, feeling guilty about it. It would not be an easy carry and I repeatedly apologized to my carriers as they worked their way uphill.

"Thanks, guys," I said one last time when we reached the top and they helped me stand. I leaned against the side of the EMS van and demonstrated again that the ankle flexed without notable pain. One guy kneeled and slowly rotated the joint and pressed here and there.

"You're right, it's not broken, I think," he said, sitting back on his haunches to look up at me, "but I think you strained some ligaments, maybe incurred a high ankle strain. You need to ride to the hospital, have it X-rayed, and get that cut dressed again."

Because the hospital serving the area was in Uvalde, I agreed to the ride. It was a convenient way to return home. I limped to the edge of the roadway and looked down one more time on the crumpled trucks.

An Edwards County sheriff's deputy joined me, a fellow who looked to be about my age but with a belly that looked a lot older. He listened to my story, yet still insisted on a breathalyzer test. I couldn't blame him. The whole someone-shot-out-my-tires idea sounded a little fishy. I knew the test could only show I'd consumed too much mustard at Kingburger.

"You'll post a guard on this wreckage then?" I asked. He said he would. I'd apprised him of the possibility of finding holes in the tires and possibly bullet fragments as well. He'd called the sheriff with a request for a forensic specialist, who was on his way. As I climbed into the back of the van, I was satisfied we'd done everything we could to protect the evidence of a crime.

The ride was pleasant under the circumstances. Since we weren't running with lights flashing, I agreed to a stop at the hotdog place in Barksdale. I wasn't hungry but got an iced tea that I enjoyed sipping as I rode semi-reclined on a stretcher. The attendant sitting in the rear with me ate his slaw-covered hotdog and fries and we talked about cars and the NBA Spurs and his young children.

Then he got to chatting with the driver and I closed my eyes. I wasn't sleepy, I was sure of it, yet the attendant kept shaking me awake to ensure I wasn't concussed and lapsing into a coma. When we pulled into the emergency entrance, I was more than ready to check into the hospital.

CHAPTER SEVENTEEN

Doctors kept me overnight for observation. Though I complained of soreness more than anything else, they feared I had struck my head more than I realized as I thumped and bumped my way down the hillside in the rolling truck. Stepping away from that wreckage with only a superficial gouge in one arm and a sprained ankle seemed improbable to them.

I was far from unscathed. My chest continued to hurt, having been bruised by the seat belt, and my arms and legs were tender from being shaken and struck and flung about. By morning—after a night of interrupted sleep—I still was sore, even to the touch, yet everything worked as designed so I didn't complain much.

Medical science had nothing more to offer me and the hospital released me. An attendant pushed me out the entranceway in a wheelchair and I was helped into Roque's truck. Roque had volunteered to drive me to the sheriff's office.

"You look like hell, of course," he said in a snippy tone. He still was irked that he had learned of the accident second-hand from Tomas, to whom I had reported before falling into a sedated sleep. "Not that I care."

"Oh, shut up. Your feelings get hurt awful easily."

"*La opinion.* None of your best friends have ever almost died and kept it a secret from you."

I just shook my head. "So little compassion for someone who's just experienced a near-death experience. I'm still hurting, you know."

Roque shook his head. "Well, let's do a little better next time, OK?"

"I hope there isn't a next time. One shove over the edge is enough for me. It was darned scary, I don't mind telling you. And so noisy!"

"Noisy?" Roque looked at me, puzzled by the statement and forgetting his annoyance.

"You'd be surprised how much racket a truck makes when it's tearing itself apart."

We both got serious. I was glad to be alive and having him there for me, and I told him so. He acknowledged the sentiment. Then I began to worry how Emma would take the news because I had neglected to call her, too.

The sheriff expected my visit. I had told him in response to his call that he needn't come to the hospital. I would visit his office. I moved like an old man, though, as I climbed the stairs into the courthouse and crept down the hall into the sheriff's outer and inner offices.

Sheriff Rodriquez was deferential as I entered. He helped seat me in a soft chair that I didn't remember being there on our earlier visit. He probably had it brought in just for my comfort. I tell you, our sheriff's quite a guy.

"Where do you hurt?" he asked after seating himself behind his desk.

"Everywhere. The better question is, where *don't* I hurt. The spinning and bouncing tested all my ligaments and tendons and joints and whatever else held me together. The good news is they didn't fail me. I'm grateful."

"You should be grateful. You are very, very lucky to be alive. I drove out yesterday afternoon to the spot where you went over," he said. "Wow. What a mess. That truck has hauled its last load."

I nodded at that.

"More to the point, if your seatbelt had given out, or you hadn't snapped it on, you'd have been tossed around and out the door and rolled over and squashed. We'd all be getting ready to attend your funeral."

I shifted in the chair and settled myself more comfortably. "I like to think, sheriff, that you and your counterpart in Edwards County would have investigated my death as more than an accident, given my recent run-ins and all. I like to think you'd have found the bullet holes in the tires. There *are* bullet holes, aren't there?"

Indeed, there were, he assured me, although state forensics specialists would have the last word on the tires. They hoped to find bullet fragments from where the projectiles struck the wheels inside the tires. "And, yes, I would have called for an examination of the tires precisely because of the earlier attack on you. Running off the highway would have been too coincidental to dismiss as an accident."

He asked for a full report then and I gave it to him after an aide came in to record what I said. I told him about spotting the Ram 3500 as I entered Rocksprings, about its trailing me from town and declining to pass me. I described the loud reports of the tires blowing out, or being shot out, and the sight of the Ram being steered directly into my truck with the passenger in the Ram holding a rifle. I described the truck in as much detail as I could remember.

"You didn't happen to jot down the license plate number before you rolled down the mountain?" he asked in jest.

I told him what my memory recorded about the two men in the Ram. They looked Latino, I said, and on the small side. The driver wore a full-brimmed hat. The other man was bareheaded, with dark hair. Neither had facial hair or at least I didn't remember any. "The rifle in the man's lap seemed to be a single barrel model, a hunting rifle, rather than a carbine or something like that. The barrel was poked out the window, so I saw it clearly."

Rodriquez asked follow-up questions intended to fill gaps in my memory, but I couldn't add much to my statement. He dismissed the aide.

"There are some worrisome elements in all this," the sheriff said. He raised his eyebrows to emphasize his concern. "We're searching motor vehicle records for the model of truck you described. As yet we haven't found any on this end of the state. Of course, the men might have driven here from the other end of the state, so that doesn't preclude anyone."

"It's not an everybody-has-one kind of truck," Roque said.

"That it isn't, so we'll be asking around to learn if anyone has seen something like it in the area. A late-model brown Ram 3500 with a big grille. I mean, how many can there be? We ought to be able to locate it. I'm hopeful." Rodriquez leaned back, resting his arms on the sides of the chair. "But that's not what worries me."

I raised my eyebrows. "I think I know what does."

Roque hiked one leg up on the other and looked at me with a quizzical expression.

"What bothers you is how did the men know I was going to be in Rocksprings yesterday morning," I said.

"*Exactamente*," the sheriff said, leaning forward again. "I refuse to believe they just happened to see you there and decided to take the opportunity to get rid of you. They had the rifle. They had a pickup powerful and heavy enough to push you over the edge, one with a heavy-duty front grille to push with. This was premeditated all the way."

Roque looked aghast. "How do you figure? No one knew except Tak and the two guys who work for him. You surely don't think Tomas or Billy had anything to do with it?"

"You tell me, Tak. I know Tomas and I know his family. His involvement in anything like this seems unlikely to me. Billy seems to be a nice kid. So, who else knew of your trip?"

"No one really," I said, then paused, and had to add, "except for Emma. I told her and her mother where I was going."

"Emma Townsend?" Rodriquez asked. I nodded. He half-smiled. "She isn't known to be a killer. That's not her momma's reputation either."

"Could they have told someone with a different kind of reputation?" Roque suggested. No one had a response to that. We decided I'd have to ask her. I wasn't looking forward to the conversation.

A few minutes later, Roque and I left the courthouse, an able-bodied man and a semi-invalid, and he drove me home. Not much chit-chat passed between us.

• • •

"You WHAT?" Emma screamed into her phone after I informed her of my tumble down the mountain. I snatched the cell phone away from my head and brought it back in time to hear her follow-up comment. "You were nearly killed, spent the night in the hospital, and I am just NOW hearing about it!?"

"That was sort of my fault," I said. She wasn't mollified by my admission. "You THINK?"

I sighed and she did, too, it sounded like, anger spent. The silence lasted for several seconds. "Yow, I'm sorry, Emma. I wasn't thinking clearly yesterday afternoon. I didn't call Roque either and he pouted all morning about it." I instantly knew "pouting" was a poor choice of word.

"Well, I'm not *pouting*. I'm disappointed. I thought we had come to be closer friends than that," she said. More silence. "Anyway, the good news is you survived what sounds like a horrendous accident. The scarier part is that you say it *wasn't* an accident. That you were pushed off the road. Here we go again."

My thoughts exactly. "It's getting old."

"Tak, listen to me. Now just sit still on your lounge chair or wherever you're calling from and listen a minute," she said. I was in my uncle's rocker on the front porch, but I didn't interrupt her. "Pablo's death was unfortunate and sad. Terribly sad. Obviously, your continued investigation of the death has drawn the attention of the murderer, or murderers. They've convinced themselves you need to go away. Are you with me so far?"

I told her I was.

"Why don't you do just that! Go away. Pablo's family and the whole community appreciate what you've done so far, but there are professionals who can carry on without you. Let them." She lapsed into silence, but I offered no response, so she continued.

"Concentrate on your business—you have a new truck to buy! Let your body heal—you nearly lost it under the crushing weight of a truck! Let's you and me do some more swimming and fishing and just forget this sleuthing business. Please."

I said nothing for a moment, moved by her earnest concern and plea. "I think that would be characterized as quitting, wouldn't it?"

"And what's wrong with that?" she said, almost yelling. "You're a volunteer sleuth. A lay detective. You don't even have a badge, let alone an official duty to capture the bad guys. You've done more than anyone else in the county to solve this. Turn it over to the pros. They're grateful for what you've accomplished."

I had to admit that Emma made giving up sound a whole lot like declaring victory. I *was* tired. Unfortunately, I was *not* a quitter. "Thanks for your counsel, Emma. I'll think about it. Seriously. I have a question for you now."

This time she didn't respond, so I continued. "The sheriff is persuaded someone must have been tipped off that I was going to Rocksprings. He doesn't believe they just happened to run into me there. The problem is that I don't know anyone besides Billy and Tomas who knew I was going to Rocksprings...except you. Did you tell anyone?"

She said nothing. "Hello?"

"I told no one, Tak," she said in an icy tone. "You told Mom and me and the subject never came up again till right now when you called."

I sighed. "I just had to ask. The sheriff and I can't figure it. I suppose it *could* have been a coincidence they were in Rocksprings and acted impulsively. I'll never know until I catch them."

"No," Emma said, "that's not right. You're going to let someone else catch them."

"Right."

Chapter Eighteen

Tonight, I would go after them. I didn't know who "them" was, but that was an inconvenient detail. Starting tonight, I was dogging them. I hadn't said anything to Emma, of course. After she'd told me to let law enforcement take over, I knew I couldn't let her in on my plan. I had to try to finish this. Today, for the first time in several days, I was hopeful I would.

It was simple: My attackers had gone to great lengths to silence me. Permanently. They wouldn't have bothered unless they believed I was onto something. After all, they were not trying to kill salvage yard operators all over Texas, were they? Of course not. It was me they wanted. Why? Because I was on to something. Simple deductive reasoning led nowhere else.

What concentrated my mind was that I could be "on" to one thing only: the shed. It was the only puzzlement I had and, hence, my interest in it was the only possible threat to them. Nothing else made any sense. The problem was, the shed made little sense to me either.

Driving up Hwy. 55 an hour after dusk blanketed the valley, I imagined all kinds of incriminating evidence waiting to be discovered in that little building. Narcotics. Weapons. Women being smuggled into the country for the sex trade.

It was only my imagination going crazy, though, and I knew it. The fact was, the sheriff and Roque had inspected the inside of the building and found nothing. It contained what Ruskey said it contained—supplementary feed, salt blocks, maybe some fence-fixing materials. It was legit. The sheriff himself acknowledged it.

"So why are you driving there tonight?" I asked myself aloud, sitting quite alone in the cab. I thought the question deserved an answer, so I yelled one in a mocking tone: "BEATS THE HELL OUT OF ME!"

I jested. I wasn't driving to the crime scene to go through the motions of surveillance. I had a purpose in keeping an eye on the shed, an operating theory, and it was this: Something indeed was kept in that building... *periodically.* Something besides cattle feed. That something wasn't there when the sheriff visited it, but it was in that shed... *sometimes.* Something that must be carried to it on a four-wheeler or carried away from it the same way. Tonight, I hoped to see this "something" come or go.

I still ached all over from the roll downhill. My ankle was tender, the discoloring around my bruises not yet numb to the touch. I moved well enough to surveil, however, and hoped I wouldn't have to do anything more strenuous than that, like arm-wrestle an assailant.

As expected, the Zamarripa ranch gate was open when I reached it. Roque only closed it when cattle were in the front pasture, and I knew there were no livestock there now. I drove through the gateway entrance, turning off the headlights as I did so, there being no point in alerting the family to my nighttime visit. Without headlights on, I counted on the light of a nearly full moon to let me see my way to the solar field.

I drove the lane slower this time. I turned off on the side road and parked the truck in the bottom of the swale that cut through right before the road rose to meet the fence separating Zamarripa land from NewAge solar property.

I switched off the engine, slid from the truck as silently as I could, clicked shut the door with the same noise-aversion mindset, and walked the road toward the fence. With each step, I scanned the ground for anything slithering across my path and listened for a rattle. Getting snake-bit tonight would not be a perfect outcome. Staying alert was my best defense against that happening.

The 9-mm Taurus handgun on my right hip wasn't there to defend myself against snakes. The magazine was loaded, with a shell in the chamber. It was cocked with the safety on. I was prepared to defend myself against whoever it was that wanted me dead.

Nearer the fence. I slowed my walk, having decided to approach the scene as if someone were standing guard at the building, the plywood sides of which I could make out in the moonlight. Nothing moved anywhere near the building. I lowered myself to the ground and scooted under the bottom wire on the fence. My bruised body protested the maneuver.

I moved to the edge of the solar panel field and crossed through the field parallel to the fence, crouching all the while. When I reached the field's far edge, well past the building, I squatted beside one of the panels.

Nothing moved on the hillside. Nothing glinted or made a noise. The dying sounds of the day—an occasional vehicle passing on the highway, the lowing of a cow—were the only disturbances riding the night air. While the stillness was unnerving, it also would help me hear anything approaching the shed.

I moved toward the hill on the other side of the solar field, pausing every few steps to listen before moving again. A mesquite tree maybe fifteen feet tall stood on the hillside about twenty yards upslope from where the ground began to rise from the level solar field. Small bushes were scattered between the tree and where I stood. I moved from bush to bush until I squatted next to the tree.

I leaned against its trunk and peered around it. I had an unobstructed view of the shed. After listening and scanning, I felt certain I was alone. I moved to the front side of the tree, sat, leaned back against the trunk and settled in for a night of watching.

I soon found myself fidgeting more than I would have liked, drawing up my feet to rest my arms on my knees, then stretching out my legs flat again. I removed the dark-colored hat I'd worn to reduce the glint of moonlight from my hairless head, then resettled it.

I supposed someone more practiced at surveillance could shift his mind into neutral and let all the other parts of his body rest while his eyes remained on alert. My mind had too many gears, too many moving parts. I fidgeted.

For the first hour, I watched and listened for the sound of feet scuffing against dirt and rock, a signal that an assailant was creeping up on me. I drew the handgun from its holster and rested it on my lap. Sometime later, I re-holstered it.

I stared at individual bushes arrayed against the hillside and tried to differentiate between thick branches and rifle barrels, between the closely clumped center of a bush and the head and chest of a sniper. In the end, I heard only fluttering wings. I saw only branches.

The degree of nervousness surprised me. I had new respect for lookouts and anyone else assigned to peer into the night for hours on end. Shortly before midnight, something caught my eye ten yards in front of me and I watched entranced as a snake of some kind slid uphill in search of a large insect or a small lizard. After it passed, I drew up my legs to keep them out of the path of anything else slithering by.

And the night drew on. *Is this the best use of my time?* I thought and lay the back of my head against the tree trunk. I might have been enjoying Emma's company at that hour and perhaps enjoying it deeper into the night. The thought of being snuggled with her at my place insinuated itself in my mind and I entered a dream zone, though still alert.

Of course, if Emma knew where I was and what I was doing at that moment, she would not want to snuggle at all. She seemed adamant about me ending my sleuthing and getting on with my life, perhaps making her life a bigger part of it. Tak Sweedner playing detective did not seem to be something she wanted to be part of.

The disheartening truth was that our relationship was not sustainable as things stood at the moment. We were at odds in a critical way. While her concern for my safety *touched* me, her wanting to dictate what I could do *irked* me. So, there I was at the juncture of touched and irked. I needed to decide how much this woman meant to me and how much I was willing to change.

As the sky began to lighten, I began to question what I was doing. I had nothing to show for my hours of sitting on a hill, nothing except serious soreness. There I sat watching a makeshift building in a pasture while everyone else I knew was finishing a night of deep sleep. If I nodded off right now and Roque discovered me, he'd probably feel sorry for his obsessed friend who looked for something criminal in an ordinary line shack.

Dang it, this is not a frivolous exercise! I was not imagining evil in ordinary. I was not seeing criminality where there was none. Something *was* going on here—right here in this pasture—even if absolutely nothing was happening here tonight.

By six o'clock, I concluded that nothing sneaky would happen with the sun about to rise. I got to my feet, aching and stiff, and made my way through the solar panel field to the fence, glancing back at the shed from moment to moment. I slipped under the wire again and this time dusted off the back of my jeans and shirt so I wouldn't soil the truck seat.

Otis seemed puzzled by my arrival at dawn. He was happy to see me, of course, but was uncertain whether he was greeting me or preparing to see me off. Dogs settle into routines, too. After I served breakfast in the bowl, the dog's confusion began to disappear, and it acted again like a dog in the morning.

I, on the other hand, was not ready to embrace the new day. I took off my boots, stretched out on my back on the bed in glorious comfort, and called it a night. For hours, my aching body had craved a prone position and I collapsed into total slumber within a minute or two.

At midmorning, a ragged snore disturbed my sleep. I checked my wristwatch. Ten o'clock. I resisted the impulse to roll over and turn my back on harsh daylight screaming at me through the bedroom window. I knew I needed to be at the yard. It was expected to be a busy day. I arose from the bed without enthusiasm, showered, and began what I was certain would be a long and painful day.

What made it more tiresome was knowing that, come nightfall, I'd be returning to that hillside. I had to. I had to give the shed three or four consecutive nights of surveillance before taking the next step, and the next step would be to enter the building and examine it myself. I didn't want to do that, there being laws against breaking into and entering someone else's property.

CHAPTER NINETEEN

An hour after the sun left the sky, I settled again at the base of the mesquite tree. This time I'd brought some spicy gum to chew on when my senses dulled and a thermos of icy water to sip and to splash on weary eyes. This was going to be a tougher night because I was drained of physical and mental energy. Kaput. Were I a battery, I would be pronounced dead.

When drowsiness came on, I first tried the old trick of self-hugging, reaching across my chest to pull against an upper arm. The muscle strain ramped up blood flow and invigorated my brain. This time the exercise revived me for a few minutes at best.

If someone would just take a shot at me and miss, I'd be wide awake. I joked. I didn't wish for that, but I did crave something more exhilarating than the previous night. Night watchmen needed a dollop of excitement to do their best work.

At nine p.m., my senses were jolted when a diamondback rattler crossed the ground between the shed and me, heading downhill and intent on the scent of a prey. It was twenty feet away. What startled me besides its closeness was its length, measuring perhaps six feet from fangs to rattles. I had been sitting still enough to have escaped its notice. That was a good sign. If the snake hadn't detected me, maybe a man wouldn't either.

A half hour later, my system had settled down from the close encounter with Mr. Rattler and I was fading fast, when the puttering noise of a small engine reached my ears. The sound came from beyond the crest of the hill. It was music to my ears, a symphonic invitation to hope again. My face smiled without my brain telling it to. I'd gambled and won.

I moved around behind the mesquite trunk, and the noise grew louder as the vehicle descended the slope. The rider bumped along in the dark because no headlights played along the path in front of the machine. It came into view a hundred feet north of the shed. It was a two-seat utility vehicle with a canvas top and a small bed in the rear. The person driving it was the sole occupant. The driver pulled up next to the shed, then backed around so the bed of the vehicle faced the building's door. Good. Something would be loaded tonight.

Moonlight allowed me to see the shed, but not as clearly as it had twenty-four hours earlier. I couldn't make out the facial features of the driver. It was a man, though, I could tell that by the way he moved. A stocky man. He seemed agile, so he wasn't elderly. It could be Ruskey or someone else with his build. He stepped out of the four-wheeler, unlocked the door of the building, swung it inward, and disappeared inside. The door closed.

Bring it on! Sleep supposedly is necessary to restore depleted cellular activity and trigger growth, but I've noticed tension does the same thing in a pinch. Weariness fled the instant the four-wheeler rolled to a stop. Just that quick, I felt invigorated, renewed, and ready to rock. Who needs sleep?! Though dreams are nice.

The man's movement outside the shed had not been furtive in the least. In fact, he had moseyed to the door, quite certain he was alone this night on the hill. His false confidence gave me an edge. A man with his guard down was a man about to give up a secret.

I repositioned myself beside the tree and awaited his exit. I had no intention of revealing myself unless I had to. If he stepped from the building with someone bound head and foot, I'd stride toward him with drawn gun. That wasn't going to happen, but I knew what to do if it did.

If all he carried was a package or a bundle, however, I'd watch and not intervene. A package could be bagged supplement, a square just a salt block. While it was an odd hour to retrieve ranch supplies, there was no law against ranching in darkness.

What worried me was the third possibility: If he carried out something unidentifiable, what then? I couldn't stroll up, glance into the bed, and—finding a bucket of supplement—wish him a good evening and stroll away.

Trespassers can't get away with that in the middle of the night on a lonely hillside. More than anything, I hoped for no ambiguity in what the man loaded tonight.

Noises came from inside the shed, but they were so faint I couldn't identify them. Light leaked from beneath the door, which meant he'd carried in a flashlight or lantern because no electric lines ran to the building. I listened and stared at the shed and listened and stared some more. My imagination galloped.

After twenty minutes, my patience ran out. Nothing could be accomplished this far from the shed. I had to get nearer. I looked around the hillside for a rifleman waiting to plug me. I didn't expect to see one, of course, but it seemed prudent to check. I saw nothing.

Easing away from the tree, I moved from one bush to the next, keeping one eye on the door and one on the hill. I sprinted the last twenty feet to the side of the shed and sank to the ground. I didn't want to give a shooter a well-defined silhouette against the plywood siding.

I squatted and panted, my heart pumping with excitement. If I didn't calm down, I was going to do something rash and spoil the night for myself. *Slow! Down!* I still was an amateur at this skulking business.

All I heard from the building was an occasional grunt, some clinking, footfalls. I envisioned the person moving salt blocks around and lifting bags and dropping them a few feet away. Why spend so much time moving the materials? When none of the sounds clarified anything for me, frustration spilled over.

I have to peek beneath that door. Alarms clanged in my head at the thought. Even *thinking* about peeking into the room was foolishness. If someone yanked open the door with me sprawled in front of it, I would be a dead man or forced to threaten whoever stood there with death.

Still, I felt compelled to get a closer look and took a tentative step toward the front of the shed. At the moment, the door opened, light spilling out. I froze and backtracked, listening for the sounds of someone running around the building to confront me. I gripped my handgun in two hands and prepared to spring whichever way I needed to get a drop on the person.

Then I heard the scrape of something being pushed across the surface of the four-wheeler bed. Footfalls told me the person re-entered the shed, grunted, exited the building and again put something in the bed. He was loading the vehicle. With what?! This was my hoped-for moment.

I steeled myself to confront the man and his cargo. When I heard the door close and the clank of the lock being fixed in place, I started around the corner. As I did so, the four-wheeler's motor fired up—and a shot rang out.

Crazed by the report, I jumped backward. I almost ran into the solar field, but Pablo had done that and gotten himself shot in the back. Was I hit? No. I shuffled backward away from the building and prepared to defend myself against the shooter.

No one came for me, but I didn't lower my weapon. I waited and still no one came. Then I realized what I was hearing: The utility vehicle and driver were ascending the hill, not coming around the shed for me. He was getting away! I sprinted past the corner of the building and through the darkness could just make out the four-wheeler topping the hill. It disappeared.

I groaned and held my head in my hands, gun still gripped in one of them. What had happened?! Why fire a round at me and flee? That made no sense. Then I knew. I understood with horror that I hadn't heard a gunshot at all. It was the four-wheeler's engine backfiring!. *Of course!* I groaned again.

I knew full well what a gunshot sounded like. That wasn't what I'd heard. Leaking fuel and air had combusted outside an engine cylinder and blown a hole in my plan! I'd messed up. I groaned a third time.

I peered up the hill and considered running to the top to intercept the unloading of cargo. It wasn't too late to see for myself what had been hauled away. I took a tentative step in that direction, then hesitated. The lighted dial on my watch read 12:14. Would he return tonight? He might. Tonight could be transport night. In fact, he might come back down in the next few minutes! I enjoyed a tactical advantage staying by the shed—familiar ground—so I decided to wait right where I was and see if I could salvage something from the night.

I berated myself for my actions of the last hour, showing myself little mercy. *You stupid jerk! A backfire! What a bonehead!* This was what parents and teachers called a learning moment. I called it humiliation. I could not foresee ever sharing the events of the last few minutes with anyone. Ever.

I holstered the Taurus and trudged over to resume my surveillance. As I waited by the tree, all my scurrying around behind the shed came back to me and I realized I'd left plenty of incriminating tracks. They could tell a story in the light of day.

I groaned yet again, got to my feet and walked back to the shed. After snapping branches from a bush, I swished the ground behind the building, next to it and all the way to the tree, then resettled myself by the tree.

In the next few minutes, the man didn't return on his four-wheeler, but perspective did. Emotions settled down. My usual good sense showed up. I began to feel much better about the incident, if not about me.

Had I rushed around the corner with gun drawn and found salt blocks in the bed, I would have opened myself to an armed assault charge. I'd have placed myself in legal jeopardy. But I hadn't done so—not for lack of trying!—and the nighttime visitor had driven away still ignorant of my presence in the pasture. In other words, I retained the upper hand.

The backfire had saved me. It had been a blessing, albeit an embarrassing one. Within a few minutes of reaching that conclusion, I got to my feet and began the walk to my truck. I'd return another day with a better plan.

CHAPTER TWENTY

"I have a lock-pick kit. I can get in that shed and I'm desperate to do so," I told Roque, who sat across the table from me at Live Oak Gorditas, his face buried in a fried tortilla. He grunted. "Technically, I would be burglarizing the property, of course."

"Technically," he said between chews.

We'd reviewed my last two nights of surveillance. He'd raised his eyebrows when I began to recount the boredom of it and then squinted at me when I told him of my narrow escape from a flagrant weapons charge. "If the man indeed had been loading contraband, my 'assault' would instantly have turned into a citizen's arrest, of course. Case solved. Refulgent satisfaction. You'd have been proud of me!"

"Uh huh, but if it had been Ruskey just loading cattle feed, you'd have been in deep guano."

I had Roque's full attention. "I want to return tonight, Roque. I want to pick the lock and turn the inside of that shed upside down. If there's something there worth killing me for or any kind of evidence of contraband, I want to find it. Tonight."

Roque finished the tortilla, sipped his coke, and leaned toward me. "You are telling me this...why."

I gave him my friendliest smile. "I want you to come along with me."

He sighed. "*Pides mucho.* You want *both* of us to go to jail. That's what friends are for, I guess."

"No jail. I just want you to stand guard up the hill with a two-way radio and to whisper in my ear, 'He's coming' so I can get out, lock up, and find a hiding place. You can run away and hide, too. No confrontation. I just don't want to enter the shed without a backup. Whaddya say?"

• • •

After nightfall, we rendezvoused in the swale below the fence and made our way to the mesquite tree. On the theory that nighttime visits to the shed happened at the same approximate hour, we waited together by the tree. We whispered a little to puncture the boredom but remained attentive to the night around us. Time slipped by quicker when two people huddled in the night.

When no one showed by midnight, we discussed the next step and decided I should enter the shed. We both were armed. Though the weight of the handgun on my belt was reassuring, we weren't looking for a firefight.

"See that clump of trees against the sky straight up the hill," Roque whispered. I made out the outline of the arbor against the night sky and nodded. "That's where I'm headed. Give me five minutes to get settled there. I'll check in when I'm ready."

He scuttled away. Soon I couldn't hear his movement nor make him out in the dark. I felt for and found the lock pick in my pocket. If the pick failed, I planned to kick in the door and let Ruskey wonder who burgled his building.

"I'm ready whenever you are, partner in crime." Roque's whisper seemed loud.

"Roger. Ten four. Over and out... Let's see, what other radio jargon do I know?"

"*Solo ve!* You waste time."

I ran to the shed without fear of detection. It's wonderful to have a lookout. Inserting the picks, I fiddled for a few seconds and the lock dropped away. I swung open the door, stepped through and closed it behind me. My LED flashlight beam illuminated the interior and reassured me that no one was poised to pounce.

The room was as Roque had described it. Stacked near the wall to the left of the door were twenty-five or thirty bags of Southern States pelleted supplement, each bag with an image of a staring cow and calf. I could feel the pellets through the paper bagging. Eleven other fifty-pound bags of a different color and labeled "Mineral" were stacked by the right wall. Filling the center of the room were a dozen or more brownish salt blocks. Each of them also weighed fifty pounds. No wonder I'd heard so much grunting in the building the night before.

I licked a finger, rubbed it across a surface of one block and tasted it. Salty. The blocks were what they seemed to be. I moved the top three bags from the stack of supplement and determined that beneath them lay more bags and nothing else, so I restacked them as before. The bags of mineral felt pellety from the outside, but I took out my pocketknife and made a short slit in one bag. The pellet I extracted indeed seemed to be extruded cattle feed.

I replaced the pellet and stood to take in the room, running the beam of the flashlight along the walls and floor. Studs were exposed, so there was no interior paneling for hiding anything inside the walls. The plywood floor was screwed in place so that footfalls wouldn't loosen them. Dust covered most of the visible floor along with the crushed remains of feed pellets. Lower-traffic areas of the floor on the far side of the room were cleaner.

I stomped around the room testing the flooring and it sounded the same from wall to wall. I sat on a stack of bags and let the light flit up and around the room. Two buckets stood in one corner, right side up and empty. A metal fence post leaned against the wall in a front corner next to a pile of emptied paper feed bags.

All in all, the room appeared to be what it was purported to be: a line shack, a feed storage building, an outlying cattle-operations facility for use as needed. There was nothing in this room worth killing anyone over. Not tonight.

If the little structure indeed was a contraband transfer station of some kind—and I increasingly doubted that it was— and if someone had dumped something there for someone else to pick up and carry away, I was a day late in intercepting it.

I fumbled the radio from the clamp on my belt and raised it to my lips. "OK, Roque. Let's go home. I can't find a dagnabbed thing out of the ordinary here."

. . .

I called Emma that afternoon. We hadn't seen one another for several days and I felt guilty about not checking in with her. She was in town partly because of me and had a reasonable expectation of her friend paying attention to her. I didn't believe either one of us thought of our interaction as courting, but we were friends of the opposite sex who at the very least were attracted to one another at some level.

"Whatcha doing?" I asked as casually as I thought believable.

"Excuse me, sir. Do I know you? Your voice sounds vaguely familiar."

"Gotcha. I've been derelict in my calling. I apologize."

"Apology accepted. What have *you* been doing?" she asked. I decided to tell her later after making amends, so I spoke in generalities. We finally agreed that a *Planet of the Apes* movie would be a good way to escape our work-a-day worlds for at least an evening. I arranged to pick her up at her mother's home at five o'clock for dinner at the Steak Barn, afterward crossing the highway to the movie house.

She wore a white collared cotton top over simple blue cotton slacks. It was an unadorned manner of dress that, by its very simplicity, backdropped her personality—open, bubbly, clear-eyed, fun. It was all there on display as we sat down at the restaurant. We were a happy couple, good friends at least.

Over steaks, the ebullience evaporated the instant I confessed to my midnight snooping. The news was not well-received. Emma appeared stunned and lay down her fork to listen as I recounted the nights of surveillance, close encounters, and ultimate frustration.

The way she set her jaw and glared at me was my first clue that she was upset at the news. The second clue was the fist she slammed onto the tabletop hard enough to warrant startled looks from a couple at the nearest table.

"You are so stupid!" she said only a little quieter than she had struck the table. At that moment, I felt more embarrassed than stupid, but she had a point. "Tak, I really thought you were smarter than that. I really felt I had made the case for law enforcement being left to people in law enforcement uniforms. I'm *so* disappointed."

"Well," I said, with a smirk, "I'm disappointed, too. I'm disappointed that all I have to show for my nights of snooping is a tired body and fresh evidence that I *have* no evidence. I'm disappointed at being a failure."

Emma wasn't amused. "This isn't funny. You're fooling around with something that could take your life! Someone has tried to kill you twice and you're still playing Little Detective. Little Sherlock. You and Watson, your fellow sleuth. You both *deserve* to be shot."

"That's a little harsh."

Emma took a deep breath and looked down at her plate. "I didn't mean that." She ran one hand through her hair and sat back in her chair. "Did you leave things in the shed as you found them? Did you give Ruskey or whoever is making night-time trips to the shed any more reason to want you dead? What aren't you telling me?"

I smiled at her, enjoying her rant, though I dared not admit it. "I've told you all, Emma. All I've done. All I've found, which, in a word, is nothing. And listen closely because here is where I'm going with this: I'm ready to accept your recommendation that I retire from the case. I'm licked."

After a moment to absorb what she'd heard, she smiled, reached across the table and rubbed the back of my hand. "Good. Now you can concentrate on me." That brought a smile to *my* face. She quizzed me another minute or two to reassure herself that I was serious about pulling back. The rest of the meal was quite pleasant.

As we walked from the restaurant, Emma took hold of my arm and leaned her head against my shoulder. It was the first act of affection either of us had demonstrated and reaffirmed the correctness of my decision.

What I had confessed to her in the restaurant minutes earlier was true: I *was* done. *Finis.* My focus on the shed was too speculative to justify continuing it. I'd grasped for straws and found none. It was time to give up the hunt and to admit defeat. My solace was that Emma's companionship was a sensational consolation prize.

We drove just across Hwy. 90 to the Uvalde movie complex and were snuggling like old friends and maybe future lovers as we entered the theater. Neither of us was hungry but I bought popcorn anyway. I could never really enjoy a movie without popcorn. The snack food made a so-so movie entertaining and a boffo movie sensational. Exorbitant theater concession prices were predicated on people like me.

The apes quickly won us over—Emma especially loved the compassionate but brave leader of the gorillas. "Did you know that a group of apes is called a shrewdness?" she declared.

We were leaning toward each other, our noses inches apart. "Shrewdness? As in shrewd?"

"As in clever, calculating, smart. Yep. That's why no one will ever mistake you for an ape." She laughed and leaned away. I loved it.

CHAPTER TWENTY-ONE

The next several days were so much fun. A burden had been lifted from my shoulders, my mind, and maybe my soul. Yes, I'd become a failed detective. I did not know who shot poor Pablo and admitted as much to Roque and Tomas, informing them that I'd dropped my investigation. They seemed happy that the self-imposed burden of solving the crime no longer pressed on me.

I did think Roque dropped his eyes too fast when he heard the news, trying to shield me from the disappointment he felt and might have conveyed to me in a look. But heck, *I* felt let down, too. The amateur detective had been stumped.

Failure left a bitter taste in me even when sweetened with the memory of how hard I'd tried. Emma's embrace of the new me didn't completely erase the feeling that I'd failed the family of Pablo. Nevertheless, I was ready to move on.

I was helped along when a broker called to say he had a buyer for the sixty aluminum barrels that had been stacked way too long behind the office. He'd even wrangled a better price than I'd been prepared to accept. As the two truckloads of barrels left the yard, I opened and closed the cash register several times to celebrate the infusion of cash.

"You're not gloating are you, Tak?" Tomas asked, looking at me over reading glasses before returning to the computer screen in front of him.

"I am, actually. Another shrewd buy and an even shrewder sale. Speaking of which, did you know a group of apes is called a shrewdness?"

"Nope," he responded without even looking up.

Having caught up on my sleep, I was full of energy and expending it each evening with Emma, Eating out. Playing Monopoly with her and her mother. The two of us taking Otis for a walk up and down the hills of Garner State Park. Good times. Emma would leave next week, and I struggled to make up my mind how much commitment I felt toward the woman. Quite a lot, it seemed. But was it enough to continue to see each other long distance?

I was hung up on her. I admitted as much to myself. She seemed similarly stranded between wanting more and all-out committing to the relationship. Didn't courting used to be easier than this? I couldn't remember.

When Roque invited me to a Sunday afternoon lunch at the ranch, I accepted without reservation. I needed space to weigh my future. Because Emma and her mother were obligated to visit a cousin that afternoon, I went alone to the Zamarripa ranch.

Driving the lane to the ranch house, the turnoff to the solar field caught my eye. A mix of emotions bubbled up. Yet by the time I reached the ranch house, they had settled again. That was then, I thought, and this was now.

Pele Zamarripa and his wife Grizelda were perfect hosts. Smiling. Generous. Interested in everything a guest had to say while under their roof. I'd been in the home numerous times before. It was a sprawling adobe-style one-story residence with open post ceilings, slate floors, several ornate crucifixes on walls, and many pieces of heavy wooden furniture, some of it carved from mesquite. The home echoed with friendliness and smelled of fried foods and bubbling bean pots.

Roque and Maria greeted me at the door, Roque with a big smile and Maria with a hug. His parents soon appeared near the entranceway and the five of us strolled through the living room and into the dining room where pots and platters filled the table.

"Sorry the girlfriend couldn't come, Tak. She have better things to do?" Roque asked as we settled around a heavy wood table. I explained her absence.

Maria scooted her chair to the table next to Roque. Her dark bright eyes always shone when she looked at her beau. She patted his arm now, sort of reassurance that she was there for him. I imagined Roque indeed felt reassured.

"Well," she said across the table, "I was looking forward to seeing Emma today. But seeing you *almost* makes up for her not being here."

"Almost...?" I asked. We grinned at one another before bowing our heads as Roque's father blessed the food. During the short prayer, I reflected on being adjacent to Maria and felt a twinge of discomfort. Roque had said she was close to Pablo's widow. No doubt she'd heard from Roque that I had given up the search. I dreaded dinner-table conversation veering onto the subject of Pablo.

But by the time apple empanada desserts were passed around the table, I had relaxed. The unfortunate demise of Pablo never came up, probably because my perfect hosts had forbade it for fear of embarrassing me. We somehow talked about the solar panel field next door and my unfortunate tumble down the mountainside in my truck and other subjects tied to the death of Pele Zamarripa's employee without once talking about Pablo himself or his killer. It was a first-class show of consideration for a guest.

After lunch, Pele and I retired to his den, which opened on a patio filled with numerous varieties of flowering plants, most of which I couldn't identify. Ignorance of the names of plants didn't take away from the pleasure of viewing them. Roque joined us after helping clear the table. He said Maria had decided to take a short nap and hoped it wasn't an affront to me that she did so.

I laughed it off. "She's quite a gal, your Maria."

He nodded. "If we don't get married soon, my father has threatened to throw me out with only the clothes on my back."

Pele smiled and shook his head. "*No cierto*. I told you could take your computer with you." A teasing and happy family.

I sat across from Pele in a comfortable soft chair and told him, probably not for the first time, that he was the only Pele I had ever heard of besides the legendary soccer player from Brazil. He smiled. "The famous Pele wasn't even Pele when he was born. It was Edson, a shortened version of Edison. He was named for Thomas Edison. Kind of odd for a Brazilian boy to be named after an American inventor, but he was. Edson Arantes do Nascimento. Pele was a nickname."

"And were you named for Mr. Nascimento?"

"I was," he said with a satisfied smile. "As I grew up, it turned out I could play a little soccer myself. I was actually pretty good at *futbol* in high school, so my name wasn't an embarrassment to me. It was a challenge, one that I never really lived up to, I suppose, but I did all right."

Roque waved his hand to dismiss his father's self-deprecation. "He did better than all right. He made all-state and could have gotten a scholarship somewhere had he wanted to leave Uvalde County. But he didn't. The ranch called."

"And I suppose I am going to die here now, on this old ranch," Pele concluded, pulling a long face, "a sad old man, my son having squandered his good fortune in finding Maria yet never marrying her, instead going off to live on the streets of Uvalde, writing stories on his computer. A sad ending for all of us."

Roque grimaced and rolled his eyes. His father wasn't going to give an inch in insisting that his son scoop up that gal.

We settled into quiet conversation about people we knew and ranch trends and whether Mexico would ever get its act together and become a safe place for gringos in general and Texans in particular, a place we could explore like in the old days. Chit-chat is all it was. Finally, I felt compelled to bring up what we'd been avoiding.

"I want you to know how sorry I am that I wasn't able to help find justice for Pablo," I said, looking across the room at Pele. "I never was able to get any traction. I must have stirred up *something*, of course, or else I wouldn't have been targeted. Yet if they'd known how little I *knew*, they wouldn't have bothered.

"Anyway," I continued, "I'm disappointed. I'm sorry for Pablo's family and friends. I appreciate both of you steering conversation in another direction over lunch."

Neither man responded. I wasn't sure what that meant.

"Ah, Tak," Pele said, after a moment more, "don't feel bad. Pablo's family appreciates what you did and feels guilty about you being assaulted.

They feel responsible for you getting hurt, though I assured them that you're your own man."

"Thanks."

Pele continued. "And you may have come closer to solving the mystery than you realized. If I were you, what I'd do now is just what you're doing: Let it be. Put it on the shelf. Take a deep breath. Step away. Your instincts are pretty good. Let your mind percolate on the murder without public pressure."

He uncrossed his legs and crossed them the other way, straightening the sharp crease in one pant leg as he did so. "You'll figure it out one day. I have confidence in you. It may come to you in the middle of the night, and you'll think it's indigestion. But there it'll be—the solution. A relaxed mind is a great problem-solver."

I was astounded by the soliloquy. It was obvious he didn't believe I had given up the search for Pablo's killer. He didn't understand that I wasn't resting and letting my mind "percolate" on the matter. I had withdrawn and put the matter out of my mind. I had done so because Emma was adamant that I end the investigation. If I renewed it, I didn't know what her reaction might be.

I said none of this to Pele, of course, who re-crossed his legs once more and smoothed the fabric of his pant leg. "A final thought," he said then. "Crooks love to misdirect us. They'll steal a plate of cookies, and you'll gripe on and on about the stolen food and not realize it really was the plate they were after. Things aren't always what they seem in a crime."

"How do you know so much about the criminal mind, Dad?" Roque asked, looking at his father across steepled fingers.

"I raised you," he said and stared at his son, "and what you are *not* doing with Maria is a crime. *El crimen!* If you don't propose to her pretty danged quick, Tak is going to have to figure out who shot *you!*" Then he dropped the severe expression and beamed at a son he loved.

CHAPTER TWENTY-TWO

Tomas and I talked cars the next day. We each had owned a few of them over the years—in Tomas' case, dating clear back to the 1950s—and we wished we still had some of them sitting in our driveways. In truth, the remembered cars might not have possessed as deep-throated a roar as we recalled, nor turned as many heads as we boasted, but they had brought us pleasure and we loved to revisit the feeling.

He and I were unloading a 1959 Cadillac Eldorado bought at auction. It was an eighteen-foot-long, black convertible with dramatically sharp tailfins, bulbous headlamps and more chrome in its grille than on a hundred Smart cars. The Caddy was a beast, albeit with a blown engine and a missing hubcap. I had visions of refurbishing the soft-top, dropping in an overhauled engine and making two-hundred percent profit.

I eased the car off the rollback and into the shade of a long open shed where we stored convertibles. Keeping the hot Texas sun off convertible fabric always was a good investment. I set the foot brake and closed the door. "Big but beautiful."

"That it is. Looks like it ought to be on a launching pad somewhere,' Tomas said as he operated the truck's hydraulics and slid the truck bed back in place. I removed my leather gloves and admired the replacement truck, which was a few years newer than the wrecked one. My insurance agent had responded faster than I ever imagined he could. I'd been able to put it into service within a week.

When Tomas finished, I climbed in the cab with him to ride back to the shop. We rambled through the rows of cars without speaking, then a glance

123

at an older model Ford sparked a memory. "Tomas, did I ever tell you about the time I bought that Edsel? The one the guy parked and forgot about?"

"Don't remember any Edsel stories."

"Well," I said, rolling down the cab window for some breeze, "it was a find and a half. The Edsel was a sales bust for Ford, you remember."

"A big bust."

"Right, so not many of them were built. In my view, it was a good-looking car, at least the original models. It got junky-looking quick, but the original '58 and '59 design, with that horse-collar grille, wasn't a bad-looking set of wheels." Tomas agreed as he parked the truck next to the office.

We moved the conversation inside where Billy was working on a carburetor at a bench in the shop. He looked up when we entered but returned to his project. The young man could be a role model for how to work at an entry-level job.

In the office, I resumed my story-telling. "Anyway, I heard from someone, I can't remember who it was right now, someone who said he knew of a guy who bought one of the original Edsels, supposedly drove it till it was about give out, and parked it. That was significant news at the time because there was a flurry of interest in Edsels. I think it was the fiftieth anniversary or something. I decided to find that Edsel."

The phone rang and I answered it. Bishop Castillo wondered if he could stop by and see me later in the afternoon. I told him he was welcome any time. I ended the call.

"Good guy, Bishop Castillo. Never gives up on me. Probably going to be rewarded one of these days when I clean up and go back to church. I'm trying to remember why I ever quit attending."

"Wouldn't hurt you to get a little religion," Tomas said. "What about that Edsel?"

* * *

The story...

Finding the car was not easy. My original informant could only offer me third-hand information. He'd heard of a man in Del Rio who owned an old

Edsel he bought new and who might be willing to sell it. After hearing the story, I mulled the idea and decided to search for the car. I made numerous calls to friends in the automotive retail industry in Del Rio and drew a blank. They'd never heard of the guy nor the car he was said to own.

So, I'd taken to rolling through selected Del Rio neighborhoods that might have old cars parked in back yards or in garages open to the street. I spotted nothing in those neighborhoods except a lot of old, rusting cars of zero value. After I noticed several people looking back at me with suspicion as I peered into their yards, I ceased the neighborhood searches altogether.

Someone suggested I place an ad in the Del Rio newspaper, but I didn't heed the advice. It was never a good price negotiation tactic to advertise how desperate you were to locate a vehicle. I estimated I'd have to pay twice as much for the Edsel if I found it through such an appeal. I wanted the car, but needed to make a profit off it, too.

Weeks of periodic searching went by. I was nearly to a point of quitting when a friend of a friend of a friend recalled that *her* friend's father had owned an Edsel. Because this was a childhood memory, it wasn't the most reliable clue I'd ever received. However, the woman said she knew where her friend had once lived and suspected the father still lived there. Turns out it wasn't in Del Rio at all, but on a ranch road almost as close to Brackettville.

After I located the home, I felt as if I'd found the proverbial needle in the haystack. The place had a haystack, or, rather, a stack of big bales. The house was situated on a hillside a quarter mile off the road. As I drove the lane, my hopes began to evaporate. For one thing, the one outbuilding looked to be a horse barn and ill-suited for storing a car.

For another, no machinery was parked in sheds or under a tree. It didn't look like anyone at the address had a fondness for old cars or tractors or anything else on wheels.

The west-facing house itself was a two-story wood-frame structure with a high front porch that was roofed in a way that suggested it had been added on. Four rocking chairs were grouped at one corner of the porch floor. It looked like a terrific place to enjoy a sunset.

A ten-year-old Chevrolet half-ton pickup sat in a parking area next to the house, suggesting someone was home. I parked next to the truck, walked a faint rut toward the house, and climbed a dozen stairs to the high porch. I knocked and turned to admire the view. The scene was spectacular in a southwestern Texas sort of way.

When I heard the door open, I'd looked around and seen a gray-whiskered man in jeans and a collared shirt standing in the doorway. "Are you Mr. Graves?" I'd asked. He'd nodded and I introduced myself. Before I could say anything else, he suggested we sit in the rockers.

He moved across the threshold in mincing steps, eased shut the door behind him, and shuffled over to the nearest rocking chair. I pulled a rocker closer to him and we both sat. "What can I do for you?"

I'd laughed. There I was in the midst of a long and fruitless search and he made it sound as though I'd just been driving by and pulled in on an impulse. I explained the laughter, hoping I hadn't offended him. As I rocked in the comfortable chair, I told him of my Edsel odyssey that had ended at that moment on his attractive porch.

I assured him that if he didn't own the car I sought, it didn't matter. It was worth visiting him just to sit on his porch. He'd smiled at that, kind of enigmatically, it seemed to me. "The Edsel. You're after the Edsel," he said, and my heart leaped. I stopped rocking.

I'd found it! While my search hadn't been a truly monumental quest, the buzz I felt in head and stomach at least matched that of Lewis and Clark upon seeing the Pacific Ocean. *"Oh, the joy!"* as Clark wrote. I pulled myself together and into a negotiating frame of mind.

"So, you have an Edsel?" I asked with the nonchalance of a man only asking out of courtesy. "I might be interested in it. Depends upon what kind of condition it's in. What year is it?"

It was a 1958, he said, or believed it was. He hadn't thought about it in a long time. But he had bought it new—yes, it was '58, he said then, because he'd purchased it one year before he and his Sarah had married. He said he used to joke that Sarah really married him for the car. They'd driven it for ten years before he'd parked it. "That's the whole story. It's still parked."

"Out of the weather?"

"Oh, yes. Hasn't been a drop of rain fall on it, nor a ray of sunlight shined on it, not in many a year."

This was sounding better every minute and I struggled to continue to feign mild interest. I went so far as to fake a yawn and to apologize for it. "Well, I just thought I'd drop by and take a look. Is it in the barn over there?"

The man looked at the barn and then at me. "That's a horse barn. Guy who rents the place from me still keeps his riding stock in there from time to time. Wouldn't be room for a parked car in there. None of the stalls is big enough."

I waited but he just looked at me with a noncommittal expression. The thought passed through my mind that the guy was senile. He had no car, only memories of once having owned one. The thought troubled me. I sighed then and asked the question he seemed to want me to ask. "So, Mr. Graves, where *is* the car?"

• • •

Tomas had leaned back in his desk chair during my recounting of the search. He'd become quite absorbed in it, as I knew he would. It was a good story. He tapped a ballpoint pen on the keyboard next to him and waited now for me to reveal what the old man had revealed. "All right, all right. I'll ask. Where was the car?"

I looked up, as if startled by the question. "What car?"

He groaned. "*No es gracioso.* I don't have time for this."

CHAPTER TWENTY-THREE

I always liked telling the story because of its punch line. For that reason, I tended to drag out the telling. Clearly, Tomas was nearing the end of his patience with me. Denouement time.

"OK. Enough joking around, Tomas, but first, I want you to guess. Where do you *think* the car was?" Tomas showed a poker face. I couldn't tell if he was thinking or just waiting. I raised my eyebrows at him. He made a rude face in response.

"He gave it to his daughter and she had it parked in *her* barn," he said. I appreciated him playing along with me.

"Nope. This is what Mr. Graves told me." I paused for dramatic effect. "'You're sitting on it,' he said. I said, 'I beg your pardon. You turned it into rocking chairs?' And we both laughed. Then he explained."

Tomas wrinkled his brow, so I hurried to the story's conclusion. "Mr. Graves had parked the Edsel at the front of his house. Some months later when the couple decided to build a high, full-width porch across the front of their home, they chose out of fondness for the car to leave it where it sat and to build the porch around it. The Edsel was under the porch floor."

Tomas shook his head and leaned back to look at the ceiling before responding. "You're kidding me."

"Nope. Under the porch floor. A couple of days later, another guy and I returned, disassembled one end of the porch wall, extracted the Edsel, and put the wall back together. Other than having the little dents and faded paint of a car driven for a decade, the Edsel was in wonderful condition.

Push button transmission worked great. I did very little to it and sold it for a pretty penny."

Tomas slapped the arm of his chair. "Well, you're right, that's a heck of a story. I'll enjoy retelling it."

"Just don't give the ending away," I suggested, as the phone rang. Back to business.

• • •

It wasn't till the end of the day when I was heading home from Whataburger with a bag of goodies for me and for Otis that the revelation arrived. It came as a mind-cleaving epiphany that left me confused for a moment. The mental experience was so discombobulating that I pulled the truck to the side of the road. I sat there, truck motor idling, both hands on the wheel, eyes fixed on some distant point.

A true revelation is like a slap in the face. A gentler analogy might be that it is like a first sweet kiss. It electrifies, clarifies, brings a rush of emotions that resist interpretation. A revelatory moment is a mental high and as this one struck, I felt on top of the world. "What do you know about that!"

Telling the Edsel story had reordered my frame of thinking. Somewhere in the back of my mind, things shifted and the rearranged thoughts had jumped to the front. I was staggered when they landed. It was just as Pele Zamarripa had said. A relaxed mind is capable of solving a problem that seems insoluble under pressure. I felt new respect for how a brain works, as well as additional regard for Pele Zamarripa.

"The Edsel was *under* the porch," I said to the windshield. "Right there under my nose. That's the answer: The incriminating stuff in Ruskey's shed is *under* the floor."

The longer I sat there on the shoulder of the highway and explored the possibility of having figured out the mystery of the shed, the more excited I became. Clues started piling up in my mind and morphing into something that felt very much like proof.

Things like the shed, built on a slope, must have at least two or three feet of open area under the lower end. Things like the siding on the building running clear to the ground, not to keep rattlers from cooling themselves in the shade but to hide something.

In the hiding space was a cache of something too large to remove in one or two trips. I was sure of it. What that something was I still had no clue, but it was there and the man on the four-wheeler was retrieving it, bit by bit, in the dark of night.

The man I nearly confronted that night wasn't in the shed for an hour moving bags and blocks around on the floor. That never made sense to me and the nonsense of it stumped me. He may have moved a few sacks of cattle feed stacked on the floor to expose and remove a sheet of plywood flooring, but the bulk of his work that night was *under* the floor.

The plywood sheeting, I recalled now with a tiny shake of my head, was *screwed* down. Which means it could be *unscrewed* and removed to give access. I replayed my time standing outside the shed with the man inside. I tried to recall hearing the distinctive whirring sound of a cordless drill working on screws. I couldn't capture the aural memory. Perhaps he'd used a screwdriver.

"Gotcha!" I said aloud. "Case solved!" Well, maybe "solved" was too sweeping a conclusion to assert at that moment, but I felt *this* close to puzzling out the mystery. I had to look under that floor. That was the thing. No question. Tonight. Under the floor.

I eased the truck back onto the highway. Minutes later, as the truck rattled across the railroad tracks, I found myself in full celebration mode and singing "Happy days are here again…" Otis was, of course, excited to see me and I had no way of knowing if his excitement was a combination of having me home and smelling the burger in a sack, or if he sensed the excitement in me and simply joined in.

We danced around each other, me holding the sack high and him jumping for it, me hooting and him barking. What a pair of dingbats we were and how happily I conceded the condition. It was a dingbat moment and we lived up to it without reservation.

I calmed the dog and myself, pieced his burger, poured his water, and retreated into the house. Grabbing a tall glass of tea, I headed for my chair, bag in hand, and plopped down, almost spilling the tea. I began to consume the double-burger, my forehead wrinkled in concentration.

I had two pivotal decisions to make, one perhaps life-altering. The lesser one was whether to return to the shed alone or ask Roque to return with me. I was anxious about the idea of being inside the building, dismantling the floor, and peering underneath with no one covering me outside the building. This was not a game. If I were discovered in and under the shed, I would be killed. That was certain. What other choice would the discoverer have? The answer was none.

I couldn't undertake this without backup. I couldn't imagine that Roque would refuse. He more likely would become incensed were he to find out I did it without asking for his help. I glanced at my watch. Quarter to seven. I took another big bite of the burger and pulled out my phone.

"Hello?" sounded in my ear.

"Roque Racoon, I presume," I said.

"Speaking." Roque and I had our routines down.

"Listen, whatcha doing tonight?" The silence that followed was not unexpected. He surely sensed what I had in mind. My best friend knew me well. Our connection was a plus most of the time.

"I'll reserve comment until I know why you are asking."

"Uh huh. We've got to get in that shed tonight. I've figured it out. I know where to look now," I said in a rush.

Silence. "Do you know what you will *find* where you look?"

Got me. "Well, no. That part still is a mystery. But I'm certain that what that building contains of interest is *under* the floor. Ruskey is hiding something under there that he has to cart away at night, a little at a time. That's what the guy was doing the other night, maybe Ruskey himself. He was removing a sheet of plywood flooring and crawling underneath. I'll stake my life on it."

"Good choice of words there."

I admitted to him that the possibility of something being hidden beneath the floor had occurred to me once or twice but had seemed implausible. The flooring was tightly fixed to the joists wherever I'd looked. Furthermore, the bags of supplement hadn't covered full sheets of flooring, only parts of individual sheets. Had an entire piece of plywood been covered, I would have moved the bags and investigated. A subfloor solution just hadn't seemed likely to me.

"I guess I was looking for a trapdoor, I don't know. I feel chagrined and a little stupid for not looking under there," I said. "But I will now.

"You still don't know there is anything there."

"True, but we will know, one way or the other, after tonight... if you're willing to help," I said. "I don't like asking you to place yourself in jeopardy. I really don't, but who else can I ask to cover my rear end while I'm in there?"

"Oh, I don't know. Emma?"

"Definitely not. Absurd idea. Too dangerous."

"Plus, she'll probably divorce you, so to speak, if she ever finds out."

He hit on the nub of my second and most pivotal decision: to tell or not tell Emma. She would not like it. In fact, she was apt to dislike it so much that she would say goodbye a final time. She had clearly signaled to me that I needed to choose between chasing after a murderer or chasing after her.

"I know. I know," I said. "What I've decided—or maybe I'm just deciding it as we speak—is that we need to do this thing and tell Emma afterwards, especially if it pans out as I suspect it will. She can't handle the idea in the abstract. Only if we succeed in finding something would she accept it."

"If she loves you, she'll understand. If she doesn't love you, she's not right for you anyway."

Roque, counselor of the lovelorn and incomparable friend. I *loved* him! "Thanks, guy. You're absolutely right, unsettling as it is to admit it. How soon can you be ready to go?"

We decided to meet at the turnoff on his lane at 8:15. We also reminded one another to come armed. As I ended the call and reached for the remnant of my burger and fries, everything seemed in order. It seemed that way for a whole sixty seconds, right up until the moment someone rapped on my door.

I had no idea who would be visiting me at that time of day and quickly dumped the bagged Whataburger trash on my way to the door. I swung it open in high spirits, my excitement about the night's impending search still rising. Then, in one swoop, my heart took flight and crashed. Emma stood there, Otis sitting next to her, panting with seeming delight.

"Hi, Tak. I bet you're surprised to see me. Am I right?" She had the broadest smile on her beautiful face that I believed I'd ever seen. I think it was the embarrassment she felt for driving out there uninvited combined with undisguised pleasure at seeing me. I was stunned and must have shown it because her smile began to fade.

"Emma," I responded, "I'm blown away. I, uh, I'm speechless."

She scrutinized my face. "I can leave. I should have called."

"No! No! Come in," I said, reaching for her arm to draw her through the door. She resisted at first before yielding. I closed the door behind her, frowning at Otis as if to say, "This is all *your* fault!"

She walked into the kitchen, first looking around the room and then at me. She had no way of knowing how disconcerting her presence was to me.

CHAPTER TWENTY-FOUR

I recovered quickly, stepped over to where she stood, took her face in my hands, and kissed her. It was chaste as kisses go but felt erotic, standing as we were in my house, alone, the whole evening before us. She responded by grasping my wrists and extending the kiss after I began to pull away. What a powerful moment.

"That was nice," she said as we moved apart, her still holding my wrists before dropping her arms to her side. "Maybe you *are* happy to see me."

"I am," I said. I waved my hand then as I looked around the room, inviting her to tour the house with me. We visited every room but the bathroom and evaluated the furniture sense of my Uncle Portis. We concluded the furniture was sturdy and serviceable and that I needn't feel embarrassed about it.

We sat on my "stylish-in-a-masculine-way" couch—her description—both of us sitting sideways to better accommodate a conversation. I reached over and took one of her hands in my own.

"How was your day?" she asked. Some time-honored conversation-starters never fail.

But my mind tumbled as I considered how to respond. I had no time for this. Roque was expecting me at his place in less than ninety minutes. I couldn't divulge my plans for the night, but I had to tell her *something* because she planned to spend the evening with me. Too much, too much.

"Uh, it was a pretty good day," I said and knew as soon as I said it that small talk wasn't going to get the conversation where it needed to go. I had to speed things along, so I added, "In fact, it was a great day."

"Oh? How?"

Plunging ahead, I said, "Emma..." Something in my voice must have warned her of a looming change in the weather for our relationship. Her face clouded ever so slightly. "Emma," I said, again, "I have something to tell you that's apt to unsettle you a tiny bit."

I supposed she expected me to break off the relationship at that point, notwithstanding the tender kiss of a few moments before. What else could she be thinking? Her summer with Tak Sweedner was coming to an end. Slipping her hand from mine, she changed her position on the couch, moving both feet onto the floor in probable anticipation of springing up and walking out the door.

"I hope you'll understand," I said. "I really do. But... I'm returning to Ruskey's shed tonight. I know what I'm looking for now."

So dramatically did Emma's expression cool and harden that a *craaack* surely sounded in the atmosphere of the room. I didn't hear it, but I felt it when I watched her face transform itself. Gone was the composure of a lover in gentle communication with her loved one. The guileless countenance of a trusting and confiding woman morphed into something grim and threatening. Her face reddened and I anticipated a full-throated shout.

"Let me explain," I said to head off an explosion. "Please, Emma. Let me explain. I really must do this because I've had a break-through in my investigation. It's important that I act on it. I can't *not* do it, even though I know it upsets you."

Emma jumped up. "Oh, for God's sake," she shouted, walking away from me and then turning back. Her profane outburst surprised me. "You are such a twit. You're determined to get yourself killed over *nothing*. A great *big* nothing that doesn't even concern you!"

"Pablo's murder concerns me."

"Pablo's murder concerns everyone, but is everyone lurking in the shadows and breaking into other people's property? No!" Her voice grew louder. "Besides you don't know that the shed and whatever it contains is related to Pablo's death at all. It's just some sophomoric theory you've come up with while playing detective."

She paced back and forth in the room as she shouted, her voice not releasing near the energy she needed to expel. "And what, pray tell, do you think is in the shed? What's so important about it?"

"I can honestly say I have no idea what's in there," I said, my voice much softer than hers. "I really don't. And if I go into the building one more time and find nothing, I promise you I will walk away once and for all."

"You've promised that before! You've *been* in the shed! You've seen what's there—cattle feed! Are you going to rip open the bags and examine the contents of each one? This is foolishness!"

Enough. "Sit down, Emma," I said with conviction. Then I said it again, more-or-less ordering her. "Sit down. I'll explain in excruciating detail what I plan to do and why I feel driven to do it. Sit down and just listen for a minute."

Nothing in her face or posture suggested she was on the verge of yielding to my plea for calm. If anything, her tirade appeared to have hardened her resolve. I half-expected her to wheel around and stalk out the door. If she did, I'd have to let her go and hope to smooth things over another day.

I was surprised when she walked into the kitchen, pulled out a chair from under the table, and sat down hard, arms crossed on her chest. I followed her to the kitchen and sat across from her, leaning my elbows on the tabletop. My arms were apart and hands open as I appealed to her.

"Whatever's in the shed is enough to kill for. I don't know what it is, but it must be valuable or incriminating or something. And I believe it's *under* the floor, that a panel of plywood is taken up each time a person goes there."

Emma closed her eyes for a heartbeat or two and then opened them. Her face showed both anger and sadness. I anticipated either a scream or a crying jag. I decided not to mention that Roque was accompanying me. No sense dragging him into it. "I'm leaving in half an hour. I have to see what's under that floor."

"That's so dangerous," she said then, more softly than I'd anticipated. She looked more grieving than angry. "You'll be discovered and, if you're right that something valuable is there, you'll be killed." She reached into the air and pantomimed the reading of a marquee. "'Tak Sweedner: Dead Before

He Ever Had a Chance to Live.' I should say goodbye now while I have the chance."

I dropped my hands to the tabletop. "That's sort of macabre. Don't write me off so easily. I'll be armed. I can defend myself."

Emma leaned forward and buried her face in her hands. I was touched by her strong feelings for me. A moment before, she'd been ready to write me off and walk away forever. Now this. Her emotional oscillations confound me.

She looked up. "I can't let you do this. I can't. You're going to get hurt. Someone has tried to kill you twice and will stop at nothing to keep his... *whatever* from being found. If you go up there tonight, you're a dead man."

"Maybe, maybe not." I felt stubborn.

She sat back and looked at me with narrowed eyes as if trying to see into my mind. "So, I guess there's nothing else I can do. I'm going to the shed, too."

I sat back in my chair then. "No. You're not."

"Yes. I am. You can yell and tell me to go home but at the end of the conversation I'm either riding there with you or I'm following you there in my car. If you insist on putting yourself in danger, I'll do the same. You've left me no choice."

"No. You're not!" I said again, firmer than the first time.

"I'll meet you there," she said and scooted her chair away from the table. This was *not* what I'd wanted.

"Emma, there *is* some danger, no question. If everything goes wrong, yes, I might have to pull my gun. I don't want you there if that happens."

"What you want for me is irrelevant. I want you to stay away from the darned building, but you're going anyway. Now you want *me* to stay away, but *I'm* going. You see the pattern? We're each doing our own thing. It does not bode well for our relationship."

I shook my head and looked around the room for a new argument, getting to my feet then and walking in a tight circle. Whatever I decided, I needed to do it fast because there was somewhere I needed to be. Emma sat motionless, except for her eyes, which were locked on mine.

"Dang, girl. You're headstrong, you know it?"

"I'm smart enough to see that going up there tonight is a bad idea. It's not going to turn out well. I can feel it. I don't *want* to go. More important, I don't want *you* to go. You'll probably be dead this time tomorrow and so will I. Oh, well....." She stood. "Let's go."

We looked at one another, sober as rocks. I tried one last appeal.

"This isn't the night you'd envisioned, Emma. I'm sorry. But I wish you'd listen to me and go back to your mom's place. I'll call as soon as I'm on the road back to Uvalde."

She offered no response. I waited for what seemed a long time before turning and stomping into my bedroom. I came out with the Taurus strapped to my side, an extra clip in my pocket. A small plastic bag held my lock pick. I'd pick up a cordless drill at the salvage yard.

She hadn't moved. I grabbed a ballcap and we walked together out the door. We would leave her car at her mother's house. As she drove out the lane ahead of me, I saw through her rear window that she had her cell phone to her ear, probably calling her mother.

I made a call, too, punching in Roque's number. "Emma's coming with me."

Silence. "Why is that a good idea?" he asked.

"It's not a good idea, but it's Emma's idea and she's coming up there tonight whether I bring her or not. I didn't mention that you were going to help me. She may be be upset when she sees you."

"May I ask," Roque said, "why you told her about our plans?"

"Long story. In a nutshell, she showed up at my place, presumably to spend some quality time with her man, a pleasurable prospect from my point of view. I had two choices: Put off the shed visit and call you or tell her our plans and send her home. I chose wrong. Now she tells me she has no other choice than to accompany me. According to her, we're all going to die, which means she's coming along at some sacrifice."

"Sounds like love to me."

"I don't know what it is," I said, "but we'll be there at eight-fifteen. Bring your gun."

CHAPTER TWENTY-FIVE

When I eased the truck to a stop in the low area on the Zamarripa ranch near the solar field fence, tension remained high. Emma and I had spoken little during the trip. She had stared out her window and clenched and unclenched her hands. When I'd reached over to cover one of her restless hands with mine, she gave me a doleful look and pulled away.

I had rolled to a stop in the lane just inside the ranch gate to let Roque approach and enter the truck. "What's he doing here?" Emma had exclaimed when she saw him. "You didn't say Roque was part of this!"

"I hoped to keep you from being angry at him, too."

She exchanged nods with Roque when he climbed in the truck. We were a grim trio—Emma especially, her mouth clenched even tighter after Roque joined us. I would have thought she'd have found his presence somewhat reassuring. Nope. Her fears for our safety outweighed everything else.

As I parked the truck, it felt like a consequential moment. In the next hour or two, I either would call the sheriff in triumph, or I would restore the sheet of plywood in the floor, re-lock the door and slink away. Either scenario appealed to me more than an armed confrontation.

Emma remained a glum companion. She dragged along with us unrelieved in her gloominess, clearly expecting nothing from the night but disaster and death. Her relentless sense of doom was a liability. The more effort Roque and I made to assuage her fears, the less alert we were to threats around us. I so wished she had gone home.

Roque and I each chambered a round and clicked on a safety. The three of us moved as cautiously as Roque and I had on a previous night, sneaking through the solar panel field, and darting from bush to bush on our way up the hill to the tree. We squatted there and surveyed the scene for five minutes, long enough to get used to the sounds around us so we could sense any change in them.

Without preamble, we then hurried to the shed. I carried the tool satchel. Standing next to the door, I pulled out the pick and went to work. In a few seconds, the door swung open.

"I'll stuff an empty sack against the bottom of the door to block the light," I told Roque. "If you get *any* inkling that something is stirring out here, give us a heads-up. OK?" He nodded and handed me a lantern. He gripped his gun in his other hand.

Emma and I stepped inside and closed the door. I flicked on a flashlight, retrieved a paper bag from a pile, and wedged it loosely under the door. Then I switched on the electric lantern and the room filled with an eerie, whitish light. Shadows danced around us as I carried the lantern a few steps away to set it on the stack of bagged feed.

At the side of the room away from the door, I kneeled and used the flashlight to scrutinize a sheet of plywood and the screws fixing it to joists beneath. The sheet was clear of bags and buckets and seemed clean, probably from being lifted. I should have picked up on that on my last visit.

"Phillips head." I whispered to myself and handed the flashlight to Emma. Tightening the appropriate bit in the drill, I listened for a moment and then placed the bit on a screw head. The drill's sudden whining shattered the silence and I winced, though I suspected the sound hadn't carried too far. I was willing to bet the man I'd stalked in the shed had used a drill, too, and I hadn't heard it running.

The screw came out without hesitation, likely from being backed out several times. My excitement grew. Emma held the light steady for me. When I dropped the last screw in my pants pocket, I set the drill on the floor and stood up. I looked at Emma. Her visage remained grim, but I thought I saw a flicker of expectation in her eyes.

"This is it, Emma. We'll know in a second if I'm dumb, or utterly brilliant," I said, hoping she would respond with an encouraging word. She offered no riposte, witty or otherwise. Instead, she sighed and shook her head.

"You're both, Tak, dumb *and* smart, and it's probably going to get you killed." Her certitude about my demise rankled me. *This isn't some kind of teaching moment, dang it, Emma! It's a time to reassure me, to partner up!*

I turned away, opened my pocketknife, and slipped the blade through the crack near a corner of the sheet. It lifted without much resistance. I raised the sheet till it rested on its opposite edge on four floor joists running perpendicularly beneath. After I leaned the plywood against the shed wall, Emma pointed the flashlight beam into the gap. We both were transfixed by what we saw there.

A stout two-step ladder screwed to the side of a joist dropped three feet to the hillside soil enclosed by the shed. More startling to us was a natural opening in the earth a few feet to the left of the ladder. It appeared to be about three feet long and two and a half feet wide, an oval slit in the rock at the base of the hillside.

I took the flashlight from Emma's hand and played it on the opening. A wood ladder descended into the hole, the bottom of it lost in murk. I realized with regret that we'd have to drop into the sub-floor area and climb down the ladder. The idea did not thrill me.

We were looking at proof that this was no ordinary line shack. It was a cover for an underground operation of some sort. At the bottom of the ladder was something of natural value like a vein of gold, or something manmade like a drug manufacturing set-up. Whatever was down there was precious enough to someone to kill anyone else who discovered it.

"It's a karst cave opening, isn't it?" I asked Emma. She nodded. "Any idea what we're going to find down there?"

"Why would I know?" she asked. "I don't really care what's in that hole."

From the quake of her voice and her fixed, wide-eyed expression, Emma's pure fright was evident. I'd never seen her so uptight. I rested my hand on her shoulder, but she shrugged it off. "I think we ought to get out of here. Right now. I don't want anyone shot."

"We can't do that, Emma," I said with as much gentleness as I could. I was anxious, too, but we had to finish what we'd started. "We can't leave without at least seeing what's in that hole."

I walked across the room, nudged the paper bag aside with a foot and cracked open the door. Roque looked at me through the crack. "I think you ought to come in here and see this. Just for a minute or two."

He looked around, holstered his handgun and pushed open the door to join us. I again sealed the bottom of the door against light leakage. Roque walked across the room and stood next to Emma. He stared at the hole and whistled. He gave me a pat on the shoulder when I joined him. "Congrats." Emma smiled at him without warmth.

"I hate to say it, but I think we all better climb down and see what's there," I said. "We need to witness what's there, put the plywood back in place, and get the heck out of Dodge."

"Why all of us? Why go down in the hole at all?" Emma asked, legitimate questions both.

"We each should see it to back up our stories. I want more eyes on whatever's there, and I suspect the sheriff will, too. Don't you agree, Roque?"

Roque jerked his head up and down. "But we need to do it *rapido*. I've not heard a peep out there, but someone could ride down on us quick. I don't want to be in that hole when someone does."

Emma sighed yet again. She seemed to be falling apart right before my eyes. I gave her a hug. She didn't respond at all. I glanced at Roque, moved past her, bent over till my hands rested on adjacent joists, and dropped into the underfloor area next to the hole. Ducking under a joist, I cleared a space for Roque, who dropped down beside me.

Emma just stood there looking at us. I feared she was going to turn and run out the door. For an instant, I wished she would, as long as her flight carried her all the way back to the truck and relative safety. *Go or stay*, I thought. She sat on the edge of the opening and hopped down to the ground.

Whoever did this had engineered the shed's flooring so the hole would be accessible. The ladder in the hole was situated between joists so a person could climb onto it. A flat, irregular and weathered piece of limestone lay on the ground on the other side of the hole.

"That must have hidden the opening before the shed was built," Roque said as I shined the flashlight on the stone. It appeared large enough to have entirely blocked the opening. "And I bet it covered the hole for a long time. What do we have down there, a gold mine or something?"

I turned to Emma. "Good thing we have an archaeologist. This discovery could give your career a boost, get you a professorship for sure." The stab at humor was lost on her. She said nothing and chewed on a fingernail.

Leaning on joists on either side of the ladder, I climbed onto it first. Flashlight in one hand, I backed down the rungs. The coolness of the air in the cavern greeted me. I didn't smell any guano, more evidence that the hole had not been long exposed. After several steps, I stopped and beamed the flashlight at a limestone wall ten feet or so away behind the ladder. In the other direction, where the karst cavern ran back under the limestone hillside, I could see nothing but blackness. This was not a small cave.

The ladder shuddered and I looked up to see Emma mounting it. I shined the light on the rungs below her and she lowered herself step by step. We continued our descent and soon I stood on a limestone shelf that jutted out perhaps forty feet from the rocky face of the cavern behind the ladder.

By the time Emma and then Roque joined me on the shelf, we knew the story. We were surrounded by very old wooden kegs. It was buried treasure.

CHAPTER TWENTY-SIX

I counted about forty of the round barrels, each formed of wood slats fixed to iron bands, each barrel two feet or so high and sixteen inches in diameter. About a quarter of them were empty and tipped onto their sides. One stood upright with an end bashed in. The flashlight beam revealed that keg still was half full of what appeared to be pancake-shaped slabs. I reached into the barrel, lifted out one, and guessed its weight at a pound.

"Splashes. That's what they called them. Crudely poured silver ingots." Emma spoke with a calmness that had eluded her for the last hour, her scholarship kicking in and overcoming her anxiety. "When Spanish explorers mined silver in the New World five hundred years ago, they sometimes made shallow depressions in the dirt and poured molten silver into them. They called the poured slabs 'splashes.'"

Roque picked up on it. "So, these are old Spanish barrels full of silver? Hidden here for safekeeping and never recovered. That's what you think?"

Emma nodded. "Perhaps being transported somewhere and offloaded here temporarily. They dropped someone into the hole on a rope, lowered the barrels the same way, and then rolled this stone in front of it to seal the hole. That's my guess. I have no idea why they weren't retrieved."

My imagination began to run. I envisioned conquistadors traveling the land with iron helmets and narrow swords and muskets, some on horseback, some on foot plodding along behind the mounted ones. The kegs of silver would have been hung across the backs of donkeys, one keg on each side, silver being carried back to the Old World. When an Apache scout or some other armed threat was encountered and the soldiers realized they could be overcome in an attack, they had hidden the treasure. That it was never recovered suggested their attackers showed no mercy.

It was all speculation, of course. How the silver ended up in the cavern never would be known. It was doubtful any records of the cache even existed, in this country or in the Old World from which the Spanish adventurers had ventured. It was untraceable treasure just waiting to be claimed.

I walked past the bunched barrels and approached the edge of the ledge. Shining the flashlight down into darkness, I saw nothing. The depth and length of the cavern was too big for my little flashlight to reveal. I returned to the base of the ladder where the others stood.

"Now we know how Ruskey got his gambling money," I said.

"We don't know it was Ruskey," Emma said. "Maybe one of his hired hands discovered the hole and built the shed."

Roque laughed. "*Vamos!* I think you're a better archaeologist than you are a detective, Emma. If this isn't Ruskey's cache, I'll personally sign over my share of the family ranch to you. You can *bet* he found this treasure somehow and is trying to sneak it away."

"Why do you suppose he sold the property?" I asked.

"I would guess he discovered the hole after the sale," Roque speculated. "It must've been the worst day of his life, finding the treasure and realizing he'd just signed over title of the land it was hidden under."

"You're imagining all that!" said Emma. The tone of her remark was contentious. Roque and I looked at each other. *What's wrong with her?*

"Well, let me say this," I said with a certain edge to *my* voice. Emma had gotten to me. "Let me say that I am very, very happy we found something under the floor tonight. I feel personally vindicated for being so stubborn. Now let's each grab one of these 'splashes' and go tell the sheriff what we found. The treasure isn't going anywhere tonight."

I picked up one of the crude slabs of silver and so did Roque. Emma didn't, being contrary to the end. She turned to the ladder and began her climb toward the glow from the lamp above her. I followed, shining the flashlight upward to help her locate the ladder rungs. Roque said he'd wait till we were off the ladder before starting his climb. "The last thing we need is for the ladder to collapse and strand us here."

Emma ducked under the joist and moved over toward the short ladder to climb up onto the floor. I stepped off the ladder and turned to look down the hole when I heard the door bang open. It startled me and I fell backward against the plywood sheet that leaned against the wall. I wasn't so surprised that I didn't comprehend what was happening: We'd been caught in the shed.

Emma gave a startled cry and threw up her arms. I reached for my holstered semi-automatic.

"If you touch that gun, you're dead!" Peyton Ruskey shouted. In the whitish light of the lamp, I could make out Ruskey looking down the barrel of a rifle at me. My right hand froze with my palm resting on the handle of the Taurus. I saw little chance of using the weapon with the rifle trained on my chest, so I raised my hand. After a moment, both arms were in the air, the flashlight grasped in one hand. Emma was whimpering and looking back and forth between Ruskey and me.

I imagined she felt as vindicated at that moment as I had felt a few minutes earlier in the cavern. We both had been right. There *was* something under the floor and, sure enough, I might be a dead man. What bothered me more was that Emma would die tonight as well and it would be my fault. Our eyes met and I tried to convey to her my regret at putting her in danger.

"Sweedner, you're a real brickhead, aren't you. I tried to take you out twice and you still didn't get the message." Ruskey stepped away from the door to approach us. Emma and I stood in full view of him from our waists up. "You just wouldn't quit. I bet you're wishing you had."

No, I was betting Ruskey had no idea Roque was in—or *under*—the shed. I was certain my buddy was listening to Ruskey, standing on a rung about two-thirds of the way up the ladder, gun in hand, safety off. All he was thinking about was how to get a shooting angle on Ruskey. "Yow, I was stupid," I admitted, looking at Emma. "I should have come out here by myself instead of dragging you along. I'm sorry, Emma."

Her eyes were wide open as she stared back at me. I hoped her mind was running along the same track as mine. *Please don't glance at the hole and give*

Ruskey any reason to think we're not alone. She blinked once or twice at me, looked at Ruskey and back to me.

"Touching," Ruskey said. He jerked his rifle at me. "I want you to reach around with your left hand and lift that handgun from your holster, using just two fingers. OK? Lift it out and place it on the plywood in front of you. Do it now."

As I complied, I kept talking, hoping to cover any noise Roque might make as he climbed into position to fire on our intruder. "I'm betting that's a .270 you're holding there, the very gun you told the sheriff you'd sold to a Mexican last year. Am I right?"

"Right as rain. Get that gun out." He glowered and stared at my hand as I tugged the handgun from its holster and dangled it in front of me. I pitched it onto the plywood then and it slid a foot or two toward him. As I tossed the gun, I caught a glimpse of Roque nearing the top of the ladder, his gun held near his head, almost ready to jump up and squeeze off a round or two at Ruskey.

"So, tell me, I can see why you might want to shoot me, but why shoot Pablo? What did that poor guy do to get himself killed?" I lowered my hands as I spoke and Ruskey didn't object. Emma already had returned her arms to her side. She hugged herself now and stared at her feet. I hoped she was regaining some composure. She might need it in a couple of minutes.

The lantern light was dim enough to obscure the expression on Ruskey's face, but he seemed to have smiled when I mentioned Pablo. His smile angered me.

"The stupid Mex stumbled onto something he shouldn't have. I'd taken a load to the truck and was coming for a second one when I saw him leave the shed and run away. I'd forgotten to close the door. My mistake. He'd seen a pile of ingots near the door and skedaddled. Just glad I had my rifle with me."

"So, you killed him," I said and shook my head in disdain. "He was a peaceful bird-lover who stumbled onto your shenanigans and you just shot him. That's pitiful."

Ruskey actually laughed. "Hey, it was good shooting. Danged good shooting. What's pitiful is how lucky you are. Twice you dodged death. I sent a boy to your yard to kill you. My mistake. But when I did send a man, you survived rolling off a hillside. Hey, if Pablo had just half your luck, he'd still be alive."

I needed to keep him talking. In my peripheral vision, I saw Roque poised to spring upward and fire in Ruskey's direction. He couldn't see his target, of course, but he could tell from my eyes approximately where Ruskey was standing and approximately would be good enough.

"On the other hand," I said, "your luck abandoned you at the casino. I heard you dropped five grand. How long before people start wondering where you get your money?"

Ruskey laughed again, though I detected no merriment in it. He was not a happy man. "I still have pretty good reserves down in the hole. I think I'll get by till my luck changes. Your luck, on the other hand, has run out."

"I'm going to move over next to Emma," I said as I bent over and squeezed under the joist separating me from her. I slipped my cap off as I ducked under and then resettled it on my head. The goal was to get out of Roque's way and pull Ruskey's eyes away from the ladder, which had been almost in front of me.

I had moved as I spoke, so the changed position was a fait accompli before Ruskey could object to it. When I stood upright next to Emma, I put an arm around her. It was a protective gesture without really offering her any protection. It was the best I could do. She looked from me to Ruskey and back to me, confusion in her eyes.

"Doesn't make any difference where you stand, Sweedner," Ruskey said. "You're ending up down in that hole. Way down deep in the hole."

"You're going to shoot us and dump us in the hole, is that it?" I asked, as Emma trembled against my arm.

"Well, you're half right," he said. "I'm going to shoot *you*. Say goodbye to your girlfriend."

CHAPTER TWENTY-SEVEN

The sentence had barely cleared Ruskey's lips when Roque sprang up and twisted around to face the room. Ruskey staggered backward at the appearance of someone else in the building. In the lantern light, Roque must have seemed like a Spanish apparition. But Ruskey quickly regained his composure and swung the rifle barrel away from us and toward Roque. The two men fired in the same instant.

I pulled Emma to me and collapsed, dragging her to the ground and out of the line of fire. Roque fired twice more in rapid succession before sprawling onto a joist and slumping to the ground.

I pushed Emma off me and grabbed for Roque's gun, which had fallen to the ground between us. I poked it upward, pointed it in the general direction of the door and fired three times, the gun kicking in my hand. Then I lay back and waited, handgun pointed up into the room.

When Ruskey didn't rush into my view and I heard no movement, I got to my knees and darted my head up past the floor edge and back down, hoping to get a glimpse of the scene. Ruskey didn't seem to be there, so I raised my head again more slowly and confirmed he was gone. The door stood open.

Roque groaned softly next to me. "You hit bad, partner?" I asked, keeping my eyes on the door.

"*Un poco,*" he grunted. "My shoulder. Is he gone?"

"I think so. Hold on a second." I aimed at the lantern and shattered it with a shot. It clattered around in the darkened room. If Ruskey stood outside, we didn't need to give him illuminated targets.

Were Ruskey thinking clearly, of course, he'd be pumping bullets at us through the plywood siding. Random shots through the wall in the corner of the building where we crouched would almost certainly hit something. I counted on Ruskey being too shaken up to have that much sense.

"You OK, Emma?" I felt in her direction with my left hand and found her sitting up and crying. She didn't answer me, but the crying told me what I needed to know.

I peered past the edge of the floor at the opened door. Nothing seemed to be stirring. Ruskey could be standing on the hill twenty feet from the shed ready to pick us off as we exited the building, but for now we had a stalemate.

"Stay down, Emma," I said, leaning toward her and putting an arm around her shoulder. "I think we're OK. I'm going to get closer to the door and look around. Maybe you could scoot over there and see how badly Roque's hurt." She shuddered, coming off her cry, and nodded.

I scrambled up from the dirt onto the edge of the flooring and scuttled across the floor toward the front wall, picking up my Taurus along the way. Squatting next to the doorway, I peered outside. With the lantern light gone, my eyes were able to penetrate the murkiness of the hillside.

Nothing in the shapes I made out in the darkness seemed a threat to me. I jumped across the space in front of the doorway and evaluated the hillside from that position. Again, nothing.

A splotch on the floor caught my eye then and I knelt beside it. A touch confirmed it was a splatter of liquid. "Emma, slide that flashlight over to me, over here at the left side of the door," I said in a low voice. "It should be there in the dirt somewhere."

In a moment, the durable flashlight came scraping across the floor, stopping just short of where I knelt. I grabbed it and put the lens close to the floor. When I clicked it on, the light revealed a splatter of blood. Roque had hit the shooter. I played the light across the floor away from the door and saw a second splatter.

"Roque, you hear me?" I wanted to hear his voice to reassure me he wasn't unconscious or worse. "You hit him. There's blood on the floor."

"*Por supuesto!* I never miss." His response was in a firm, if tired-sounding, voice. I loved hearing it.

"Thanks, buddy. Stay put just a bit longer and I think we can get out of here."

How bad was Ruskey hurt? That's what I was desperate to know. Was he incapacitated, maybe sprawled on the ground a few feet from the shed, barely conscious? Had he limped away to find treatment? Or was he injured just bad enough to be angry, resolute and determined to end this as soon as we exposed ourselves?

I checked my watch. Not even midnight yet. I jumped back across to the other side of the doorway and closed the door. In pretty short order, five blocks of salt were snugged up against the bottom of it. Two hundred and fifty pounds. No one would be opening that door without expending some effort. I so wished I had taken that precaution earlier. Because I was so excited about finding the treasure, I'd dropped my guard—with disastrous consequences.

I repositioned the bags of feed to form a waist-high bunker enclosing an area maybe four feet wide. The remaining salt blocks were stacked alongside the bags as an additional barrier, though there were only enough to fortify two sides. I pieced together the bunker as quietly as I could manage, not wanting to give anyone outside the shed any indication of what was happening inside.

"It will be safer to stay hunkered down here, I think," I said just loud enough for Roque and Emma to hear. "We'll wait for daylight. I don't know where he is out there and don't want to chance it." Neither Roque nor Emma responded.

• • •

Remaining in the shed was scary because it gave Ruskey time to call for help and come down on us harder. I banked on the blood on the floor. He'd been hit by at least one bullet. There was nothing like being gunshot to re-order a man's priorities.

Getting as far away from us as fast as possible had to have made the most sense in his condition. He was outgunned. He had to assume we'd cell-phoned the sheriff, so the cavalry was coming. Leaving the pasture and going on the run must have seemed his wisest course.

The truth, however, was I'd called no one. In Hill Country, cell phone service was intermittent. Most carriers offered spotty service here at best, and my carrier was not the best. I pulled out my phone and checked again. Nope, no service. Rescuers would not show up tonight. In the morning, the solar field crew would be back and give us cover. We'd wait for them.

Roque got to his feet without assistance. Emma had torn off the bottom of his shirt and wadded it in the wound near his left clavicle. The bullet had exited high on his back. In short, Ruskey's bullet hadn't hit a bone nor a vital organ. It was a flesh wound, but the bullet had plowed through enough muscle and tissue to warrant concern. Emma had ripped off the bottom third of her blouse and was pressing it against the exit wound.

"He's bleeding, but it's slowed. If he lies still, he should be OK," she said.

She and I lifted him up onto the floor and I gave her a hand up. We eased Roque onto the pile of bags and helped him slide down to the floor inside the surround. I crumpled an empty feed sack and Emma made a pillow of it under his head. "*Gracias, los chicos,* for the loving care. If I don't bleed to death, I'll treat you both at Live Oak Gorditas."

Emma and I sat side by side inside the bags, squeezed next to and against Roque's legs. I could see past her to the door. If someone tried to enter the shed, a few rounds through the door would discourage the attempt. I hoped someone *would* try.

Emma and I talked in undertones, not wanting to give away our position to anyone outside. Every couple of minutes we'd direct a comment to Roque and expect a reply. If none were forthcoming, we roused him. Blood stains on the material pressed against Roque's wounds didn't appear to be growing larger. Roque seemed in good spirits, everything considered.

"In a few hours, I'll be the hero of the Gun Battle at Ruskey Shed. You, Tak, will be the Great Kahoona Detective," he said in such a strong voice that I shushed him.

"And you, Emma," he continued, softer, "will be enshrined forever as Nurse Townsend, Savior of Wounded Detectives. You might think about entering medical school."

Emma didn't respond in the same vein. She gritted her teeth and hung her head. "I'm not a heroine, or a savior of any kind," she said in such a low voice I wasn't certain we were supposed to hear. "I'm feeling like a chump. Tonight was not my finest moment as a human being. You each were very brave. You kept your wits about you and overcame a deadly situation. I'm very proud of you. I..."

She leaned forward and began sobbing loud enough that I put my arm around her and whispered that she needed to grieve more quietly. She nodded and tried to stifle her full-out crying. I pulled her over against me and this time she didn't resist.

The entire night had been a strain on her. First, she'd been disappointed that I was doing what she'd begged me not to do. Then she'd been threatened at gunpoint and seen a friend shot. Now the terror continued as we wondered whether we would survive the night.

These things were all outside of Emma's natural orbit, which consisted of an academic and formal existence. Dealing with bad guys to her meant rebuffing unwanted advances by faculty members and listening to the whining complaint of a student who'd just received a D on his paper and deserved it. Being shot at? Not so much.

Of course, she hadn't *been* shot at. In fact, Ruskey never even pointed his rifle at her during the confrontation, not considering her a threat. He would have had to end her life, too, though, before night's end.

I gave her shoulder a squeeze and fretted anew about endangering her. I should have called Roque and postponed the search for a day. One more night wouldn't have made any difference. I'd been selfish and I knew it.

Emma sat up, leaned away from me, and sighed, her crying at end. She took a deep breath. "Do you think he's dead?"

I shrugged. "No way of knowing till we go outside and see either a body or more blood. He *might* have stopped breathing by now. On the other hand, he could have bound up his wound and positioned himself out there to snipe at us."

Emma sat back against the bags and looked down at Roque, who offered a wan smile. "I hope he's dead," she said. "It would be a perfect ending to this whole nightmare. The confessed murderer of Pablo dead from a gunshot.

The silver recovered and displayed in a museum. The mystery solved and you, Tak, a public hero able to return to your chosen life's work as a salvage yard operator."

The little barb announced the return of the Emma I knew, a wry, teasing woman. Emma was becoming herself again. Her remark provoked a chortle from Roque, and then a wince as the wounds reasserted their immediacy.

CHAPTER TWENTY-EIGHT

The hours passed much slower than we wanted. I could testify of their creepage because I'd checked off each one, constantly peering at the dial of my watch and hoping it was later than it was. Roque slept through much of the night, his bleeding stanched for the most part.

I had gotten comfortable at one end of the bunker and pulled Emma over onto me and she had fallen asleep after a while. It was pleasant having this woman snuggled against my chest, one hand resting on my belly as if she were my lover.

To stay awake, I concentrated on listening for disturbing sounds of activity outside the shed walls. I heard none, except for coyotes yipping and yelping somewhere close to the building. I mused about them being attracted to the hillside by the body of a man with a fatal gunshot wound.

As the night wore on and adrenalin stopped flowing, I got sleepy. I stayed awake by reviewing the night's developments. I knew for certain now—and could prove it with the testimony of my compatriots—that Pablo was killed after stumbling on the silver recovery operation.

Poor guy. Had he dodged Ruskey's bullets and made it to the Zamarripa ranch home, the news coming out of Uvalde County would have been about the discovery of a Spanish treasure and the trial of a local rancher for attempted murder. That would have been scandal enough and Pablo would have been the hero.

But had it played out that way, I thought with some embarrassment, I wouldn't have called Emma. She and I wouldn't have gotten closer as friends. We wouldn't have spent a delightful night together camping by a pristine river and developed what had begun to feel like the beginning of a permanent romantic relationship.

Pablo's death made all that possible. I shook the thought from my mind. Poor Pablo.

That wasn't all that prickled my brain as the night drew on. Emma's behavior had disappointed me. From the moment at the house when I'd confessed my plans till an hour ago when she finally fell asleep using me as a pillow, Emma had been way out of sync with her usual demeanor.

I could understand some of it. Her disappointment in me had rocked her. I'd let her down big time. My mistake had been to let go of the case before I was ready to do so. I should have said, "No, Emma, if you respect me, you'll let this investigation run its course."

That's what I *should* have said. I regretted not doing so.

I also was disappointed by her resistance to the idea of Ruskey involvement. Up until the moment he burst in ready to shoot us, she disbelieved what was self-evident. Were the Ruskey and Townsend families close? Was he an old family friend? He wasn't, that I knew of. Yet she'd refused to ascribe guilt to him. It was a case of poor judgment writ large.

Then there was her behavior during the anxious minutes Ruskey held us at gunpoint. It was at variance with the Emma I'd come to know. She'd exhibited none of her poise. Her self-confidence normally verged on flippancy. Under stress, she'd been nonplussed and bewildered by what was happening to her.

Yet all of that notwithstanding, I didn't think one whit less of Emma. Not a whit. I'd just learned she wasn't quite the person I thought she was. Beneath her strutting and quipping, she was more vulnerable and tender-hearted than I'd realized. In a way, she was a *stronger* woman than I'd assumed, covering up her fragile confidence while functioning at a very high level.

I stroked her arm where my hand rested on it and felt closer than ever to the woman.

. . .

We were all awake at half past seven in the morning and had been for a couple of hours. Rocky and I sat side by side, facing the door, guns in hands. I'd torn my T-shirt into a long strip, feeding it under Roque's left arm and across his shoulder, giving his wounded shoulder some support and pinning the two compression cloths in place. He was sore and, to be honest, irritable.

"A wounded warrior has every right to be a jerk," I'd admonished him after he barked at me from lack of sleep and his aching shoulder. He'd smiled and apologized.

"You suppose your folks heard any of the shooting over here last night?"

"I wondered that myself. Dad's a pretty deep sleeper, but Mom can hear a sneezing mouse. I hope she didn't hear the gunfire, though, because when she learns today it was her son shooting and *being* shot, she'll feel awful for not coming to my rescue."

As soon as we heard the solar panel trucks being driven up for the day's work, our plan would be set in motion. My two companions would stay put in the feed bag bunker while I jumped out the door and raced around the shed, gun drawn. If I wasn't fired upon and found no one lurking behind the shed or elsewhere on the hill, I'd run to the solar crew for help.

What we all hoped was that as soon as I stepped out the door, I would see Ruskey's body on the ground where he'd collapsed. We would exult at the discovery.

So, the morning wore on. Not until fifteen minutes after eight did the sounds of approaching trucks disturb the silence. I winked at Emma who mustered a smile for me. "Here goes nothing," I said.

After moving salt blocks away from the door and giving my two friends a reassuring glance, I snugged my cap on my head, threw open the door and stepped outside. Nothing seemed changed from the night before. I didn't stumble on a body, sad to say. I sprinted around the shed with the handgun pointed in front of me and was relieved to find no one there. I ran several more steps before turning and scouring the hillside.

No shot came. No one stood on the hill to shoot at me, not that I could see. I holstered the nine-mm and ran toward three parked trucks and startled workers still sitting in them. I waved my arms as I approached, yelling for them to call the sheriff. They just sat there and stared at me, no doubt put off by the sight of a bare-chested man with a gun at his side running at them and shouting.

The superintendent stepped out of a van then, and I headed for him. "Boy, are we glad to see you!" I shouted. I could tell he didn't share my feelings.

• • •

An hour later, Roque sat on the bumper of an EMT vehicle parked beside the solar crew vehicles. Before the emergency personnel arrived, I'd gotten a bottle of water from the work crew's cooler and a bologna sandwich from one of the crew members. Roque had consumed both.

His father and mother had driven over from the house after being notified by the sheriff. Mrs. Zamarripa sat next to him on the bumper now, looking shocked. Roque, of course, hadn't told his parents the night before where he was going.

"So, you figured it out, Tak. *Felicidades,*" Pele Zamarripa said and gave me an awkward hug. "I knew you would."

"I almost got your son killed, Mr. Zamarripa. I'm not happy about that."

"Hey, he's a grown man. He wanted to help. You both did what you had to do to get to the bottom of things," he said. "I'm glad he wasn't killed though. I want to do that myself if he doesn't marry Maria."

Emma, who stood beside me, paled at Pele's joke. Men and their sense of humor.

She was more relaxed now—we all were, of course—yet she still exhibited more reserve than usual. The night had taken a lot out of her. I hoped she would bounce back from what must have been a traumatic moment in her young life. Most people live their entire mortal existence without once being threatened with violent death. She had experienced it now.

Sheriff Rodriquez and a deputy arrived in separate cars moments later, their red and blue lights glinting off the sides of the other vehicles parked there. The sheriff stopped to speak to Roque and his mother. He watched as Roque was helped into the EMT van and strapped down on a gurney for a ride to the hospital. Pele walked over to join his wife. They soon drove away in their car to follow the emergency vehicle into Uvalde.

Sheriff Rodriquez then approached Emma and me. He almost glowered at me. I suspected he was torn between feeling glad about the turn of events and irked that I'd pushed things so far. "What have you done now, Tak?" he asked without much teasing in his voice.

"Other than almost get myself and my friends killed, quite a lot actually." I showed him the silver "splash" I'd carried up from the cave. "The story is in that shed, sheriff."

"Let's take a look," he said after examining the ingot. Emma and I led him and his deputy to a building we had come to know better than we had ever wanted. I tersely confessed that I'd burglarized the building because I'd felt certain the answers we all sought were under the floor. I'd been proven right, I said, but Peyton Ruskey had caught us there and a shoot-out had followed.

The sheriff stopped walking and, after a few halting steps, so did the rest of us. "You and Peyton Ruskey shot at each other?" he asked.

"He started it. He came in with his rifle pointed at us—the same rifle he told you he'd sold, by the way—and Roque got the drop on him. Then the shooting started. We were all lucky we weren't killed. I realize that now. We were very lucky."

The truth was, I *did* feel lucky. It could have turned out so much worse. I looked at Emma whom I could tell shared my feelings at that moment. "Very lucky."

We stepped inside—moving around blood stains on the floor that would prove Ruskey was the shooter—and I explained to the sheriff what he was seeing and the ancient treasure below ground. He peered into the hole and turned back to me.

"You've done well, Tak. At some point, I'll have to charge you with burglary, of course, but we can work that out. You've really done well." He reached out his hand to me and I gratefully shook it. Boy, I liked this man.

"Now we need to find Mr. Ruskey and get his side of the story."

CHAPTER TWENTY-NINE

Rodriquez instructed his deputy to radio the courthouse and get forensics personnel headed up to the scene along with two more deputies. "Have Marjorie contact area hospitals and clinics and tell them to be on the lookout for a man coming in with one or more gunshot wounds. Then apologize to the solar crew superintendent and tell him his crew can't work around here today."

The deputy turned to walk away. "One more thing," the sheriff continued, and his deputy turned back. "Tape off this area using outlying bushes, going out maybe fifty feet from the building on each side." The deputy strode off. The hillside once again had become a crime scene.

"Are you up to walking up the hill with me and see what we can see," he asked me. I told him I was feeling fine and readily agreed. He turned to Emma. "You can stay down here, Emma. We'll be right back."

She started to object, I could tell, but agreed with some reluctance. "Be careful," she told me, and grabbed my arm with both hands. That didn't surprise me. The kiss to my cheek did. Then she was gone, and the sheriff was smirking.

"Bonded under fire, I see," he said. I shrugged.

Rodriquez drew his semi-automatic from its holster and I did the same. In the daylight, drawn weapons seemed unnecessary, yet under the circumstances it felt right. We didn't yet know if Ruskey was still around. We worked our way up the trail in no haste, splitting our attention between obvious hiding places for a man with a rifle and the ground immediately in front of us.

It was a safe assumption Ruskey had struggled up the same path last night and I hoped to find additional evidence of blood loss. I wasn't disappointed. Some thirty yards from the building, the sheriff and I each spotted something on a rocky outcrop. Rodriquez bent over it. "It's blood, if I'm not mistaken," he said. I had begun to believe he seldom was mistaken.

Another eighty yards brought us near the top of the hill and in sight of a fence line just beyond the crest. More to the point, we saw a familiar four-wheeler parked by the fence. We both crouched. "That's Ruskey's machine. He didn't ride it down to the shed last night because he knew we'd have heard him coming."

The sheriff looked at me. "So how did he know you'd be there?"

That was a good question. Why *hadn't* he ridden down to the shed? The better to sneak up on us, of course. "Sheriff Rodriquez, I'm reminded once again why you're the chief law enforcement officer in the county. You see what most of us don't. How *did* he know we were down there!"

The sheriff looked up and down the fence line and back to me. "Ruskey seems to have been in the loop. So, who kept him there? Maybe someone saw you guys heading for the shed last night and tipped him off. I wonder who."

Me, too. I'd known about the plan to look under the floor. Roque had known. So had Emma. Someone else was keeping tabs on our movement.

We stood and walked ahead to the fence and the machine. A portable fence-climbing stair was positioned near the four-wheeler. Perfunctory examination showed no blood on the four-wheeler, but several smears of blood could be seen on the stile. Ruskey hadn't been on the machine at all last night. He'd limped up the hill, climbed up and over the fence, and driven away. Whatever vehicle he left in would be bloody, too.

We holstered our handguns and descended the slope. Rodriquez piled some rocks at one point to help forensics people find the splatter of blood. Lights still were flashing on the sheriff's vehicles as we approached the shed. Two more law enforcement units had arrived.

Emma walked over to greet us. We told her we'd found the four-wheeler but nothing else. She looked stressed and I suggested she return home and get some rest.

"No, I'll leave when you do. Mom's gone for a few days to visit her brother, so she's not sitting and stewing about me," she said. "What are you going to do now?"

"I'm giving the sheriff a tour of the cavern. Want to come down with us?" No, she said, she didn't. So, Rodriquez and the deputy who had arrived with him followed me into the shed, once again stepping carefully past the blood. We all dropped down into the dirt under the opened floor—the sheriff exhibiting more agility than I'd expected from someone his age. Each of us carried flashlights as we descended into the cavern.

"Wow!" Rodriquez said, stepping off the bottom of the ladder. His deputy echoed the wondrous sight. They walked among the barrels, not touching anything except the cave floor with the soles of their shoes. At one point, the sheriff leaned down and closely examined the top of a barrel. "You know, I'm going to have our forensics guy dust a few of these barrels. It'll be fun if we can lift some 500-year-old fingerprints."

We moved farther out on the shelf, staying well back from the edge. None of our flashlights penetrated the darkness to show us a far side of the cavern or even its rubble-filled floor.

I looked up at the rocky ceiling over the shelf. It might have collapsed during the hundreds of years since the silver had been deposited there, crushing and covering the kegs of silver. It hadn't, though, to the ultimate misfortune of Ruskey.

"How much of this silver did you carry out, just a couple of pieces?" Rodriquez asked. I nodded. "Once we get this all examined and cataloged, it'll need to be sent to Austin for safe-keeping. Maybe they'll let us keep one piece as a souvenir."

We walked among the barrels some more, each of us hoping to find a piece of eight or a conquistador sword or some other memento. We could hear deputies and forensic specialists talking above us as they worked on the blood on the floor and on any bullet holes in the walls.

Between the ladder and the wall behind it, the sheriff stooped and carefully picked up an object his flashlight beam had illuminated. A leather glove. It must have fallen from a climber's hip pocket on the climb out and not been missed.

He held it out to me. "This yours?" I shook my head.

"Sergio!" the sheriff called upward. His forensic specialist responded. "Drop me a plastic bag. We're got a glove here." The light in the opening faded as the specialist complied, leaning into the hole and dropping a bag. It floated sideways to where I was standing. I caught it and handed it to the sheriff. He put the glove inside and sealed the bag.

"If Ruskey's DNA is in this, he can't deny being down here."

We were fascinated by the kegs and began to speculate why the rancher had taken so long to empty them. The solar crew had moved onto the site at least 45 days ago, so he couldn't have done much work in the daytime, except on weekends. But working at night, he could have finished removing all the silver by now. Yet he appeared to be extracting no more than a few pounds of silver each week.

"Why didn't he make a business of it?" I asked. "Take out a hundred pounds every night, for gosh sakes, and cart it away to a safer place. When I was outside the shed the other night, I heard Ruskey loading the four-wheeler. As I think back on it, it couldn't have been more than fifty pounds or so. He could have moved more *that* night. I don't get it."

"We may never know, if he's bled to death somewhere," I heard Rodriquez say from across the cavern. His light roamed among the barrels. "But if he worked by himself, it was going to take a while. We haven't come across any evidence of partners, have we?"

I told him we hadn't. "So," the sheriff continued, "working alone meant a lot of trips up and down this ladder and in and out the door and up and down the hill. If the four-wheeler had been spotted repeatedly making that trip, night after night, someone was going to wander over and ask him what the heck was going on."

"Greed, then," I said. "He didn't hire help because he would have had to split the revenue. He decided to do it himself and not have to share. How much money are we talking about, by the way? What's the value of silver?"

Rodriquez rubbed his chin. "If I'm not mistaken, a ton of silver, a full 2,000 pounds of silver, is worth something like half a million dollars. Probably more. We're talking a genuine treasure."

Silence followed. I thought we'd dropped the subject when the sheriff spoke again. "He didn't want to split the revenue, but how could he *earn* revenue from this stuff? He couldn't just walk into Bank of America and ask for cash in exchange for a pile of old mined silver. It doesn't work that way. It has to be assayed, its value determined. Who does Ruskey know to do that?"

Now I was unresponsive. How could a rancher with little networking find a buyer for his silver? "Sheriff, you've done it again. That's a brilliant deduction."

I heard him laugh. "Not brilliant. Pretty rudimentary, actually. But it is a good question, I'll admit that."

Back in the sunshine, I found Emma sitting on the ground in the shade of a sheriff's van munching on a doughnut and drinking bottled water. Sitting beside her, I selected a chocolate doughnut from a box of assorted baked sweets perched on her lap.

"I bet this is going to taste pretty good," I said and bit into it. It did. "How are you feeling?"

She shrugged her shoulders and pursed her lips. "I'm tired, of course. Bet you're even tireder. I'm also feeling disgusted about the way I behaved last night. I wasn't much good to you and Roque. I apologize."

I reached around behind her and pulled her toward me. The box of pastry almost fell from her lap. While she was grabbing it, I leaned over, kissed her on her forehead, and leaned away again. "You don't need to apologize for anything, Emma. You did fine. My gosh, you put yourself in danger—after warning us again and again it was going to *be* dangerous. You faced down a gunman and patched up Roque. Just what are you apologizing for?"

"I also bitched and cried and acted pouty when I didn't get my way and generally was a real pain in the ass for you and Roque," she said. "I wouldn't blame you if you walked away from me and never looked back."

"Hah!" I felt good about the conversation because it showed Emma's self-awareness. She *had* been something of a pain in the rear end, but having owned up to it, annoying memories of her behavior were evaporating. "I'll take you in a crisis any day, woman. I'm not walking away from you."

At the request of the sheriff, a deputy offered me a light department jacket. I accepted the garment, feeling a little self-conscious at being shirtless amid all the uniformed personnel. He offered Emma one, too, since her midriff was left exposed when she sacrificed the lower part of her blouse to doctor Roque. She declined.

We ate then, not a nutritious repast, but we needed nourishment before we joined the sheriff in one of his vans for a debriefing session. Normally such reports were given in an office, but Rodriquez wanted to get a preliminary accounting of all that had transpired. The information would be dispatched to other agencies waiting to launch a manhunt.

"Well, do we have our stories straight?" I asked her. "We were taking a late-night stroll through the pasture, just minding our own business, when this nut-job jumped up and started shooting at us and we took refuge in a little shed we found and stumbled on a silver mine. Something like that?"

She gave me a conspiratorial smile. "You left out the part about finding the leprechaun in the shed who told us about his pot of silver under the floor. I hope he didn't get hurt in all the shooting."

CHAPTER THIRTY

We decided to leave the leprechaun out of it. It was a good decision because the sheriff wasn't in a jesting mood. He was all business. Though I had wrapped up my part of the investigation, the sheriff still was in the middle of his. Each moment was critical now in his pursuit of a fleeing killer.

To be honest, there was no reason to believe Ruskey was *in* Uvalde County at that hour, or even in the United States. He may well have crossed over into Mexico by now. I just hoped he was lying dead somewhere—it mattered little whether it was in this country or that one.

"I know the back story on this, of course," Rodriquez said to us as well as to the electronic recording unit he'd switched on. "You've suspected for some time that Peyton Ruskey was hiding something in the shed, even though I'd inspected the building after being admitted by Mr. Ruskey himself. You were unconvinced and subsequently staked out the building on, what, two occasions?"

I nodded.

"For the record, you need to actually say something," he admonished me.

"Oh, yow. Sorry. I staked it out on three occasions, actually. Twice by myself, once with Roque." I went on to explain what I had found on each night-time visit, including when the shed had been visited by someone on a four-wheeler, presumably Ruskey though I couldn't identify the driver. I also admitted to being inside the building on one previous occasion and, like the sheriff, finding nothing incriminating.

That brought us up to this morning. "So, tell us what happened last night," the sheriff said.

I related the hurried decision by Roque and myself to re-enter the shed because it had occurred to me that what we sought might be *under* the floor. To explain my inspiration for that judgment, I recounted a short version of my Edsel story. I could see the sheriff enjoyed the telling. Emma even seemed to like it. I then explained how Emma had joined us at the last minute after learning of our decision.

"You hadn't been in the shed prior to last night, is that right?" the sheriff asked Emma. She said that was correct.

We entered the building, I continued, with Roque staying outside as a sentry. After I removed the plywood flooring and discovered the entrance to the cavern, Roque had joined us to explore the underground area. Finding the silver, we had grabbed a couple pieces of it as proof of our discovery and climbed the ladder.

"Then Ruskey made his entrance with his rifle. Because Roque hadn't finished climbing the ladder, he was out of sight. It was our good fortune that Ruskey didn't know he was there," I said, and smiled at Emma.

"After a few minutes of bantering with Ruskey so Roque could get into position, I moved over next to Emma to draw his attention away from the ladder. That was when Roque jumped up with his handgun. He and Ruskey fired at each other."

"How many times?"

"Once. That is, Ruskey fired once. Roque fired twice at least." I stopped talking to pick up a bottle of water from the floor beside me and take a sip.

"After the first bullets were fired," the sheriff continued, "and Roque was hit, you say you grabbed his gun and fired blindly in the general direction of where Ruskey had been standing. You don't know if your shots struck him?

"No. Either Roque hit him or I did. I suspect it was Roque because Ruskey never returned fire after he pulled the trigger on that first round."

"None of you saw Ruskey again, is that correct?"

"Correct," I said. "We doused the lamp for the cover of darkness. I closed the door and built our little bunker in case Ruskey start firing through the wall at us. He never did."

The sheriff nodded. "That was good thinking, Tak. The 'bunker.' The bags and salt blocks *might* have stopped a .270 round after it spent some force powering through the plywood. Maybe. It did offer some protection, in any event. But no shots were fired from outside?"

"None."

Rodriquez turned to Emma, who nibbled on the end of a thumb. "Is that how you remember it, Emma?"

She nodded, then remembered she had to speak for the recorder. "Yes. It was loud. That's mainly what I remember. The gunshots were so terribly loud in that little building. I thought my eardrums were going to burst. Before the shooting started, I was so scared I just stood there in disbelief. I didn't even know Roque was going to spring up when he did."

"What did Ruskey say to you as he stood there?" Rodriquez inquired.

"To me?" Emma said, sounding a little startled.

"To the both of you."

After she hesitated, I jumped back into the conversation. I told him Ruskey admitted to sending a man around to batter me in the salvage yard and someone else to run me off the highway. "He also admitted to shooting Pablo after the poor guy had happened upon his cache of silver. Ruskey smirked about the shooting. He joked about what good long-distance shooting it had been."

The sheriff considered that, removed his hat and scratched his head. "He's a hard one." He then asked Emma if that was what she remembered Ruskey saying. She said it was.

The law enforcement officer said nothing more for a moment. "Did he threaten you both with death?"

"You bet," I said. "He said he was going to shoot me and dump my body, quote, 'way down in the hole.'"

"And Emma, too?" He looked at Emma.

I hesitated. "It was implied. I asked if he was going to shoot us and he said I was half right, that he was going to shoot *me*. I hate to think about it, but maybe he had something else in mind first for Emma."

I looked to Emma and was startled by her expression. She looked both mortified and frightened. Before that moment the thought might not have occurred to her that Ruskey had intended to sexually assault her. While her death was inevitable, it might not have come soon enough. I reached across the table and touched her arm.

"Just a couple more questions and you all should head home," the sheriff said, recognizing the state of mind Emma was in. He asked more details about our entry into the shed, noting for the record that while my intentions were good, I had committed burglary in picking the lock to enter the shed. It followed, he said, that Emma and Roque were accomplices to burglary. His comments were given as sort of an aside, but I supposed he needed to get them into the record.

"Emma, you're a trained anthropologist or archaeologist. Tak told me you immediately identified what you found in the barrels as "splashes" of silver. Small, crude ingots of silver. It was lucky that Tak and Roque had you there with them last night to identify the cache. Did you immediately recognize the artifacts as genuine?"

Emma didn't reply for a moment, staring in front of her. "Yes, they were genuine," she said in a monotone. "They were five-hundred-year-old silver ingots." She looked at the sheriff then. "I say five hundred years as a rough estimate. I don't know exactly how old they are. I just saw them for the first time last night. They could be older."

"Of course. How would Mr. Ruskey have cashed them in? He couldn't have done so easily, could he?"

"How would I know?" she blurted with some energy. The recorder was preserving a very uneven performance by this exhausted woman. Waiting to interview her tomorrow might have been a better idea.

"Well," the sheriff continued, "I just meant that archaeology is your area of expertise and therefore you might have some idea of the degree of difficulty Mr. Ruskey faced to unload hundreds and hundreds of pounds of old silver ingots."

Emma closed her eyes and shook her head. "I'm sorry. I'm not quite myself. Yes, he would have needed to find an unethical broker willing to deal in unreported treasure of this kind. Such people are out there, I'm told, people who are willing to dispose of just about anything of historical value so long as they get a cut."

The sheriff took from the table top a sheet of paper. "The Texas antiquities code spells out how the state has an interest in preserving cultural materials from earlier periods of history including, quote, 'treasure embedded in the earth' or found in or under the land of the State of Texas. It requires discoverers of such treasures to report their discoveries."

He lay the sheet on the tabletop. "It's a misdemeanor to not comply with the law but violating the antiquities code seems the least of Mr. Ruskey's problems."

The interview ended and Emma seemed relieved as they stepped down from the van. She needed to go to her mother's house, pull the blinds in the bedroom and sleep the day away. We were taking our leave when the sheriff walked over.

"I'm wondering if you want to take just one moment more, Tak, and accompany me back down into the cavern?"

"Whatever for?" Emma blurted, clearly out of patience. "Can't we just leave?"

"Of course, you can," the sheriff said apologetically.

I frowned at Emma. "Just a second. What do you want to see, sheriff?"

"Oh, nothing, probably. Ruskey was so threatening, talking about dumping your body in that hole. Because he's now an admitted killer, I'm wondering what we might find at the bottom of that cavern. More bodies? I'm taking in a high-intensity light for a better look."

I looked at Emma. "I'd like to accompany the sheriff. Can you wait a few more minutes?" She looked resigned, closed her eyes, and nodded.

Fifteen minutes later, Rodriquez, a deputy, and I moved toward the outer lip of the shelf in the cavern. The deputy held the bulky high-intensity spotlight. He pointed it out into the darkness and switched it on.

Some fifty yards away we could see a huge stone column, perhaps fifteen feet in diameter, the result of dripping limestone-laden water forming a stalactite on the ceiling of the chamber and a stalagmite directly below, the two projections growing together over many, many years. Beyond the column, the light didn't reveal an opposite wall.

"A huge place," the sheriff said. We echoed his awe.

Dropping to our hands and knees, we crawled the last few feet to the edge of the shelf. The deputy lay on his belly and pointed the light downward. In its rays, we found the floor of the cavern possibly fifty feet below us. It was a field of rocky debris, large and small pieces of limestone jumbled together, the remnants of a fallen ceiling.

As the deputy swung the light around, a patch of color appeared near the edge of the light close to the base of the shelf. He turned the spotlight on it. None of us spoke. Among the rocks lay the body of a man. One foot appeared to be bare. The other still was encased in a boot. What appeared to be blue jeans clothed the legs. It was the shirt that caught my eye.

I turned toward the sheriff and found him eyeing me. "See that red shirt?" he asked. "I bet if I had my field glasses with me, I would see a red-*checkered* shirt." I nodded. The same kind of shirt worn by my attacker in the salvage yard.

"Ruskey said he regretted sending a boy to my place to do a man's job," I said, looking back down at the body. "I guess this is what happened to people who disappointed him."

"You know what?" the sheriff said with an edge to his voice. "I'm beginning to believe Ruskey is a mean son-of-a-bitch. That's good information for my deputies to have when they're out looking for him."

As we made our way back to the ladder, Rodriquez paused before climbing it and addressed me. "The irony is, if Ruskey had dragged Pablo's body back to the shed and dumped it in the hole, we'd have had nothing. We give up on missing persons after a week or two. Ruskey would have been home free."

Chapter Thirty-One

Yellow tape now surrounded the shed, draped on bushes in a rough circle, looking somewhat like an avant-garde piece of outdoor art. The hillside in rural Texas on which was perched a nondescript little building would never again know anonymity. A deputy had backed his car over nearer the taped-off area and gotten comfortable. The site was under 24-hour guard as a crime scene and the repository of a fortune from half a millennium ago.

State archaeologists, archivists and law enforcement personnel would walk the ground and explore the cavern under it for weeks to come. One could only imagine the exasperation felt by the project superintendent for NewAge Solar, whose schedule would fall further and further behind.

I heard Rodriquez on the radio dictate the wording of a general law enforcement alert for Peyton Ruskey, who was wanted for murder, attempted murder, assault with a deadly weapon, and violation of the state antiquities code. The last charge struck me as piling on, but Emma the archaeologist might disagree with me about that.

After Emma and I scooted under the barbed wire fence onto Zamarripa ranch property, we stood and brushed dirt from our clothes and found ourselves staring back at the place where we had spent so many eventful hours. It was an ordinary pastoral scene from that viewpoint, but our mind's eye saw the vast cavern hidden under the unremarkable hillside. I wondered if I ever again could take our Hill Country terrain at face value.

I reached out for Emma's hand as we turned away and we slow-walked down into the draw where my truck awaited. I told her then about discovering the body of my assailant in the hole. She stutter-stepped at the news and squeezed shut her eyes. I gripped her hand tighter.

After we entered the cab and I keyed the ignition, I felt overcome by a combination of exhaustion and exhilaration. Both conditions can take it out of you. I collapsed back against my seat, light-headed, and closed my eyes.

Emma asked how I was feeling. Eyes still closed, I told her I wasn't sure what I was feeling other than relieved to have the whole mess behind me. I opened my eyes then and looked at her.

"I think my body and mind are telling me that I am very, very lucky to be alive this morning," I said, almost whispering. "Both of us should be dead at this hour, Emma. Instead, we're off to enjoy a shower, a hearty breakfast, and a visit with a friend in the hospital."

I paused. "To be quite honest, I feel like praying."

And so, I did. Faced forward again, I closed my eyes and offered a short but sincere prayer, expressing gratitude for life and hope and friendship. I found myself voicing an intent to return the following Sunday to a congregation of people way more faithful than I ever had been.

When I finished, I glanced at Emma, who was staring at her hands in her lap. I started the engine and we backed around and left. We were content to ride in silence for several miles, our nerves still tingling from all we'd seen and endured in the last twelve hours.

As I drove the highway into town, my mind revisited the kegs of silver and the firefight and the sight of a body in the deepest recess of the cavern. I kept shaking my head at this memory or that one.

"Penny for your thoughts," I said, turning to Emma, who seemed glummer than I'd expected her to be after our rescue. She shrugged and wagged her head.

"Oh, just thinking. How interesting life is. How quickly it can change from a fast-track sprint to a slog," she said. "Me, I'm crawling. Not quite sure how to get back on my feet and start sprinting. Or if I can."

"Sure you can. You're whole. You're healthy. You're beautiful. You still have me as a friend. What more could you want?"

She gave me a tight-lipped, pensive look. "You're still my friend?"

"My gosh, Emma. We've just been through hell together, helped one another through it. In the words of the sheriff, we bonded in battle. We're tight," I said with more emotion than I had intended.

She just shook her head and looked out the window, speaking to me while still looking away. "I hope so, Tak. I hope that we can always be close."

• • •

I waited in the living room of her mother's house while Emma showered. I sat on the couch at first, my arms folded, still absorbed in last night's events. Soon drowsiness overcame me. I removed my boots, stretched out on the couch and watched the rotating blades of a ceiling fan in the center of the room cast distinctive whirling shadows on the ceiling. The next thing I knew, Emma was shaking my shoulder and I opened my eyes to her smiling face.

"Not tired, are you? Maybe you should take a shower."

"Nah." I pushed myself up and reached for my boots.

"No, seriously, go in there and let the hot water wash away the grime of last night. I feel refreshed and you will, too. Give me that jacket. I'll hang a shirt or T-shirt on the bathroom door handle. I'll fix us some breakfast while you're showering."

I hadn't the strength to argue. I gave her the jacket, dragged myself into the bathroom carrying my boots and moments later closed the shower door. The ordinary bathing experience seemed extraordinary that morning. The hot water seemed to give me a deeper cleansing than usual and a brief blast of cold water on my shoulders left me shivering in delight.

As I toweled, I heard Emma talking to someone, probably bringing her mom up to date. A faded burnt-orange University of Texas T-shirt hung on the bathroom door.

"That was a great idea," I said, joining her in the kitchen. She was dressed in jeans and a fitted collared blouse with snap pockets and elaborate stitching. A cowgirl. "What I want to know is what is a Texas Longhorn T-shirt doing in a Texas A&M Aggie household?

"Dad could be a contrarian," she said, scooping scrambled eggs on plates that already had strips of bacon. "If the Aggies disappointed him in a big game, he'd don the Longhorn shirt to demonstrate his personal disgust. I guess he thought it would shame the Aggies into doing better the next time they took the field."

"It's so funny how fans begin to believe a team really gives a dang what they think," I said.

Emma placed the skillet in the sink and pulled out a chair near one of the food-laden plates. I seated myself in the other place. Without further ado, we began to consume the food with the relish of people who had missed a meal. My plate was half empty before I initiated conversation.

"I hope Roque's not badly hurt. I mean, he's hurt, but if it was just an in-and-out wound, he should heal nicely and have a shoot-out scar to brag about." It was a flippant comment and Emma mumbled a reply but otherwise was noncommittal.

"The more important question," I continued, "is how much Ruskey is hurting. He lost a lot of blood on his way up the hill. If he didn't get somewhere and stanch the bleeding, he might be in bad shape, which would be all right with me."

Emma said nothing. She seemed more interested in the remnants of food on her plate than she did our conversation, which now that I thought about it was more of a monologue than anything else. I returned to eating, glancing at her from time to time. "Did you know Ruskey at all before all this?"

When she blanched, I knew I had spoken out of turn. My query had struck her as an insult or something and I tried to walk it back. "I mean, were your families ever close or anything?"

Her fork clattered onto the plate in front of her and her hands gripped the edge of the table. "Why would you ask that?! Am I suspect here?!" she shouted across the table at me. I was stunned by the vehemence of her response.

"That's silly," I said and regretted my choice of words. "That's absurd. You seem sort of reluctant to say anything bad about the guy and I just wondered if there was a family history that would make you feel disloyal criticizing him. No sin in that."

"I barely know the man," she yelled and pushed back her chair from the table. She dropped her hands to her lap and took a deep breath. "Tak, I've been through hell in the last 24 hours. You questioning my loyalty is absolutely the last thing I need to hear."

"I was not questioning your loyalty!"

She got to her feet and walked away in the direction of the bathroom. Alone, I sat unmoving and lashed myself in my head for uttering something hurtful. I decided to wash the dishes as recompense. I ate what was left on my plate and headed for the sink.

When Emma returned a few minutes later, the dishes were immersed in sudsy water and I was scrubbing on the skillet with a sponge, a towel thrown across one shoulder. I heard her enter but didn't turn around. About the time I assumed she had walked out of the room again, I felt her arms encircle my waist. I dropped the sponge and dried my hands on the towel.

"I'm sorry," she said, her head pressed sideways against my back. "I overreacted to an innocent comment. My nerves are shot. I haven't shown you much character in the last day or two. I wouldn't blame you if you started distancing yourself from me."

I swiveled around in a way that encouraged her to keep her arms where they were. When I faced her, I enclosed her in my arms. "I kind of like this distance right here, you pressed up against me." And I did.

"Listen, Emma. I've known all along that you weren't perfect. I mean, you can't even catch bigger fish than me and I hardly ever throw a line in the water."

She smiled at me, her face a few inches from mine.

"Need more evidence of your imperfection? You don't always laugh at my jokes. Yes, your flaws have been evident for a long time," I said and raised one hand to stroke her hair. "But here's the deal: I like you just the way you are. So much so that I'm afraid I'm falling in love with you."

There. I had said it and felt no regret for having done so. My feelings were obvious to me and to her and I needed to voice them. While I didn't feel compelled to ask her to marry me, something in my heart of hearts knew that a proposal would be forthcoming soon.

"I think I love you, too, Tak," she said with tenderness, "even if not all of your jokes are funny." And we kissed. Sedately, then more hungrily. Her arms tightened around my back.

She pulled her arms around to the front of me then and propped them against my chest, one hand coming up to trace the outline of my lips with a finger and playfully tug at my short, trimmed beard, then dropping back to be captured in my embrace. "You know why I came to your house last night?"

"You were hoping I would open up some cans and feed you?"

She lightly shook her head. "Wrong. I planned to spend the night with you. I decided if you weren't going to invite me there, I would just show up. I was hoping you wouldn't throw me out. Would you have?"

I squeezed her gently. "Not unless I had a midnight mission planned."

"Yes," she said, frowning, "that's true. You do have your priorities. Maybe I can change them." She paused. "I don't want to be here alone tonight, Tak. Mom isn't coming back for two more days. I want to spend them with you. I'll feel safer. I'll feel more loved. Take me home with you."

"I'll have to clear it with Otis, but it'll probably be OK," I said and kissed her some more.

CHAPTER THIRTY-TWO

Emma packed a travel bag with enough changes of clothing and toiletries to support her for a few days. She would return to her mother's house before her mother did, but the next night or two would find her living with me. It was exciting to think about, of course, and yet I had misgivings.

This wasn't a tryst, nor a lark. On the heels of the previous night's all-nighter—albeit with Roque snugged up against us—it had the feel of a... *thing*. A union. A permanent pairing. I'd grown to want just such a relationship with Emma, of course, and the kitchen sink kisses and conversation had confirmed my desire.

Yet dissonance banged around in my head. I was uncomfortable. I felt swept up and on the verge of losing control. Oh, sure, I was happy, but from the recesses of my mind, I heard myself shouting to my heart, *Slow down, buddy!*

Emma sat close to me in the truck, which calmed my fears some. Anyone paying attention when we pulled into the hospital parking lot might have noticed she was seated closer to me than to the passenger side door. That was new. Emma had scooted over by me when she'd entered the cab. That was a development.

After buying the truck some years ago, I had removed bucket seats and replaced them with a bench seat to give me the option of carrying three people. Or, in this case, carrying a second person in the middle. Emma had taken advantage of it. On balance, I was glad she had.

We walked into the hospital, down a couple of halls and around a corner or two before we found ourselves in the doorway to Roque's room. Maria was in the room, as well as Roque's mother. Grizelda Zamarripa was less tense than when I'd seen her earlier in the day and she bounced up from a chair and warmly greeted us. Emma and Maria exchanged hugs and then Maria embraced me, partly I was sure on behalf of Pablo's family.

"How's the shootout hero doing?" I asked and a jumble of conversation followed. Because Maria and Grizelda were leaving, they were pleased we were arriving to take their place at the bedside. After they walked away down the hall, the room quieted, and Emma and I stood on opposite sides of the bed.

"In all seriousness, the hero designation is not lightly bestowed in this case, Roque," I told him without a hint of levity. "You saved our lives last night. Had you not been there, had you not had the courage and taken the initiative to surprise a shooter, Emma and I would be lying on the cavern floor. That is stark reality and I want to say thank for your heroism. I mean it."

Roque was taken back by the sincerity of my remarks. He bobbed his head in embarrassment. "*Bastante,*" he said, showing me the palm of a hand. "Enough. I'm just sorry he got away. Looks like a real hero would have nailed him so we could have gone home last night instead of spending the night on a plywood floor surrounded by smelly cattle feed."

I glanced at Emma, who blinked her eyes at Roque's reference to killing Ruskey. "It's true, Emma," I said to move along the conversation. "Roque's not a very good shot."

I walked around to her side and we both sat in straight chairs next to the bed. Roque hadn't heard about the sheriff's discovery of my attacker's body on the floor of the cavern. His jaw dropped. "The guy is a real killer," he said.

"I want to apologize to you and to Emma for putting your lives at risk," I said, slipping an arm over the back of the chair, my hand on Emma's shoulder. "It was foolhardy. I really didn't see how much danger there was in that situation. But Emma had. She warned us *repeatedly* that we were treading on very, very thin ice. I insisted on doing it, anyway, and I'm sorry."

This seemed to be my morning for serious speeches, but I'd needed to make each of them. We had come *this* close to being killed because of my willfulness.

"We survived it, Tak," Roque said. "We solved a mystery that needed solving. Pablo's family feels a lot better. They feel justice has been served. It was all worth it, I think. Plus... I'm going to have a scar I'll be able to brag about the rest of my life."

We all laughed, and the mood lifted. Roque said the doctors told him he could go home that afternoon. The slug hadn't struck any bones. His shoulder would be sore for some time as the muscle healed, but he could resume his ranch work almost immediately, though wearing a sling. Life felt good for all of us.

Emma and I had one more stop to make before retreating to my home. I pulled up next to the shop at the salvage yard and noted the number of pickups parked in front. "That means it will be a busy day," I said, which in turn meant my employees would have to hustle. Yet I had no intention of helping. I'd called Tomas and told him as much.

As Emma and I entered the building, a cheer went up. A dozen people stood by the counter, and I suspected the assembly wasn't spontaneous. The Walmart bakery cake on the counter with one big lighted candle atop it was the clincher: We'd walked into an informal "appreciation" party.

The group launched into "For He's a Jolly Good Fellow." Emma and I stood just inside the doorway until the song ended. Then we approached the counter amid backslaps and exchanged handshakes and raucous greetings. Most of them were men and women I knew. The others had come to the yard intending only to buy something and stumbled into a celebration. No matter, they seemed to exude as much cheer as did the people who knew me.

Tomas banged on the countertop and quelled the noisemakers. "If I had a cup of cheer, I would raise it in toast to the guy and gal who just joined our party. I would toast Tak Sweedner and Emma Townsend and a third person who's resting up in the hospital, Roque Zamarripa. We are proud of you, for being bulldogs in seeking justice for a family who lost a loved one. For being brave in the face of danger. And, most of all, for coming back to us so we would have a reason to enjoy this cake."

The cheering resumed. I hugged Emma whose mind once again appeared to be meandering somewhere far away. I looked forward to her return, to the moment when she could shrug off the trauma she was feeling. I dedicated myself to helping her regain her natural jauntiness.

The cake turned out to be delicious. It was slathered with sweet frosting, which is what I looked for in any pastry. Soon the cake dwindled on the plate and the crowd thinned, too. I told each departing partier that his or her greeting had warmed me, and that I was grateful they had taken the trouble to come.

"I don't suppose you're going to give us any help today, being a hero and all," Billy quipped as he wiped frosting from his fingers. "Maybe you could loan us Emma. She's better looking anyway."

I smiled at Emma. "Sure, you can have her. You do know a transmission from a wheel bearing, don't you?"

She favored the room with perhaps the brightest smile the room ever had seen. "Listen to this lug nut. I've forgotten more about transmissions than he *ever* knew." Her quip was well received by us car guys.

We were a happy couple as we climbed back into my truck and rode through the salvage yard gateway. Emma was chatty as I turned east toward home. My heart pounded with good feeling. A grin seemed a permanent feature on my face. My underlying doubts about the relationship had dissipated. We commented on the quality of blue in the sky and the length of the boney projections on the heads of longhorn cattle in an adjacent pasture.

Our hands touched where they rested on the narrow seat space between us. She crossed her legs loosely and I occasionally rested a hand on a knee. When I did, she covered it with hers. She gave me warm and expectant looks and, yes, I began to feel aroused by it all.

We waited at the tracks for passage of the tail end of an eastbound Burlington Northern-Santa Fe freight train, its double-deep container rail cars swaying as they rolled by. I told Emma the train was a symbol of commerce and industry that I hoped would never cease to exist in America. "It inspires me as a businessman. Can you understand that?"

"You don't sound like a salvage yard operator, Tak," she said. "I think you're going to become a captain of industry before you're done." The comment further convinced me how much I needed this woman in my life.

• • •

Otis didn't greet us as I pulled to a stop in my usual parking place. I waited an instant to see if I could hear him running toward us, barking excitedly, but midday silence was all I heard.

"Where's your dog?" Emma asked.

"That's what I was wondering. A few times a year he doesn't greet me because he's out inspecting something at the other end of the pasture. Otis is not a lazy dog. He makes his rounds," I said. "Plus, we're coming in at midday when he had no reason to expect anyone."

I banged shut the truck door to signal our arrival, but Otis still didn't trot up, tail wagging, barking. That was OK. I just didn't want him to come scratching at the door when Emma and I were otherwise occupied.

She carried her overnight bag to the porch and waited as I emptied the dog's water bowl and refilled it. When I unlocked and opened the door, I felt an impulse to pick up the woman and carry her across the threshold but decided I was getting ahead of myself.

"I haven't been in your place for all of, what, eighteen hours. It hasn't changed much," she said. She carried her bag over near my bedroom door. I hung the ballcap on the hat rack and slipped my handgun and holster from my hip, setting them on the counter by the sink along with my extra clip.

"So here we are," Emma said and plopped into my easy chair. I pulled out a straight-backed chair by the kitchen table, swiveled it toward her and sat. After crossing my legs, I pulled off my right boot. While standing by the salvage yard counter eating cake, something in the boot started poking the ball of my foot. It had shifted a moment before and become a real aggravation. I felt around in the boot, dumped out a tiny pebble, showed it to Emma and sat the boot on the floor.

I leaned back and rubbed my eyes. The restorative effects of the shower and the cheerfulness of the conversation at the yard were wearing off. Weariness was surging back. If Emma and I moved to the bedroom any time soon, I was confident my exhaustion would disappear.

"Yep, so here we are," I echoed. "Should you check in with Mom? Or did I hear you talking to her when I was toweling off after my shower?"

"I've not spoken to her. I'll call her in a few minutes. She wasn't expecting to hear from me, but I should call before she hears about everything from someone else."

A voice came from over my shoulder, from the direction of the hallway that led to a second bedroom and the bathroom. "We wouldn't want her to be worried."

Emma stared past me. I jumped to my feet. Peyton Ruskey stood at the end of the hallway, his rifle once again pointed at me.

CHAPTER THIRTY-THREE

The man brimmed with spite. His eyes bulged. He almost shook with rage—or perhaps needed a blood transfusion after being wounded. More to the point, the barrel of his Remington wasn't shaking. It was fixed on me, unwavering and threatening. I'd no doubt that a .270 slug would rip through my chest an instant after he pulled the trigger.

Emma had sprung to her feet and flung one arm across her chest as if to still her heart. She stood apart from me and, if anything, edged farther away, which seemed like a good idea. She might yet escape this maniac.

"What are you doing here, Ruskey?" I said, fighting to regain some composure after his re-emergence into my life. He didn't respond and I evaluated what I was seeing.

His shirt was unbuttoned and what appeared to be duct tape was wound around him horizontally between his upper chest and his belly button. A round from Roque's gun must have struck him in his side. He had doctored himself, put some absorbent cloth on the wounds and taped it together. How much blood Ruskey had lost, I couldn't say, but he didn't look energetic. He looked mad.

"I'm here to show you how it feels to be shot, Sweedner, to let you see your blood flow out between your fingers while you try to stop it. If I live just long enough to see you suffer, I'll be happy," he said. His voice was rough.

Yet for all the fierceness he tried to convey, Ruskey sounded weak. He was only one big exertion away from collapsing. That thought restored hope that I could get out of this.

"Why don't you let Emma walk out the door. She's not done anything to you. You haven't a snowball's chance of getting away with all you've done, so it doesn't make any difference what she knows. You're as good as caught anyway. Just let her go."

As I spoke, I took a step sideways, away from Emma. More important, it was a step toward the counter where out of the corner of my eye I could see my loaded semi-automatic.

"She's not going to walk *out* that door right now any more than your dog is going to walk *in*. Your dog likes hamburger a lot. Did you know that? Even when the meat is poisoned."

The announcement froze me. I instantly felt loss. Otis, my friend, was dead. My fun companion gone. Yet the terribleness of the news motivated me. Ruskey had just given me one more reason to stop him from killing anyone else.

"You're a real brave guy, aren't you, you jerk. A real killer, specializing in gentle Mexican bird lovers and happy little dogs. I have no respect for you whatsoever."

"Your respect is of zero interest to me. I just want you to sit back down in that chair. NOW!" He poked the air with his rifle to punctuate his command.

I didn't want to sit. Remaining on my feet gave me a better chance of crossing the room and grabbing his rifle before he could use it on me. I had no idea how to accomplish that, but I wasn't going to die without trying. That I knew. I didn't sit, per his order, and hoped he was more interested in prolonging my agony than he was in ending my life.

"I'll sit if you'll agree to let Emma walk out of here," I said and repositioned my feet to lunge at him. I moved deliberately, fearing a quick movement might startle him and cause him to jerk his trigger finger. That would not end well for me.

"I don't know why you display so much concern for this woman," he said with a look that almost was smug. "Do you really think she has any interest in hooking up with a junk dealer? A junk dealer! Her dreams are bigger than that, junk man. You haven't a prayer of giving her the life she deserves. Actually, you don't have a prayer at all."

I looked at Emma, who blanched at Ruskey's remarks. It must have unsettled her to hear this killer siding with her, as if he were bargaining on her behalf. The guy was nuts.

"You're the one who ought to sit down, Ruskey," I said. As I did so, I shifted ever so slightly and slipped my stockinged toes under the rise of the sole on my empty boot. I hoped to use the boot as a distraction. "You're the one who looks worn out from our run-in at the shed. I'll sit down if you will."

He must have felt a wave of exhaustion sweep over him at that moment and staggered ever so slightly before catching himself. Taking a step toward me, he sighed as if shooting me were the last thing in the world he wanted to do but I had left him no choice. As he steadied himself, I felt we'd entered a final act in this little standoff. It was now or never.

I kicked my foot forward, sending the boot flying toward Ruskey. He flinched and fired the rifle as the boot struck the ceiling and bounced down against him. My arm stung but I was too busy scrambling past Emma to care, hoping to reach Ruskey before he could throw the bolt on the rifle for a second shot.

I tripped on something and almost took a nosedive to the floor but managed to stagger up and throw myself into him. We collided as he completed reloading the weapon's chamber and swung the barrel toward me.

We crashed against the wall on the back side of the room and the rifle *cracked* a second time, this time close enough to my head that all sound disappeared except for intense ringing in my ears. We struggled silently. I could feel the blows, but I couldn't hear them

Ruskey kept trying to bang the rifle barrel against my head and I kept thrusting it away. He was weak from loss of blood but was still a stocky, strong man. Furthermore, he was fighting for his life. If he didn't prevail against me, he knew he was at the least going to prison for the rest of his life. He had nothing to lose and fought like it.

Each of us gripped a part of the rifle with one hand and pummeled one another with our free hand. Our fists bounced off our heads and our legs kicked for advantage. We fell to the floor, with me on top for a moment before he bucked me off and rolled on top.

I landed on my back with my feet planted against the wall and my arm cocked. When I saw an opening, I slipped a punch that hit him in the throat. The blow proved decisive. Ruskey tried to keep fighting but struggled for breath as he gagged from the impact. Then I slugged him hard under an eye and he fell off me.

I wrenched the rifle free, kicked him away from me, and stood up, gasping and coughing. My left arm was bleeding enough that the back of my left hand was covered with blood. The bullet wound was superficial, though, gouging out flesh as it zipped past me. I took a handkerchief from my back pocket, and held it against the wound, trying to stem seepage.

Ruskey recovered quickly and sat up, but when he saw me throw the bolt on the rifle and point it at his chest, he sagged backward. He coughed hard and eased himself onto the floor on his back. His chest rose and fell in short, abrupt spasms and he closed his eyes. I thought maybe he was dying, but after a moment he opened his eyes and gave me a hateful look.

I stepped back farther. Emma had moved away from the easy chair and stood next to the counter. I was happy to see her standing there because the second bullet Ruskey fired had been in her general direction. What a Pyrrhic victory for me had Emma been fatally wounded during my struggle. Instead, the errant shot had blown an ugly hole in Uncle Portis' wall.

"Are you all right?" I asked Emma. She looked stricken. I wondered if she finally had come to the end of her ability to cope. How much death and near-death can an ordinary person face in twenty-four hours and still keep a sense of balance?

"Grab that holster and gun and bring them here, will you? He might only have one more round in this rifle. I might want to put more than one round in him," I said, with a malevolent look at Ruskey who still lay on the floor. "C'mon, try to jump me. Please."

He struggled to sit up, and then surprised me with a smile. His face was badly bruised. He had a cut under one eye, and the wound in his side had begun to seep blood around the tape. Yet he was sitting on the floor smiling up at me. It was unnerving.

"What do you have to smile about? This your lucky day or something? Sure doesn't look like it." I backed toward Emma, the rifle still pointed in his direction.

My ears still rang from the rifle's explosion next to my head, so I almost missed the distinctive sound of the slide on a semi-automatic weapon being levered, chambering a round and cocking the trigger. I was confused by the sound, looked nervously at Ruskey and started to turn to Emma when I felt something hard pressed to my head behind my right ear.

The synapses in my brain normally react as swiftly as anyone's. Not this time. I couldn't piece together what was happening. The combination of hearing a weapon cocked and then feeling what might be the front end of a handgun against my skull suggested to my brain that someone had gotten the drop on me. What puzzled me was...who?

"Tak," I heard Emma say, "Dad taught me how to fish, but he also taught me how to handle a semi-automatic. Please point the rifle at the floor and hand it to Peyton."

Peyton? The voice was Emma's, and she was referring to this killer by his first name? She was holding a gun against *my* head? *Emma?* I started to turn my head to face her, but the gun was pushed harder against my ear, and I stopped.

Ruskey struggled to his feet, groaning, and staggered over to me. He took the lowered rifle from my hand and half-turned away. Without warning, he swung around and backhanded me with his fist. I fell sideways and ended up on my hands and knees. I remained on all fours, stunned by both the blow and the revelation about Emma that preceded it.

"Get up and get in that chair," Ruskey demanded and poked me in the small of my back with the barrel of the rifle. I sat back on my heels, got to my feet, and collapsed onto the kitchen chair. Ruskey retrieved my boot. "And put this back on."

Emma stood next to Ruskey, pointing my gun at me. I looked her in the eyes, searching there for something to explain the inexplicable. Her eyes didn't convey hate, nor even triumph. I saw pain there, maybe some confusion, certainly sadness. Yet the dominant characteristic was resolve. I didn't know what her plan was, but it was clear that she was going to do it, come hell, high water, or me.

Chapter Thirty-Four

"You good? You got him?" Ruskey asked Emma. She nodded. "I'm going to the bathroom to change the dressing and tape myself again." He looked at me. "Your damned fighting has bought you a couple more minutes of life, junk man. After I get patched up, we're taking you out back and you're history."

I heard him talking but my eyes were fixed on Emma. I heard him leave the room, but I only saw Emma as she pulled out another chair across the table from me and sat. The working end of the Taurus never wavered from its alignment with my chest. Gone completely from her countenance was the listless vacuity that I'd worried was evidence of psychological damage from the stress of the last eighteen hours.

"You appear as if a terrible load has been lifted from you, Emma, and that you're on track again with your life." I almost whispered, perhaps the last intimate conversation I would have with this woman for whom I had begun to feel passion. "Somehow I'd believed you were on an altogether different track. You're a good actress."

Her expression was resolute. "It wasn't all acting, Tak. I do love to be with you. I think we could have become quite a team. But this situation had come up for me, this opportunity, and you stubbornly kept putting yourself in front of it, risking everything. How many times did I plead with you to stop? How many? I pleaded and pleaded, but, no, you wouldn't stop. I'm so sorry you didn't."

Her words didn't square with her determined look. "I don't believe you're sorry. I don't believe you ever believed we would make a good team. I see now I was just someone you had to manipulate and move out of the way. I suppose you came up from the university to throw me off the track. What if I hadn't called you in the first place?"

"Then Peyton would have taken care of matters himself. Your call gave me a chance to work against discovery from the inside."

My heart felt heavy, but my brain was regaining its quickness. "You set me up. You knew when I might be alone at the yard so the guy could jump me. You knew I was driving to Rocksprings. Ruskey knew he could find us at the shed last night because that wasn't your mother you were calling as we drove out the lane, it was him. And I bet you called him this morning from your mother's house, didn't you? You told him he could catch up with you here."

She offered no response and for the first time since I sat down, I took my eyes from her, and lowered my head, leaning forward on the table. The arm with the wound throbbed, and probably bled, but I didn't care. It wasn't painful enough to distract me from my intense disappointment.

My conclusions about Emma were true, but I still couldn't square the truth with my memories of the woman. Swimming with her in the river, a happy, seductive gal. Eating lunch with her and her mother, me courting each of them. Cuddling and comforting her in the shed after the shooting. Tenderly embracing her and being embraced in return just a couple of hours ago. The same woman?

I sat up. I had more questions. "How in the world did you get mixed up in this?"

"How do you think?" I did think and then I knew.

"I get it. He contacted you about finding a buyer, one of those unscrupulous people who treat buried treasures like just another commodity to be bought and sold. He knew you were an archaeologist and hoped you might have the right connections. He was right. What was your cut?"

She frowned, probably at my crude description of her reward for finding a buyer. I was sure she preferred "commission." Thieves have such delicate feelings. "I needed the money. College bills. A worn-out car. Taxes on Mom's home. College faculty members don't make a lot of money or have much security till they're granted tenure and I was years away from that. The sudden possibility of getting a commission for moving the silver changed all that."

Uh huh. Commission. "And you had no compunction about stealing? You had no second thoughts about being complicit in a murder?"

She shook her head at that. "Pablo's death occurred later. I actually was very shaken by it."

"I can tell. The money canceled out the guilt, didn't it. You miraculously got over it. Had Ruskey killed me, I'm sure you'd have gotten over that, too."

The dreadful conversation had no effect on Emma. Her hands held the gun steady, as if she were on valium. Her expression was cool and calculating, undisturbed by my recounting of events.

I hadn't expected her to be shamed. She was too deeply in the game to pull out now. But I had thought she might exhibit some small degree of embarrassment for her flagrant duplicity. It was clear she was not uncomfortable at all.

My very first observation had been dead on. Emma *was* a good actress.

Ruskey returned. He moved as if he had taken a bullet, all right, but didn't appear to be on his last legs. I wondered if he had gotten a blood transfusion, corrupting an underpaid worker at the hospital to do so. He'd discarded his bloody shirt now and the taping around his stomach looked clean, if not antiseptic.

"Hang on. I'm going to scrounge through Sweedner's drawers and see if I can find a loose-fitting top," he announced and disappeared into my bedroom. I noticed Emma's suitcase by the bedroom door, a reminder of what might have been.

OK, Tak. Do you want to die today? Quit feeling sorry for yourself! What are you going to do? Whatever I did next, I knew I could do it easier than I might have a few minutes earlier. My gunpoint conversation with Emma had blown away the last of my mental confusion. She was the enemy, a formidable one, and I understood now that she had been all along.

My whole new perspective was an advantage only if I disguised it. Emma and Ruskey had to believe I still was moping about my lost love, too crushed to give them trouble. I had to appear a helpless lamb on its way to slaughter. How good an actor was I?

Under Emma's watchful gaze, I leaned over, picked up my boot and tugged it on. I needed two shod feet under me. Ruskey returned wearing a zip-up tan jacket that had been loose on me but would be tight on him. He shrugged it off as he approached the table and started pulling out drawers by the sink. He held up a serrated knife, which jangled my nerves just a bit, before dropping it back in the drawer and bringing out scissors. He lay the jacket on the counter and snipped off the sleeves.

"OK, boy detective, let's get that phone off you," he said, walking to me and pulling my cell phone from its holster. He tossed it on the counter. "Maybe we can plant that somewhere and misdirect a search."

Emma had no response. Ruskey turned back to me. "Let's go meet your maker, junk man," he said. Emma and I stood and he looked at her and my gun. "You have any compunctions about using that thing on your boyfriend. Maybe I should handle it."

For an instant, I thought I saw a flicker of regret flash through Emma, but it passed so quickly I couldn't be sure. If Ruskey had seen it, her response immediately reassured him. "He's covered. I can pull the trigger."

Ruskey picked up his rifle and opened the door, which I noticed now featured a ragged hole from the first bullet fired from the rifle. He walked ahead through the doorway. I followed. Emma was close behind with the semi-automatic aimed at my spine.

The day had turned partly cloudy, but the air was warm as we walked out from under the porch roof. Ruskey leaned the rifle against the side of my truck and walked on ahead. Emma nudged my back with the handgun, so I followed. I idly looked around and wondered where Ruskey had hidden his car or truck, though it didn't matter much. Moot point. I hadn't seen it and here I was.

We were headed across the open area next to the house toward the pasture gate on the other side. I supposed they wanted to leave my body somewhere out of sight in case anyone came looking for me. Less than a mile away, an engineer on a passing freight blasted the air with his horn as he approached the road crossing.

I stopped and turned to Emma. "So, tell me, how will you explain my absence? You're the last person seen with me. How will you not be a prime suspect in my disappearance?"

She stopped and stepped back, keeping her distance and the gun trained on me. "Oh, I don't know. I guess we had a lovers' quarrel and I insisted you take me home. That was the last time I saw you."

"And the bullet holes in the house?"

"I know nothing about them. Someone must have fired a weapon in your home after I left it. Now, move on." She wagged the gun in the direction of the pasture.

I turned toward Ruskey, who stood with hands on hips, clearly impatient with the interrupted death walk. "And what about you?" I asked. "Your treasure is gone. You *are* suspect number one. A man on the run. Do you think you can disappear?"

He took a step toward me, fists clenched. "Shut up! I won't be *dead* like you! Now, shut up!"

I shrugged, but added a taunt over my shoulder to Emma, "Do you actually believe this man won't turn you in when he's caught, Emma? Or... are you going to shoot him, too? That's probably your best hope of getting out of this mess."

Ruskey was on me then, knocking me down with a blow to my head and then kicking me. I tried to roll one way and then the other to avoid the blows, but some of them connected. Emma was screaming and he was yelling back at her. He backed away then, gasping for breath and swearing at me.

"Get up, Tak!" Emma yelled. "Get up and shut up, like Peyton said. Just shut up!"

I got to my feet hugging my right arm in front of me. "Screwed up my arm," I complained and turned to follow Ruskey, limping a little. What they didn't know was that my arm was all right and the curled-up hand that I carried with tenderness held a fistful of dirt. I hoped for a chance to use it.

The gate was open, which surprised me. I should have noticed that when I'd arrived with Emma. It might have warned me that something was amiss. I wondered if I would have entered the house more warily having seen the open gate.

Our destination was the well, I understood that now. That was why the gate was open. The body of Otis probably already was at the bottom of the well.

I felt more and more desperate for a distraction, anything to divert Emma's attention long enough for me to jump her. Then Ruskey himself supplied it, emitting a *whoop*! He'd spotted a rattler just a few feet from where he stood. It was coiled to strike and was close enough to be a genuine threat. He jumped sideways.

I whirled around to find Emma perhaps six feet behind me. Her eyes darted back to me from Ruskey. The gun she held in two hands swung back as well. I had reacted too slowly to take advantage of the snake's sudden appearance. I glowered at Emma, who seemed as determined as ever. I fought off the panicky thought that I had just missed my last chance to make it out of this situation alive.

But then something caught my eye in the sky behind Emma's head and I looked beyond her. One of my buddies in his crop duster was bearing down on us. Emma heard the approaching plane, too, and knew in an instant that it posed a danger.

Her eyes darted between Ruskey and me as the noise of the plane's turbine engine grew louder and louder. She looked frightened. Was the path of the plane going to bring it so close that the pilot would see her holding a gun on me? If so, there went her alibi about a lovers' quarrel.

Emma and Ruskey froze in indecision. They'd been exposed. The noise from the plane's turbine engine grew louder and Emma had to try to disguise her intent. She stepped to her right, lowering the gun till it pointed at the ground and turning her head to look for the plane in the sky. Before she'd completed her turn, I stepped into a throw and heaved the handful of dirt and dust at her head.

CHAPTER THIRTY-FIVE

A few ounces of granular dirt and dust are not weaponized when thrown. Their effectiveness lies in their being in the air instead of underfoot. And my timing was good. Emma must have sensed my movement and turned back toward me just as the leading particles of dirt splattered against her face. The dust hung in the air. When the dirt struck, she closed her eyes by instinct, turned her face away again, and ducked.

The bad news was that, with the same instinct, she had raised the semi-automatic in my general direction and pulled the trigger. The gunshot was almost drowned out by the roar of the plane as it barreled past us perhaps thirty yards away and above our heads. I was aware of all the noise but was intent on reaching Emma before she could recover well enough to draw down on me. I felt no impact of a nine-mm round and continued my headlong lunge at her.

She'd staggered back at first but had not lost her wits. Aplomb under pressure. You gotta admire it. She regained the semblance of a shooting stance and the Taurus was inches away from zeroing in on my head when my outthrust left hand swept sideways against her arms.

The gun kicked out another bullet just as I struck her, so my poor ears again took the brunt of an explosive discharge from a weapon. For the second time that afternoon, I found myself fighting a silent battle.

My momentum carried me into Emma, who stood her ground. My left hand grabbed for the gun or her wrists or whatever it could find. My right fist smacked against her check. As we collided, my legs kept churning and

Emma fell backward, landing on her back with a grunt. I landed on top of her, still grabbing at the gun and her arms.

She tried to kick me and to knee me in the groin, but nothing short of castration was going to deter me from getting hold of the weapon. She released one hand from the semi-automatic and reached for my face, scratching my forehead in a futile effort to poke my eyes. I was learning that hell hath no fury like a woman fighting to get away with murder.

I got a firm grip on the gun, then, wrenched it from her hand, and rolled off her. I rolled a second time to put some distance between Emma and myself and jumped to my feet with the semi-automatic pointed in the direction where I expected to see Ruskey charging me.

Instead, I saw him kneeling on the ground. Blood streamed from one shoulder, one of Emma's shots having sent a round ripping through it. He saw me and gave me an anguished look as he realized the tables had turned. His head sagged and he shouted something at the ground that my ringing ears couldn't quite make out.

The ears were regaining some of their function, though, and I heard the plane engine again. It wasn't approaching us this time, however. It circled us at low altitude, the pilot concluding that what he was seeing in my pasture warranted interrupting his passes across the nearby farm field. I waved at the plane and hoped the pilot recognized me. He must have: The wings wagged.

My attention was drawn back to Emma then. She apparently wasn't feeling vanquished. She rose from the ground, took in the plight of her partner, put her hands on her hips, and threw me a discouraged look. To my surprise, she walked toward me exuding confidence, her hands half raised. I couldn't tell whether she was surrendering or beseeching me. I held the gun in one hand and dropped it to my side as she approached. She read my mind.

"You're not going to shoot me, Tak," she said, favoring me with a beguiling look, as beguiling as one can look with one cheek reddened from the blow I'd given her, a tiny trickle of blood leaking from a nostril.

She must have felt the blood flowing and stopped. Pulling up the bottom of her blouse, she dabbed at the blood, knowing full well she exposed her stomach and part of her bra in doing so. Ever the temptress. She let the blouse drop back in place. "You might hate me at this moment, but you're not going to use that gun on me."

My breathing slowed after ramping up like crazy during the height of the struggle. I took a deep breath and settled it some more. "You were prepared to use the gun on *me*, Emma. In fact, had you been just a little quicker or stronger, I'd be lying at your feet right now. Bleeding. Please don't try to appeal to my better nature. Right now, I don't *have* a better nature."

In the corner of my eye, I saw her partner trying to get to his feet. "Ruskey," I yelled, turning to him, "if you persist in trying to stand, I'll be obliged to put a round through one of your legs, so just stay the hell where you are."

Emma hadn't hesitated while I addressed her partner and was within a step or two of me when I turned back to her. She reached out both hands, apparently still convinced she held some power over me. The things women get in their heads.

An instant before her hands touched my chest, I raised the gun out away from my side and then jerked it in and clunked the top of it against the side of her head. She didn't even have time to register surprise, falling sideways and landing on her face.

After taking a moment to assess her condition, I walked around Emma and approached Ruskey. "You can't possibly know how close to death you are at this moment. When I think of Pablo and Roque and how you turned that woman over there into a scheming killer, I really *really* want to shoot you. Turning you over to the sheriff just doesn't get it. Please... give me reason to turn my gun on you."

Ruskey was a beaten, tired man. Wounded by gunshot twice in one twenty-four-hour period. Slugged and slapped around in our brawl in the house. A fortune in silver slipping away forever. He nonetheless tried to muster bravado. Unfortunately, the best he could do was sneer and mumble about me not knowing the difference between Shinola and something else I didn't quite hear.

I kicked his shoulder just to hear him scream. "Take off your belt! If your shoulder hurts doing it, I don't care. Just take off your damned belt or I'm going to knock you in the head even harder than I did her!"

In a few minutes, he lay on his belly with his arms bound behind him by his belt. His legs were bound together by *my* belt. Ruskey finally looked as thoroughly defeated as he in fact was. As I got to my feet after binding his legs, I kicked some dirt in his face. Accidentally. "Oops," I said. He sputtered and turned his head away.

"If you hear another rattle, you might want to lie real still," I told him, though I was sure the snakes were all curled up in shade somewhere. I headed for the well. As expected, at the bottom of the shadowy, deep hole was the body of my four-legged buddy.

After landing in a heap when dumped without ceremony, the body of the dog had settled into a graceful position. Otis lay on one side, legs outstretched as if in slumber, head stretched forward in comfortable, dignified repose. An undertaker couldn't have arranged the body with any more eye appeal.

I decided on the spot to come back the next day and drop several wheelbarrows of dirt down the well to cover the body and leave the animal just as it was. If I sanded and polished a two-by-six, burned "Otis" into it and attached it to the bucket-raising winch, my four-legged friend would have a fine headstone. I had given myself a happy task to anticipate.

I leaned against the top edge of the well. Then I turned away and slid down the outside of the wall to sit on the ground. Dropping the Taurus to the dirt, I rested. The spray plane continued to circle. I waved a weary arm at the pilot once more and the plane banked away toward the airport.

Emma lay across the way, unmoving, but I was pretty sure she was resting the rest of the unconscious. A headache awaited her upon her return to this world, that and handcuffs.

"Un. Be. Leeevable." I muttered just loud enough for my battered eardrums to hear. What a rollercoaster. Kissing that woman and preparing to climb into bed with her one moment, the next moment slugging her in the face and clobbering her in the head with my gun.

A grackle swooped in and landed on the ground not far from where Emma lay. I guessed the black bird had spotted a morsel from the air. It pranced across the pasture for several yards, its majestic tail trailing, and stopped to peck at the ground. It took flight about the same time a roadrunner landed nearby. The sleek bird dipped its head and sprinted across an expanse of pasture, as only a roadrunner could, before returning to the air. Just showing off.

My musing was interrupted by Ruskey, who moaned where he lay in the dirt and coarse grass, turning his head from side to side, wondering when someone was going to come patch up his wounds. "Hey, Sweedner, damn it! I'm hurting here," he yelled in the direction of the house. He didn't see me relaxing behind him at the well. Let him yell.

After another minute of reflection, I heaved a sigh. I wished never again to experience the variety of pains running through me at that moment— physical, emotional, psychological. Even a shudder of relief at avoiding death made me wince. I was close to tears, so inconsolable did I feel.

Yet it would pass. I knew, and I really needed to get moving. Adrenalin wouldn't sustain me much longer. I struggled to my feet, hurt running pretty much the length of my body. Ruskey had delivered some decent blows in his attacks and Emma had done her best to batter me.

I walked over to where she lay. Ruskey saw me then and yelled some more about needing attention. "I'm hurting here!" It was so ludicrous for him to think I cared. I flashed a smile at him, turned my back, and looked down at Emma, whose face lay sideways in the dirt. I knelt and lifted a couple of strands of brunette hair from her cheek. *Girl, girl. What a good life we might have had. I'm gonna miss you.*

I felt for a pulse in her wrist. It was steady and strong. Satisfied she was OK, I got to my feet and headed for the house to retrieve my phone and call the sheriff.

The spray plane pilot had saved my life. Without his arrival, I suppose I might have figured out a way to get a drop on Emma. I would have tried. I knew that. Yet had he not zoomed onto the scene at low altitude at a critical moment, the greater likelihood was that my lifeless body would at that moment be sprawled atop Otis at the bottom of the well.

Trudging past the gate and nearing the house, I wondered what car or truck at the yard would be the best reward for the pilot. Maybe the '59 Cadillac.

Chapter Thirty-Six

Maria looked lovely in a long and ruffled white dress that stopped a scant quarter of an inch short of the floor. I wondered how a seamstress could hang a dress on a body with such precision. Her dimpled cheeks were rouged, her full lips a lustrous red. Her eyes danced with joy. A purple-flowered Texas sage sprig adorned her hair on one side of her head.

Roque looked of noble stock in his Western-cut dark suit that framed an oversized, pleated and hand-tied Western tie the same color as Maria's Texas sage bloom. Every inch a Mexican caballero, Roque stood next to his bride and beamed at guests who moved through the receiving line in the Zamarripa ranch home. Pele and Grizelda Zamarripa and Maria's parents greeted guests on either side of the happy married couple.

Invited guests carried conversations from room to room in the rambling ranch house accompanied by *mariachi* musicians. The quartet of strolling singer-instrumentalists blended the sounds of guitars, violin, and accordion.

The scene was pure revelry following a wedding ceremony at Sacred Heart Catholic Church that was "high church" by my ceremonial standards. Classic religious pomp was mixed with appeals for fealty to Lord and spouse, all delivered in a fascinating, choreographed ritual that was a bit long for those of us sitting in hardwood pews.

The pews were no softer at my church, yet I had again begun to find my place in them on Sunday mornings, much to the delight of Bishop Castillo. He had beamed the first morning I re-entered the building and given me a homecoming hug. I had rejoined the congregation sadder, wiser, and more grateful for the blessing of life.

At that moment, I perched on a padded stool next to the ranch home's food bar, nursed a fresh-lime soda and munched on peanuts. I don't know who else in the room was drinking so-called "mocktails," but I appreciated their availability.

Tomas Gonzales and his wife ambled past holding plates of hors d'oeuvres, a pretty, teenage daughter in a mauve dress trailing them. A suite of suitors trailed the girl as nonchalantly as they could. She glanced over her shoulder now and then to encourage their continued attention.

I decided to enjoy my lime drink on the patio. After grabbing another fistful of salted peanuts, I wound my way through the crowd and out the patio doorway. Several knots of people were laughing and conversing in separate parts of the landscaped area. A pair of lawn chairs sat empty against a wall of the house. I crossed the patio and claimed one of them.

It was a delightful Saturday in south Texas in late October, neither warm nor chilly. If a thermometer could talk, it would be saying, "Ahhhh." A few high clouds pocked the blue expanse hanging above the house.

I took a sip of lime and closed my eyes, retreating a moment from the social hubbub around me. I heard the other chair squeak when someone settled weight on it. Feeling obligated to greet the person, I opened my eyes.

It was Sheriff Rodriquez. "Hey, sheriff. Roque's big day. You do know his dad threatened to shoot him if he didn't wed Maria."

"I know," he responded after gulping down iced tea. "I told Roque there was nothing I could do about such a threat. A father has certain rights and expectations."

I loved the droll comment. "Poor Roque. Everybody ganging up on him."

The good sheriff and I had seen each other more than we would have liked in the follow-up to the summer's unfortunate events. A patched-up and unrepentant Peyton Ruskey was a noisome guest in the county jail, where he seemed bent on irritating everyone who visited his cell, from meal-servers to lawyers. He was a bitter, sour loser just as I'm sure he would have been an obnoxious person of wealth had his scheme played out as planned.

Elsewhere in the jail, Emma Townsend awaited her day in court. She, of course, faced charges as Ruskey's accomplice. In addition, I had fully informed prosecutors of her willful intent to murder me in my home and pasture. Unquestionably, I was doing the right thing in pressing charges, but it didn't always feel that way.

By choice, I was not privy to second-hand conversations going on in the jailhouse between lawyers and clients, nor to the workings of sheriff's deputies and detectives laboring to pull together the case against the two defendants. I frankly didn't want to know the ins and outs of the matter as the legal case against the pair was built. I was interested in neither legal maneuvering nor gossip. It was all too close.

Even so, one of my law enforcement friends had confided in me that the criminal partnership between Emma and Ruskey completely unraveled once they were behind bars. That didn't surprise me. He said they each blamed the other for the whole scheme. Consequently, though there was no doubt that Ruskey murdered two people, Emma's role in the affair still had not been legally defined.

She now claimed to have been deceived by the rancher in agreeing to help him dispose of the silver. Furthermore, she said she had been threatened by Ruskey and warned that if she said anything about the death of the two men, he would retaliate against her mother. In effect, Emma argued that she also was a victim of Ruskey's greed and willful violence.

I was noncommittal about the tidbit of news from my friend. It all would come out in court. The facts were clear in my mind: Nothing in my relationship with Emma in recent months indicated she had been anything but a full partner in the crimes and that she was fully responsible for her decisions. I knew my testimony would be instrumental in her conviction on all counts, and that knowledge left me feeling morose.

Her mother and I had supported each other in the weeks immediately following Emma's arrest, talking for hours at a stretch in an attempt to understand a daughter and friend who had become someone neither of us recognized. We cried some, laughed a little, and comforted one another in our mutual loss.

Mrs. Townsend and I wondered if Emma and Ruskey's relationship had been romantic as well as criminal. While we doubted it was, that might have explained Emma's woeful misjudgment. We looked for excuses for Emma, in other words. In the end, we couldn't find any.

Mrs. Townsend saw Emma every week, but I made clear early on that I wouldn't be accompanying her to the jail. Not only would prosecutors voice strenuous objections to such visits, my whole being argued against it. Our connection as a couple was severed.

"I keep wondering what the solar panel company is going to do with its cavern," Rodriquez said, nodding in the direction of the land just north of where we sat.

University archaeologists had explored the pristine dark cavern and were near to declaring it the largest karst formation of its kind in Texas. The opening Emma and I had discovered a few hundred yards away led to a separate and much smaller cavern. The larger underground formation—now dubbed the "NewAge Cavern"—was virgin except for being despoiled by the conquistadors. Not even bats knew of it.

"The county is seriously considering buying the property and developing the cavern as a tourist attraction," the sheriff continued. "Pele, of course, hates the idea."

I had no response. I took another sip of the drink and stared at a phalanx of autumn blooms in the patio area. They merged in my mind into a colorful wallpaper.

"Given any more thought to my offer to become a deputy, Tak," the sheriff asked.

I knew he'd bring it up. Rodriquez had offered me a position in his department because, he told me, he admired my ability to decipher clues, find motives, and follow trails wherever they led. He used words like "initiative" and "resolve" and "courage." I wouldn't have to give up the salvage yard, he assured me, just let someone else manage it day to day and bring to his department my gift of "puzzling out" things.

The proposal flattered me, and I was considering it. As a career, lawman was a definite step up from junkman. Yet I was troubled by the thought of becoming a law officer on the strength of having exposed and brought to justice a very close friend.

Emma would see the irony in it, certainly. I believed it would make her sad way down in that part of her that hadn't been poisoned by Ruskey, that region of her heart where I was certain she still valued love and honor and friendship.

"*Gracias,* sheriff," I said. "I'm still thinking on it."

About the Author

Gillespie Lamb developed writing skills as a newspaper reporter, editor and columnist before leaving journalism to become a freelancer and pursue less formulaic writing. He published his first novel in 2017, a middle-grades reader titled *The Beamy Courage of Gerta Scholler*. This second novel is his initial foray into the mystery genre. The setting of *The Junkyard Dick* is the rural Texas region where Lamb lives.

Note from the Author

Word-of-mouth is crucial for any author to succeed. If you enjoyed *The Junkyard Dick*, please leave a review online—anywhere you are able. Even if it's just a sentence or two. Thank you!

Gillespie Lamb

We hope you enjoyed reading this title from:

BLACK ROSE
writing™

www.blackrosewriting.com

Subscribe to our mailing list – *The Rosevine* – and receive **FREE** books, daily deals, and stay current with news about upcoming releases and our hottest authors.
Scan the QR code below to sign up.

Already a subscriber? Please accept a sincere thank you for being a fan of Black Rose Writing authors.

View other Black Rose Writing titles at www.blackrosewriting.com/books and use promo code **PRINT** to receive a **20% discount** when purchasing.

9 781685 130176